D0594334

For Conall

Text for DK by Working Partners Ltd
9 Kingsway, London WC2B 6XF
With special thanks to Adrian Bott

Design by Collaborate Ltd
Illustrator Ellie O'Shea
Consultant Derek Harvey
Acquisitions Editor James Mitchem
Designer Sonny Flynn
US Senior Editor Shannon Beatty
Senior Production Editor Robert Dunn
Senior Producer Ena Matagic
Publishing Director Sarah Larter

First American Edition, 2021
Published in the United States by DK Publishing
1450 Broadway, Suite 801, New York, New York 10018

Text copyright © Working Partners Ltd 2020
Layout, illustration, and design copyright © 2021 Dorling
Kindersley Limited

DK, a Division of Penguin Random House LLC
21 22 23 24 25 26 10 9 8 7 6 5 4 3 2 1
001–319101–Apr/2021

All rights reserved.
Without limiting the rights under the copyright reserved above, no
part of this publication may be reproduced, stored in or introduced
into a retrieval system, or transmitted, in any form, or by any means
(electronic, mechanical, photocopying, recording, or otherwise),
without the prior written permission of the copyright owner.
Published in Great Britain by Dorling Kindersley Limited.

A catalog record for this book is available from the
Library of Congress.

ISBN: 978-0-7440-2136-3 (paperback)
ISBN: 978-0-7440-2772-3 (hardcover)

Printed and bound in Great Britain by
Clays Ltd, Elcograf S.p.A.

www.dk.com

For the curious

The publisher would like to thank: Sam Priddy and Jo Clark;
Sally Beets for editorial assistance; Caroline Twomey for proofreading.

Quiz answers

1. Four

2. Person of
   the forest

3. Borneo

4. Pelawan tree

5. True

6. Rafflesia

7. Durian

8. Palm oil

A WHITE MERC WITH FINS

James Hawes

TUCKAHOE
PUBLIC LIBRARY

PANTHEON BOOKS

NEW YORK

FEB 2 8 1996

Copyright © 1996 by James Hawes

All rights reserved under International and Pan-American
Copyright Conventions. Published in the United States by
Pantheon Books, a division of Random House, Inc., New
York. Originally published in Great Britain by Jonathan
Cape Ltd., London.

Library of Congress Cataloging-in-Publication Data
Hawes, James
    A white Merc with fins / James Hawes.
        p.   cm.
    ISBN 0-679-44225-1
    1. Bank robberies—Fiction.   2. Young men—Fiction.
    I.Title.
    PS3558.A814W48   1996
    813´.54—dc20   95-33078

Book design by Deborah Kerner

Manufactured in the United States of America
First American Edition
9 8 7 6 5 4 3 2 1

To Teresa

CONTENTS

A
WHITE
MERC
WITH
FINS

1

HOW
TO GET TO
MOSCOW

Brady wanted a real gun, he insisted on a real gun, the big meathead bounced up and banged on the table with his big meatball fists and roared he was out if he didn't get a real fucking gun. So I hopped up too, I knocked my chair backwards accidentally on purpose and stuck all my knuckles on the table like a baboon and put my face within loafing distance of his and yelled back:

—Shut up and listen to the Plan!

—You can't rob a bank with a plastic fucking cap gun!

—What the fuck do you know about robbing fucking banks?

—Well I fucking know you don't rob fucking banks with plastic fucking cap guns! Great fucking plan!

This was serious. I had let myself get into the F-word thing with Brady, and now it was my round again, and we were already close to saturation.

—Is nice big heavy plastic, says Chicho.—Look!

—I don't give a fuck how fucking big it is (Brady was tempted, his eyes wobbled, but he knocked the gun away, he looked like a lobster on speed by now) and I don't give a fuck about the fucking plan, I am not fucking robbing Michael fucking Winner's private fucking bank with a plastic fucking cap gun!

I knew it.

I knew I should never have told Brady it was Michael Winner's private bank. It isn't really, I only said that to pepper things up a bit for Christ's sake, does everything have to get taken literally? Now Brady is sure the bank will be guarded by Charles Bronson, he just KNOWS everyone will have blood bags and jerk wires and stuff.

Brady is a Reservoir Dog fetishist, God help us, he thinks doggy fashion means dressing up like Harvey Keitel, if Quentin Tarantino farted in a bucket, Brady would queue for the bootleg video, he gets his Dog rig on and rides round the Circle Line with a shower of sad cronies, that is the story of his life. There is only one way to deal with a paid-up psycho like Brady, so I snatched up the plastic cap gun and prodded its red plastic snout into his big broken nose.

—You have been listening to absofuckinglutely fuck all have you, fuck you you fucking dull fucker, the whole fucking point is that it's fucking obviously not a real fucking gun, any fucker with half a fucking brain can see that, underfuckingstand you monu-fuckingmentally fuck-faced fucking fuckwit!

There.

Nuked him. Total saturation. Even Brady had to take a breath to digest that lot. Time to strike:

—Look, OK, OK, I said.—You can wear the Dog stuff.

—Yeah? says he, blushing with hope and shame.

Hope and shame.

I must give Brady his due, he is not proud of his fetishism. He is ashamed of it, except when he is actually in the grip of it and riding with his Doggies. He does not want to do it, he just has to, and when he cools down he gets ashamed. That is good, it is the one good thing about Brady, my oldest friend.

His shame shows that he has eaten from the tree of the knowledge of good and sad.

It shows he is a little fucked up but not a hopeless case, which is why I like him, I suppose. Anyway, I know he cannot resist the idea of actually robbing a bank, or at least being part of an actual bank robbery, while dressed in his Reservoir Dog kit.

—Yeah, says I, you can wear the suit, like it's some big concession by me to keep us all friends. Actually, Brady and his Doggies are part of the Plan, but I kept that in reserve because I knew Brady would cause trouble about something, he always does, he just likes making trouble, he is the kind of bastard, you know, who will say to you after three pints:

—OK, so will you back me up when those three over there start on me?

And you look round and you see these three skinheads or whatever, guzzling snakebites, going rather heavy on that spotty chimp cackle that some yoof do, it's true, and looking generally

JAMES HAWES

like they must have slept through the alarm clock on the morning
the gene pool was being ladled out, but on the whole minding
their own speedy little business, and you reply:

—Who, them? They aren't starting anything.

—They will.

That kind of bastard.

—The shades as well? says Brady.

—OK. I spread my arms out. The shades as well.

—OK, says Brady, and he spreads his long arms out in front
of him, like there was never really any problem.—OK, hey, fine,
I'll use the cap gun.

—And I? says Chicho.

—Hey give me a chance, I say.—It's all in the Plan.

But it's OK, he's not making trouble.

Chicho never makes trouble.

He did nearly get seriously mediterranean with me once, that
was when I broke up with his sister Pilar (which means pillar,
which is a funny name for a girl when you think about it), but
now he knows it was for the best, she is married to a Portuguese
baker off the Portobello Road, they cook toothbending sweet pas-
tries dusted white with confectioner's sugar, they have this machine that squeezes star-shaped tubes of sugary sludge straight
into boiling oil, like play-dough in hell, to make churros for
dunking into cups of melted chocolate. They bake what Fred the
Security Chief calls croysants stuffed with more chocolate, and
they have spicy, oily pork cutlets in breadcrumbs and stuff like
that. No wonder Chicho is so bloody fat, but that's OK too, because he is just naturally big and fat and cool, he is the kind

of man who looks right being fat, if you know what I mean, not stupid, a chubby-chaser's dream man, and he doesn't give a toss anyway about anything except his sister's happiness and his half-brother's allegedly fabulous wood-fired restaurant in Zaragoza, both of which he worries deeply about.

As far as Pilar goes he is OK now, because he realizes that she is much happier married to this Portuguese baker than hanging around waiting for a sad waster who lives in a glorified shed (me), but as far as the wood-fired restaurant goes he is slightly fucked up at the moment, since he has got to buy a half-share in it now, or never.

—All you have to do is just shout a lot in Spanish and carry Suzy about a bit and gibber at the police, I say.

—Gibber? says Chicho.—Gibber? What is?

—Laputamadrecabrondiosmio! says Suzy the Black Widow.

—This is gibber? Oh, is easy for me, says Chicho.

—I thought I was driving, says Suzy the Black Widow.

—You are, I say (Me wild with lust, say my eyes, Good, say hers).—But in the Plan you have to scream and stuff and get carried about a bit by Chicho too.

—Is easy for me, Chicho promises her.

—But how dreadfully melodram-oid, darling, says Suzy in the perfect tonsil-swallowing Upper-Class accent we need, with the chinless overbite and floppy arms to suit.

—Brilliant, I say.

—Is easy for Suzy, says Chicho admiringly.

—Jesus, just like some all-fur-coat-and-no-knickers bitch! laughs Brady.

—But I do get to drive afterwards? she insists, in her ordinary voice, which is Dundee, and with her ordinary face, which is eyeballing and Scots, and her ordinary gestures, which are straight and finger-pointing.

—That's why you're in. For the driving and the telephoning. The screaming and being carried about is extra.

—What am I driving?

—Whatever Mr. Supaservice gets us. I told him something seriously flash, a disco tank, a white Merc turbo with big wheels and fins or something, something a flash Arab would drive, something they will all remember at two hundred yards, but with room for three people and a full trash bag.

—And it has to be automatic, she reminds me.

—Trust me, I say, and make eyes at her again, and for a moment I almost stagger as I have a kind of vision with feeling, if you can have such a thing, of my hand ironing slowly down her flat stomach and into her black 501s.

Like yesterday.

Suzy the Black Widow not only does the perfect UC accent, she is also the greatest driver we know. Chicho was with her once when they were coming back from Zaragoza with his sister Pilar (who is a big friend of hers) doing 120 (miles, not kilometers) round the périphérique in Paris, which is like the M25 Meets the Wall of Death, she was just burning all the French off while skinning up with one hand start-to-finish. She drives like she is breathing through the carbs too, driving with her is like watching some wise kid belting through the been-there levels of a video game, it is just total control. She has never had any kind of accident in her life, she is the only person in the world who could actually afford to insure a legit white Merc turbo with big wheels because she has such a huge no-claims bonus, except it would have to be automatic, she cannot drive a clutch, she says a clutch is a piece of macho shit, if God wanted us to drive with three pedals She would have given us three feet, better to have two hands on the wheel so you can just point and shoot, says Suzy. Funny how all men who wet-daydream about dick-extension cars are also convinced that these same cars have to have short stubby gear levers for them to play with, it's a kind of giveaway, she says, isn't it?

—Well, I admit.—Actually there is a hitch with the car.

I see they are all thinking the same thing:
yeah yeah yeah
we knew it
there's a hitch
there always is
it was a nice idea but what the hell.

—**W**e need five hundred up front before Mr. Supaservice will even talk serious to us.

And we all look at the table, where we have pooled all the money we can get our hands on.

Suzy starts to count it scottishly, but we already know it is not five hundred. We watch her with impossible hope. When she is halfway through counting, and when we can now see, never mind know, that it is not going to make the cut, Brady hits critical:

—What's wrong with us? What has that fucking thieving black bollix got against us? yells Brady.

—We have no track record, I yell back.—That's the whole bloody point (I carefully avoid getting into the F-word thing again).—That's what I've been trying to explain. Would you all just listen? OK? That is the whole point of the Plan. Look: none of us ever got done for anything, OK, so

(a) we have no connection to the police, right? That means we have a hundred times better chance of getting away with it. And we don't live together, we never did, we're not family or anything so

(b) we are not connected to each other, right? And that means even if it all goes wrong on the day, so long as we stick to our stories whatever they say or do, none of us, on our own, has done anything heavily criminal. That's why it's such a good Plan, right? None of us has to do anything worth anything much until it has all worked out. You (I point at Brady) don't have to do anything except booze with your mates until we're actually going for the getaway, and you'll only get a fine, or three months tops, for smashing the place up and scaring people. Even if they clock on to us and get the three of us inside the bank, so what? If we stick to the story about Suzy's Story they can't do us for anything except me for fiddling the dole and Suzy and Chicho for deception.

—I am stupid Spanish man used by clever Scottish girl, says Chicho.—Is easy for me, and he makes one of those nice big cool mediterranean waves that I can never do, like he is swatting a fly in slow motion.—Nothing.

—Right I say. They couldn't even prove conspiracy. Even if we fuck up.

—Hold on, says Suzy.—You still haven't told us anything really. I mean, what's all this stuff about the police helping to shut us in the bank? Don't you think you'd better tell us?

—I'm not telling you until you believe in the Plan.

—How can we believe the fucking plan if we don't know it? says Brady.

—Is hard for us, says Chicho.

—You have to believe the Plan as the Plan, it's just a set of moves, that's all. C follows B follows A. But we have to get A sorted before we go on to B. Never mind C, I'm not telling you about C until the rest is up and running, when we've got the car sorted and when I've sorted about Fred with Dai's friend Jimmy, then we go on to C and I call Sammy. If I tell you about C now, you'll run a mile. Look, it's like taking a parachute jump or something, you have to learn the drill like clockwork, you have to believe it works like you believe Tuesday follows Monday before some bastard shoves you out the plane, or else you panic and get tangled up and splattered, right?

—Splattered? says Chicho.—What is splattered?

—Budabudabudabuda! says Brady, and he does someone being machine-gunned in one of his films.

—Oh, says Chicho.—Is very bad for us.

—OK, OK, says Suzy, shooting me a funny look like she is giving me a chance, and Chicho and Brady nod too. We now have a more solemn scary atmosphere, which is dead right considering, so I continue, but find myself unnerved by Suzy's eyes.

—Right. Um, shit, where did I get to?

—The bit where we actually come out of the bank, says Suzy, stacking the final notes.—The bit where Brady has to come in. The plastic gun?

—Oh yes. Right, so when Brady sees us coming out, it's a fair bet the police will see us too. Now, they might well still buy it whole, they will be so frazzled by then, they might let us through anyway. But this is the dodgy bit because now we do actually have the money, now it is serious. So what happens as we come out of the bank?

—The Dogs go critical at the Pizza Express, says Brady, and he twirls that plastic gun he hated so much two minutes ago round and round on his big middle finger, and he sings in his big horrible voice:—I love the sound of breaking glass.

—Right. Brilliant. And what does Brady get?

—Public disorder and resisting arrest, says Suzy.

—A couple of hundred quid fine for a quarter million! gloats Brady.

—And why only a little fine? I insist.

—Yeah, yeah, yeah, because it's only a crap plastic gun and any eejit can see that and everyone knows I'm a Doggy anyway and all I did was break a pizzeria window and fire off a few caps and sling a few bottles of Sol around Bow Street.

—Right. Stick to the story and we're OK.

—Hey, but what if they still catch you three in the car? asks Brady, like he has just cleverly spotted a big problem.

—You don't know us and we don't blame you.

—I don't mean just me, he says, all offended.—What if they do stop you and they get you, all together, in the car, with the money?

—Hey, who's driving? says Suzy.

—Is easy for Suzy, says Chicho.

And then we all laugh, that is very good, I was proud of us, and proud of the Plan.

It's funny, I'm not proud of the Plan like it's something that belongs to me, I just love it like it's something perfect, like a little jewel or something, that is all there and is all just how it has to be. I am not proud OF IT, I am just proud and happy it is there. Strange. It seems to have this independent existence now.

—But we've only got four hundred and seventeen quid, says Suzy, and she plops the wad back on the table, and us back to reality.

Sad but true.

Amazing but true!

We just do not have five hundred quid between us! What century is this? But then that's why we are in this anyway: we are trying to save our lives. London is a mincing machine, where people go in one end and money comes out the other, and we are on the wrong end of it, we are going in, in, in.

Except now the great God of Temping has shown me the way.

I am going to save our lives if it kills us.

We are going to crawl out of the mincer, and start living.

There are really only three supertribes in London: the ones who will never be able to get mortgages, the ones who live and die by the mortgage rate, and the ones who do not need mortgages. Those are the ranks of slavery and freedom, the rest is all just questions of degree.

Chicho wants half the restaurant in Zaragoza.

Brady wants a pub in Castlebar, County Mayo.

I want a flat with tall windows and a garden.

These are not visions of some heavenly life on a rocking chair on a veranda, they are not some heap-of-crap chill-out +cop-out fantasies, they are our dreams of starting blocks for a proper crack at living.

Each to his own, say I.

No one knew then what Suzy wanted.

But she was right about one thing: I had to get us another hundred quid right now, while we were still convinced this could happen, it was my Plan, it was down to me to fire us up into escape velocity, or else the whole thing would stay just another big idea, like those great big beer-fed life-saving ideas we had last Saturday night in the pub:

> Brady was going to make a TV series called The Worst Serial Killer in History, about this bloke who really is The Worst, I mean totally crap at it, he never manages to kill anyone at all, he keeps digging pits and filling up acid baths and stuff and always ends up doing people favors by mistake.

> Chicho was going to franchise out Mr. Chorizo stalls all over London, so after a year or two he could go back to Spain and sit around getting even fatter playing cards and hire someone else to just cruise around London collecting his money for him once a month. He suggested me, the bastard.

> I was going to learn to teach English and make £25,000 a year in Saudi for four years and then buy a flat in Sheps Bush and be an Expert on Middle Eastern Affairs. I thought maybe I would go Islamic so as to up my profile. It's just like being a Presbyterian really, except for the clothes.

> I didn't then know what Suzy was planning last Saturday.

And naturally, all that happened was we all woke up on Sunday in our beds and just read the papers and looked at pictures and plugs for rich+famous people.

But this week I had been shown the Way.

I was going to make this story real.

The first thing to do is the first thing.

How do you get to Moscow?

By going to Moscow.

So I nodded to Suzy and we upped and left Chicho and Brady sitting like two big owls on my bed, in my shed.

More about the shed later.

As we walked down the garden and through the back gate I flipped her my little bottle of acetone and my little tin of matte varnish and my little paintbrush.

More about them in a minute.

She stashed them without asking. Nice.

And off we went to liberate some hard currency.

More about this now.

2

A
BALD MAN
IN A WALK-UP

It was Saturday night, about 9:45, close orange sky and damp warmish streets. London was on the move, regrouping its molecules for night running, morphing itself along the neural paths of seven million phone books and filofaxes; a hundred thousand tribes, each with its own territory, rules, traditions, leaders, heroes, enemies and court jesters, gathering themselves in cars, buses, taxis and tubes. The whole world had finished working and shopping and eating, the early-evening films were emptying out, everyone was just waiting to party, raring to kick it into gear and keep it running late, this is what the city lived for and worked for Monday to Friday, nine to five, this long night that would go on until the week was buried and Sunday half dead.

This was the time to be out.

As Suzy and me came out of the back gate, we could already scent it in the wet air, a million people in the mood, an ocean of dried-out souls shifting with the pull of man-made moonlight, wailing for lasers and music and booze and drugs and sex, for just one moment that might feel like time had crashed, scanning the night for that secret alleyway we have never found but only seen in dreams, where the neon flickers and the stairs lead down and the doorman winks and the faraway beat says:

here it is
here it is
this is the land where ads come true
this is the door to the big world.

We headed due east up west in Suzy's horrible old automatic mini, she went twice round the roundabout between Sheps Bush and Holland Park, accelerating all the time, just to show what she meant by that stuff about having two hands on the wheel.

—Don't worry, these minis stick like glue, she said.

—Good, I said with my ear braced against the roof.

—And it's safe anyway, it's got a crumple zone.

—A crumple zone in a mini? Where?

—From the headlights to the back bumper.

—Nice.

Logically, we should have been pretty depressed. I mean, how sad can you get: we were about to risk totally fucking up our lives, forever, for about the take-home pay of a bus driver. This might have been a rational calculation if our lives were fucked up anyway, say we were junkies or UnderClass or whatever, trained to think of a criminal record as just another subheading in the average CV.

But we were not UnderC, or even Working Class. We were Lower Middle Class. We both went to college and got degrees, for Christ's sake. Our parents are nice decent people who have always been in work to pay off their mortgages all their lives, and not one abuser amongst them.

I once got this old hippie to hypnotize me to see if I had any Hidden Memory Syndrome that might explain why I am such a waster and would rather have my legs sawn off than do a steady job, I was sort of hoping I had been traumatized, so I would have someone to blame. It turned out I did have loads of forgotten memories, who hasn't for Christ's sake? except they were all good ones, they were all about teddy bears and Christmas and stuff: my mind was an abuse-free zone.

That's the trouble, if you have a nice LMC childhood, you hit your twenties still believing the world is really made of sugar and sunshine.

As we passed Notting Hill Gate, I banished teddy bears and sunshine from my mind, to harden myself up. I was at work, for Christ's sake, this was no time for weakness. I checked that I was dressed for work: I had swapped the normal Gap T-shirt and blue 501s for the old Oxfam tweed and the green cords and the Every Englishman check shirt from Marks&Spencer via Oxfam.

Suzy double-parked by Liberty, and I went into that pub by Oxford Street station and got two pints, like I was waiting for someone, and squeezed in between a bunch of lads in nice shirts and ties who were having a good time on G&Ts. I said:

—Just waiting for someone. I hope you don't mind? Golly, it's packed, isn't it? I said this so they would think I was some boringly unquiet person who might try to collar them, so they would ignore everything I did even more.

They had their jackets off on the bench behind them, they were having some loud+silly argument about why the Roman Empire collapsed, was it to do with slavery, barbarians, fate, chance or unsound financial institutions? They were laughing a lot and doing TV voices, it sounded like a good conversation, actually, not entirely unlike the kind of thing I used to get pissed talking about with my friends at college.

But I was here on business, so I took off my jacket too, and drank some of my pint and looked at my watch like I was annoyed at someone for being late and patted all my pockets for cigarettes which were not there and then rootled about in my jacket for them and let my hand slide under my jacket and lo and behold! I also got a checkbook and a card from the jacket underneath, which I at first just let slip under my jacket, not into its pocket, in case anyone had seen me, so no one could say I had put it in my pocket; it is vital (like in the Plan) to always keep open that little possibility that it was all an accident, to unnerve any accuser, since no accuser can ever be 100% sure. Then I just sat there for a couple of minutes smoking and thinking.

I looked at this gang of lads who had been to Colleges and were now having a good time with their suits off, and I had a serious bout of the horrors that said: How the hell did I end up like this, nicking wallets in pubs? How did the dream, the Middle-Class dream of sugar and sunshine, come to an end?

Really, they should not send people like us to Colleges. It is bullshit, they might as well be honest and make us go to work in banks when we are eighteen, or else only let us into Colleges to do teaching certs or accountancy or stuff like that. Instead, you get three years of the interesting stuff and then they tell you: OK lads and lassies, the good news is: you now have the legal right to wear a fucking stupid hat and gown (to prove you are intelligent).

The bad news is: that's it.

Yes, boys and girls, you have had your free sample of what life is like for the real MC, the taxpayer, for some mad reason, has paid you to read Shakespeare (Suzy) or Wittgenstein or Kafka or A.J.P. Taylor (me), you have studied Mies van der Rohe or Paul Klee or Astrophysics or whatever took your fancy, you have slept about and hitched around and your body clock is locked into the chimes at midnight and the long, slow summers, and now that you have just about realized who you actually are, or might be, you have to go and be an accountant or a schoolteacher or work for P&G developing brave new deodorants.

Fair enough?

What?

Suddenly, the brief yoof-socialist near-equality of College is gone: the nice guy who had the crappy old funny GTi is off to see America, the nice girl who subbed your drug experiments has gone to Mum's Spare Flat in South Ken to look up some pals in publishing, and little you are left high and dry, wilting towards teacher-training, accountancy, or the dole office.

Mum, Dad!

The Imperfectly Launched Young Adults swarm home for more money.

Except Mum and Dad have no money.

Meltdown.

It turns out that Mum and Dad have been spending nearly every penny they earn to keep the things you thought were just kind of quietly supplied at night by the nice folks at Central MC Stores. It turns out that being LMC (and not proper MC like you kind of half-thought you were) is a lifelong fight with money, and on a still night you can hear the ground slipping. There is just never quite enough money to forget about money, you can never quite look at Life's Great Menu without your eyes drifting towards the Special Offer Set Dinner, there is always the ghost of some Final Demand in the corner of your eye. You just never quite make daylight.

And so when you come out of College with your student debt gift-wrapped in a big-deal fake parchment certificate, expecting to start where Mum+Dad left off, you find Mum+Dad never actually left off, they are still fighting money day and night. There might be a little help with a little deposit on a little flat coming your way, but that is it, that is all there is, it cannot be risked because it cannot be replaced, it will not be dished out until the deeds to the Starter Unit are on the table. The long vacation of extended adolescence is gone, it is time for YOU to take over on the MC ladder, and you stagger and hear Rutger Hauer's voice saying:

Time to Work.

It hurts, it hits home, but shit, OK, OK, so we'll work, we're not too proud to work, we want to work, we want to make a mark, we'll take anything, absolutely anything, hear me, that pays about £14,000 a year to start with and lets us do something, just anything, that does not sandpaper our twenties away.

Is that too much to ask of the twentieth century?

Is Hell centrally heated?

And so about two or three years after you leave College, you wake up one Sunday afternoon with zero money in the pocket (Oh Christ! That last, useless round last night!) and old milk on the sink and nothing coming in till next Thursday's unemployment check, and as the evening slinks deadly in you realize that deep down inside you, you were still thinking, somehow, that Life actually comes with a 100% quibble-free money-back guarantee if not fully satisfied, you can't really fuck it up.

Until now.

Now you know it doesn't, and you can.

Vertigo.

The second wave of teachers and accountants ebbs in.

I looked at these blokes and tried to wonder how long they had held out, they must have stuck it out for a bit, everyone does, even if they don't admit it, no one actually plans to be an accountant or whatever, do they? No one is really cut out for suits and nine to five, you just get sliced and diced until you fit. But then, where were the marks? I could see no blood, just clean polycotton and full wallets.

I mean, it's all very well to keep on holding out, but for what? Yes, you can stand up proudly and say:

Fuck this, OK that hurt, but that noise was just my crumple zones going, I will not, not, not work my hair off and dig lines in my face in a bank or a staffroom, I cannot, like I cannot breathe underwater, sorry Mum, sorry Dad, you Never Had It So Good, you had The White Heat and JFK and full employment for Christ's sake, you knew you could change jobs every year and you thought you could change the world in the holidays between. We are the retro-people going nowhere backwards, we are the ironic generation, we can stand back and look down and laugh at it all, like it is all some crapclever ad, but irony is really balls, irony is what you do to stop it hurting before it starts, irony is a pre-emptive strike on living. We have to be ironists because we have nothing to risk hurting for, it is not the hurt we are afraid of, but getting hurt for no reason, we have no big picture of where it is all going and who is flying it by wire and why. So we will sit here, and just veg out for a year or two with our Dogs on Strings and try to get some perspectives, and wait for The Job, the real thing, to come ambling along. What is The Job? We don't know. Something that lets us say Yeah, that's what I do, that's me here, that's me in the spotlight, without having to look down at our drink and tack on Well It's Not So Bad Really, You Know. Just something to make you roll out of bed in the mornings and think, ah, yes, yumyum, off to Do Things again today, not have the alarm dredge you up and dump you down, lost and thinking Oh Fuck, not Work again! Jesus, you are young, the nights go quickly, you can take it, if it doesn't come along for a while, so what? you can just hang out and listen to the clockwork that spins the world and try to work these new maps out so you know which way to turn.

Which all sounds fine and nice and hippyish and cool and everything, except if you are not real MC what it actually means is: you live in scummy walk-ups in shitty barrios full of launderettes and porn newsagents, where the bath is always sprinkled with someone else's pubes and lost expat radio stations crackle in the night.

So I did.

Time flies, the days flip over into years.

I am 28.

28!!!

Somehow, The Job never turned up.

By the time I had got to thinking this I had almost finished the smokescreen fag and I tell you, I had the willies good and proper again, I had a headful of steam up, the blood-thumping certainty that I had to do something radical to save my life. Fear had given me back my wings and my guts.

So I plonked the half-smoked fag in the ashtray and stood up and took my jacket and the checkbook and card underneath it and walked out, with the booty still gathered up among the folds of the jacket, not in the pocket, as a final line of defense, out to the car where Suzy was waiting.

We drove to the corner of South Molton Street, to that Bureau de Change (best to park somewhere you can escape quickly in different directions), where it took ten minutes for me to practice the signature maybe sixty times:

Mr. R.H.A. Perceval

(a nice Upper-Middle-Class signature, it was a pleasure to

write) and to play at convincing myself I WAS Mr. R.H.A. Perceval, and for Suzy to put the matte nail-varnish on that particular row of dates in the calendar on the back of the checkbook and let it dry, like I told her to do. She was interested in that, it was a new one to her. My own patent, actually.

As I practiced that signature, so that I could write it like I really was this man, I was thinking how England is the absolute fucking paradise of class continuity. I mean, here we are, nine hundred years after William the Conqueror and his French-speaking, French-named Vikings came across and took England, and you show me a person with a froggish name, Perceval or Montague or Beaufort or whatever, and I will give you two to one that this person is MC or better. Old Money lasts, that is why everyone crawls to it.

Anyway, when we were ready, we trotted into the Bureau de Change and yes! the poor little permed cow in the office was tired, it was late, she was half relieved we were a nice English couple out clubbing, Mr. R.H.A. Perceval with his tweed jacket and his three initials and his snooty-looking girl in henna and leather jacket and jeans that let you see an inch or three of her noticeably flat tummy, not a bad black robber or some foreign loony with what he claims is a visa card from the Bank of Bosnia-Herzogovina, she didn't bother to make sure that the ballpoint went right through the paper, she just made a little x on the date box, so that meant we could sit in the car and remove the invisible film of nail varnish with acetone nice and carefully, which meant, of course, that the ballpoint ink, being on top of the nail varnish, went too, and hey presto! the date box had no cross on it. The paper was a little bit roughed up, but only if you looked very closely, and we made sure the checkbook was bent around that area to hide it.

We had actually done it together now, we eyed each other with that unholy light in our eyes, we were through the door of the law together and licking our lips now, so now it was no big deal to whiz automatically along to the Bureau de Change by McDonald's at Marble Arch and set another £100 free, and that was that, we would not use that checkbook again, I would give it to Mr. Supaservice as further proof of our honorable intentions, he could sell it on no sweat, it wouldn't get too warm for the organized boys and their desperate men for four or five days. We had what we wanted: £100 for Mr. Supaservice and £100 for fun tonight, and no one hurt except whoever insures Mr. UMC Perceval's bank against their losses, which means no one I care about and I hope no one you care about either, because if you care about that, I warn you fair and square, you will care about a lot more things that are coming a lot worse.

I gave Suzy our whole ton straightaway and she zipped it into the sleeve of her leather, I don't know why I did that, I suppose I was just feeling that way, it seemed the natural thing to do, like I was sure we were going to spend it together.

And she took it without thinking, too.

Nice.

Then she looked at me and said:

—My place or your shed?

You see, I do not live in a skunky walk-up anymore. Not quite. I cannot really complain, and I do not, because:

I have back-up.

That little edge.

To those that have, will be given a breathing space.

I live in a half-shed in my Big Sis's garden.

She is ten years older than me, she left College in the early eighties. This makes her a relic of the good old dispensation, that corporate state that existed from 1945 until about 1982, that conveyor belt for taking the LMC into the MC (the ones who were stitched up were the WC who paid tax but did not use mortgage relief and free universities and arts councils and stuff: they got The Sun instead). Big Sis, the lucky cow, managed to hit the tail end of this LMC Heaven, and so she has a nice house in Sheps Bush and a laughable 13-year-old mortgage.

And I get the shed.

Don't get me wrong, I like it.

I love it, it is a great big shed, tacked on the back wall of her house, I built it with Chicho three years ago, it is 14 by 14 by 9 feet high, raised off the ground on old railway sleepers, with electricity coming through the wall from Big Sis's house proper, it has a double bed on 5-foot-high stilts under which I keep my bentwood rocking chair, my music-generating equipment and a rusty, clonking fridge full of beer and cheese and Chicho's tortilla and stuff to snack at without cooking, it has rockwool insulation (after the first winter, when I froze my balls off), it has curtains and lights, it has pretty blankets hanging on the walls and bookshelves bolted to what used to be the outside wall of the house, and last summer when I had nothing to do and no money for several weeks of long nights, I even carved the gables so it looks like something from an old Russian fairytale.

I use Big Sis's electricity and her bathroom and her washing machine, and give her £30 or so a week if I am working at temping or whatever, and nothing much if I am not. I am part of the household when I want to be, and free when I do not, I am shaved, washed, civilized, and do not pay £50 a week to live in a shit-ridden walk-up in East Acton or somewhere.

This gives me a relatively high disposable income.

To go with my disposable life?

Bob (Big Sis's husband) does not mind about me living in a shed in their garden because soon after I moved in, I caught a 17-year-old burglar who was (understandably) not expecting someone to pounce on him from behind out of a shed in the middle of the night as he jemmied open the window, and I beat the shit out of him, thus saving Bob's Bang&Olufsen tower of speakers, before I realized he was only half my size and he was holding a glorified nail file to get in windows, not a knife to stick me with. He should have dropped it, but he wouldn't, I think now he didn't understand what I was yelling, I was scared too, I could see this thing glinting in his hand, I had him round the face, it had got hard-core physical already, I was screaming dropthefuckinknifeyascumbag and stuff like that, I didn't dare stop hitting him now until he suddenly gave up and went all limp and dropped it. I half tore his top lip off, I sometimes think about that at night, I can still see the skin at the corner of his lip, tearing in the light from a window over the way, and the blood squeezing out and over my hand, I am very sorry about that, I let him run away then, he even said thanks in this little voice as I kicked him back over the wall, and now I wish it had never happened.

However, it means that Bob now sees me as some Ultimate Deterrent.

Bob is a pinky-scrubbed sort of person from a real proper MC background with family trusts and stuff, he is a liberal lefty barrister, I think his political awakening came whenever it was he discovered that not everyone is allowed to drive a Volvo and browse the snack counters at Waitrose, as far as Young Bob was concerned this was a cosmic injustice, an unnatural evil, ever since then he has been a bold warrior for MC Heaven. At his dinner parties, I serve to illustrate (a) the Housing Crisis and (b) his generosity to his wife's sad family. I go along if the dinner smells very good, which it often does, because Bob is a prime-time cooking fetishist, in summer he just plucks bay leaves and basil leaves from terracotta-potted plants on his balcony and pops them straight in, and also because I like hearing his Story.

He only has one real Story, but I can hear it again and again, I mean, who cares if it's new or not, is Hamlet new? Bob's story goes like this:

After the Miners' Strike, Bob was defending a miner who had been charged with throwing a brick at the police, and denied it. Now, the police at that time had just invented those giant-sized modern riot shields we now take as normal, and the policeman concerned had been (they said) hit by this particular brick on the knee. Bob had one of these new shields brought in and he got the copper to stand there with it and he held a brick in his hand and asked how the hell the copper thought anyone could hit him on the knee with a brick when the shield came down to his ankles. The cop makes no reply, he has not been briefed for this, there is nothing in his notebook to read about this. So Bob holds this brick up and says:

—Well, I suppose it could have bounced?

—Yes, says the copper, quickly, that's it.

Bob drops the brick on the floor. It doesn't bounce. The magistrates shift their buttocks and look at their fingernails, the copper keeps looking at the brick, going very red, and quick as a flash Bob brings out a half-brick and says:

—Maybe it was more like this one?

—Yes, that's it! says the copper.

Bob drops the half-brick. It doesn't bounce either. Case unwillingly dismissed.

Apart from the great food and this story, the other reason I like Bob's dinners is every now and then a nice MC girl will assume that because I live in an eccentric shed and am (after all) Bob's wife's brother, and am always very nice to my nephews (4 and 6) who love having me in the shed, I must really be some kind of disguised MC person on extended holiday, just waiting to reveal my private income when the right girl comes along, and sweep her off to a life of insured artiness in Islington.

I would if I could.

I am the world's perfect Uncle, and I am only 28.

Some weeks ago, Bob was preoccupied at dinner until suddenly he said, out of the blue and a little bit too quickly, that he thought maybe the boys would enjoy having the shed as a gang hut when Jamie was maybe 9. Or 10, he said straight away, and went all red and immediately gave me more wine and was very very especially nice to me all evening.

Aha.

And guess what else? In three months I will be 29.

2Fucking9.

And we all know what comes after that.

I am nearing my sell-by date.

The months are starting to run by in time lapse, the sun flits across my Life On Earth in quick, short arcs.

I do not think I want to be (deep breath) 30 very much.

I do not want to be 30-very-much in a shed.

Or kicked out of one.

And still temping?

Maybe I was only ever short-listed for happiness.

Sometimes, recently, I have started to wander the streets in the evenings, in the rain, and look up at the lights in the windows of the little houses, and I could axe-murder these people just for their Chinese lampshades and their nice IKEA bookshelves and spider-plants.

I hate this in me.

I hate the way I have started to worry about how I am never going to be MC, and about money, and getting old. I never used to, I swear to God, I used to fuck and swill unthinkingly with whoever, I did not know who they were or how rich they were or how old they were, it never even occurred to me.

Maybe I was blind before?

Maybe I am getting twisted now?

I do not know, I do not know.

I suppose you are never worried about anything until you think you might be losing it.

I am in danger of losing my shed.

I am cruising towards losing my twenties.

I am starting to lose my hair for Christ's sake.

That is the worst, the hair. That is the first whistle of the scythe. You can work off a beer pot or iguana tits or love handles (I have just started to realize that I too might one day get them, I honestly never thought I could. Who does?) but you cannot work off a baldy head, you can only blow it off.

Across the other side of the garden wall, I can see the back windows of the houses in the next street. In one of them sits a bald man in a walk-up, his curtains are always open and you can watch him making model planes all evening long.

Sometimes he kind of slows up and gradually stops, then sits for a minute or two staring ahead, then gets up and whips his curtains shut (they are orange curtains, of course, I think there must be a secret by-law everywhere that says all walk-ups have to have orange curtains) and then ten minutes later he opens them again slowly and sits calmly down again to his glue and plastic bits. I assume these intervals are the physical wank breaks from his mental wanking, or maybe he is just banging his head on the wall in despair. Or both.

I have started to watch him like it is some horrible mirror into a possible future.

I have no intention of ending up like him.

But then, nor did he.

Watching him, I know the meaning of fear and the power of certainty: nothing could be worse than that, going to prison could not be worse than that.

Being an accountant could not be worse than that.

Up till now, I have been able to resist the great end-of-millennium equation (dwindling hope+looming fear = accountancy) by making sure I walk past Charing Cross in the rush hour once a week, to look at the accountants crowded in front of the Departures Board, staring up madly like peasants in front of an icon, waiting to be told they can go at last to wherever it is they do not really want to go.

But I know I am weakening.

I read an ad for Trainee Accountants last week, twice.

No, no, no.

If I become an accountant now it means I should have become one six years ago.

I cannot cop out now.

I have to rob Michael Winner's bank and save my life.

Which is why I am (now, to get us back up to speed) sitting with Suzy in her horrible mini deciding where to go next.

—**W**e've got to go and see Mr. Supaservice, I said.

—Roger, she said.

—No, Mr. Supaservice, I said.

—Ha Ha, she said.

I watched her as she stuck the shift into D and the engine lurched into rough contact with the wheels.

—We must be fucked up, I said, as we pulled away from the Bureau de Change, nice and calm around the big swing of the road.—I mean, we don't have to do this, this is ridiculous. We could still do the rational thing, you know, we could, say, get some vocational training maybe, we could still start proper careers even now.

—Yep, says she, easing us round Marble Arch, slowly accelerating all the time, both hands on the wheel.—We could. Is easy for us.

—We could have Critical Illness Benefit and Employment Protected Endowment Mortgages and PEPs and 401Ks.

—Dead right, says Suzy (for a moment we are stuck behind a night bus at Queensway).

—I just mean, you know, we aren't totally fucked up yet, look, say we had kids.

—You what?

—I mean just say. We could still just about give them a normal childhood. An idyll, like it should be. Bears and Christmas and stuff, LMC heaven.

—What the fuck are you on about?

—I just mean, we could still be accountants or something, if we bought suits and lied at interviews.

—Yep, you're right, we could still do it.

—We could. That's all I'm saying.

—OK.

—OK what?

—OK if this doesn't work we both become wee accountants. She looks round.—I mean it.

—Oh, I say.

—We are going to Last Chance City, OK?

—Sounds tough.

—It's the only place to live, she says.

And she whipped out past the bus and gave it the boot and even the traffic lights seemed to be shouting out Way To Go, because I swear to God once we hit fifty-five we never dropped under again all the way home, even in a horrible old automatic mini, it felt like warp factor 139 or something, the whole car was definitely going to fly apart, and the lights just went

RedandYellowandGreen

RedandYellowandGreen

RedandYellowandGreen

ahead of us, right down the Bayswater Road and through Notting Hill and Holland Park and round Sheps Bush Green, like we were turning them on just by wanting it to happen, and we had this kind of psycho-samba latino stuff pumping out top volume, people looked around when we went by because of the music and also because of the way a horrible old automatic mini doing fifty-five sounds like Thunderbird 1 on coke, and if you never did it you will not understand why it is that joyriders just go for it when they see the blue lights behind them, even knowing they are bound to get caught or mashed up or something. We would have done it, I tell you, colleges and all, we were just high on those 100% pure, all-natural, freshly-squeezed organic uppers that only your own brain can make, chemicals that make anything that comes in tabs or powder just fade, fade away; magic which we had called up out of ourselves by cutting out the bullshit and grabbing what we wanted out of the bright windows, just like that.

I looked over at Suzy driving and I wanted to stop and fuck right there, in the mini, because she looked so good and so hot, and she could see the way I was looking at her and she was grinning just like me, and I thought: when they invented Life, this was what they meant. I did not care if we crashed+burned right then, but I wanted us to live forever.

One hour later it was all getting out of control.

3

ARMPITS
AND
SUCHLIKE

One hour later we were talking about what we were going to do with the money and Suzy said she was thinking about going to India and, you know, sorting her life out, changing herself, you know, and I thought Oh Christ it was too good to be true and I said, maybe a little snappier than the occasion warranted:

—Oh yeah really?

—Yeah, she said.—And I'll come back just the same except forty pounds lighter and talking shit.

Which is when I started laughing.

Back to this in a minute.

But before that, we dropped Mr. Supaservice off his five tons, and the checkbook+card on top, thus impressing him with our business ability and goodwill, and he looked at us and said:

—Well well well well well.

—Ye of little faith, I said.

—That's me, little brother. But hey, I touch and now I be-lieve. So what do you want?

—An automatic GTi or something, I said.

—You don't get automatic GTis, said Suzy.

—The Spiderwoman is right.

—What was that you said? she asked me.—A white Merc with fins?

—Hey, that's nice, said Mr. Supaservice.—That's good. The lady has taste. I think I heard tell of one or two up in Southall, the guys that own the all-night stores like Mercs with fins, and these Asian guys, they like automatics, they think it makes Ealing Broadway feel more like New York Broadway. If I find one, little Miss Bad Black Widow, you got it. Supaservice will take the heat off it nicely for you, it will not even warm your eight little hands. But it isn't cheap. A white Merc with fins? Automatic too? You better hear the price first.

He told us fifteen grand, and I told him right out we would give him fifty-two fifty, but only after the job, like I really ex-pected him to agree straight away. I liked the sound of fifty-two fifty, it sounded really worked out. He did not like that at all, I knew he wouldn't.

—You trying to bullshit me, Mr. Milkybar? You think I get

the cars for free? Shit, I thought you were kosher. I got to pay Cash on Delivery, boy, and so do you.

—Come on, Supa S., I am talking venture capital here. Do you want to be just another high-street car dealer? Look, we have no capital, we need the goods, we have to offer way above market price, and who takes the risk? You? No. You are the middleman, you are in the saddle, you pass on your risks to your suppliers, see? You tell your man it's a new deal, he gets you a Merc, he gets nothing today, he gets double money or nothing on Wednesday, your man needs the money or he wouldn't be nicking cars for a living, so what does he say? He says yo baby yo baby yo yo yo.

—You have a business head, Mr. John Denver.

—We are Thatcher's children, Mr. S. It's up to you. You take a risk with us or else get out and get a kosher dealership and a little sign and take your twenty per cent, you can call yourself Mr. Safe Secure Mercedes Mart, how about that?

—Yeah yeah yeah, says he, like he's walking away, but I know that one kind of got to him.

—If we fuck up on the job, you get the car back Tuesday afternoon, no hotter than when we got it, and you've got the five ton for one day's hire.

—So how come?

—It's all in my Plan, Supa S., we have fail-safe abort mechanisms right up until the loot is in the boot. I can't tell you more, need-to-know, know what I mean?

—I aren't saying you aren't a clever man, Mr. Milkshake.

—Too clever to try to snitch you up, Supa S.

—You got to risk a little to make a lot, says Suzy.

—You call that a little, Miss Spiderbite?

—Sixty, after the job, I say.

—And automatic? I suppose you want to specify the in-car entertainment system too just while we are at it? I suppose you want an autochanger and everything?

—Do we look like we're playing games? says Suzy.

—You look great, Miss Moneyspider, says Mr. Supaservice, with a big gleam.

—You too, says Suzy, but if you can't do it, fuck you anyway. So give us back the money and the book and the visa card. Come on, she says to me.—I'll go shopping for gold tomorrow and we'll find a freelance down the House of Pies to supply us.

What instinct!

What negotiating skills!

What bluff at the very moment of Closing!

It was like Suzy had been reading Strike Out! Selling or watching gypsies deal for horses in Wanstead, which comes to the same thing. I mean, how did she know that the word freelance is what pisses Supaservice off most?

It is, because he likes to think he runs the car scene in this neighborhood, he is proud he gets a cut of everything, he hates the fast new crackhead yoof that hang around the House of Pies and don't give a fuck and don't cut no one in for nothing never nohow. He has his business to defend against these lean+hungry competitors with no overheads.

Mr. Supaservice has overheads. He needs big cash flow, because like any struggling MC, Mr. Supaservice lives very nearly above his station.

He has to pay the school fees for his many sons, and for the spoiling of his many daughters.

Mr. Supaservice is actually called Maurice, he is a big tall thinnish muscly black man, about 40 I suppose, and he knows that if he sends his sons to the ordinary school in Latimer Road they will get in with the street life and start doing bad things when they are 13 or 14, to look hard and because it's fun. And because they are not MC and black, these silly little crimes of credibility will not be treated like schoolboy pranks, the Supaservice sons will get kicked in or fitted up in Shepherd's Bush Police Station and then they will be on the conveyor belt, into the mincing machine. So he sends each of his sons in turn, between the danger ages of 12 and 16, to some dotheboys boarding school in Hampshire, where he has to pay thousands of pounds a term, which he makes by renting out council houses and pimping and hot wheels and stuff. At 16 they come out with GEDs, and the worst of the acne-time testosterone rage has been spent on the teachers, who are paid to take it. Supaservice has about ten sons by about four women, I think, sometimes I am really jealous of that. He has to support the women too. As for his many daughters, he believes that so long as you make sure a girl thinks she is the bees knees she will never sell herself cheap in any way, so he just lets them stay at their various homes and spoils them completely rotten with clothes and jewels and stuff and on their birthdays he borrows a real Yank limo, a six-wheeler with a TV aerial on the boot like a boomerang on a stalk and black windows, it belongs to some big car-dealer friend of his, and he picks them up and drives around the Bush a bit so as all their friends can see them, and then takes them to some big-noise black club in Brixton, where he has a table and champagne ready waiting, so they will never look at some bad-news street boy. All the local 10-year-olds are desperate to get in with his 10-year-olds because their dads are desperate to get in with him, so his kids have a great time because of him, and they know why they are having such a good time, other kids have to blush when dad comes by, but not the Supaservice kids, and so they all love him. Until very recently, he was the number one role model man in the neighborhood. Now he feels a little bit threatened, he is establishment, that is partly why he likes me, I think, he kind of despises me because I am a waster, I know, but he also likes to buy me a drink or just come over and say hello (which is great for my cred), partly because he likes condescending gently to a college boy, partly because he gets free legal advice from Bob, whom he calls Consiggleeairy, which Bob hates, and also partly because once someone said he was Just A Fucking Tory, and he got quite upset until I told the other man No, Supa S. is just into the Free Market and the Free Market is great, the only problem is we haven't got it, we have got Capitalism instead. Supaservice liked that one, it kind of got him off the hook.

(His hobby is bouncing out from behind or under cars when his MC liberal media white neighbors from the BBC go by, so they have heart attacks before they realize it's Mr. Supaservice, from whom they buy cheap cars and about whom they tell their friends in wine bars, and then he wags his finger at them and accuses them of being racists who subconsciously think every nigger is a mugger, and laughs ha ha.)

So he looked at the money and the checkbook with all its nice checks and its nice visa card that he was getting just as a sweetener, and he said, shit, he had known us for years, if we had no record we must be cute (it never occurred to him we just never did anything much) and he said seventy-five and Suzy said sixty again, very scottishly indeed, before I could say sixty-five and he said OK and we two shook on it, I felt kind of stupid doing the shaking because it was Suzy that swung the deal, but he didn't offer her his hand. I don't mean he didn't want to shake with her for any bad reason, he just didn't think about it, she was a girl. I was The Man. Suzy just shook her head and laughed to herself, I knew she was thinking the same.

(Once I was helping Chicho's sister Pilar buy a horrible old Fiat from this old Spanish guy in Acton who spoke no English but would never deal with a woman because he could just not get his peasant head round that. I speak no Spanish, so the conversation went something like this:

ME TO OLD MIGUEL: Pili here might want to buy that horrible old Fiat you've got out the back.
OLD MIGUEL TO PILI: What's he say?
PILI TO OLD MIGUEL: He says I might want your Fiat.
OLD MIGUEL TO ME: It's a lovely runner.
ME TO PILI: What's he say?
PILI TO ME: He says it's a lovely runner.
ME TO PILI: How much do you want to pay for it?
OLD MIGUEL TO PILI: What's he say?
PILI TO OLD MIGUEL: He's asking me how much I want to pay.
PILI TO ME: Tell him four-fifty.
ME TO OLD MIGUEL: She'll give you four-fifty for it.
OLD MIGUEL TO PILI: What's he say?
PILI TO OLD MIGUEL: He says I'll give you four-fifty.
OLD MIGUEL TO ME: Why do you allow this insane woman to mock my declining years?

ME TO PILI: What's he say?
And so on.)

And so anyway, one hour later, after we had done our business with Mr. Supaservice and called Brady and Chicho to tell them it was on and to meet us at the shed in two hours for the big news about the real Plan (OK OK, it's coming, I promise), I was telling this story to Suzy as we were sitting at a big table looking out over Bush Green, with half a reddish Szechuan Feast dead and growing sticky in front of us.

During the meal she had slipped off her shoes and played with my dick under the table with her bare foot, she could stick her leg straight out like that for as long as she wanted, that was because she had done Ballet for some years, which was also partly to do with her flat tummy. So I slipped off my shoes and tried to tickle that nice seam of her jeans between her legs, but it didn't really work because my feet were too big and stupid for that and anyway I still had my socks on which felt kind of silly and English and my thigh was killing me after about twenty seconds of holding my leg up. Try it.

But now we had stopped all that anyway, we were leaning back and looking at each other across the table and just smoking cigarettes and picking bits of prawns out of our teeth with toothpicks and yarning away while we enjoyed the mixed buzz of adrenaline, Tiger beer, chili, monosodium glutamate, tobacco and sex to come.

Which was when she said that stuff about going to India and coming back forty pounds lighter and talking shit.

Now she had me laughing out loud too.

You know that head-back, holy-god way of laughing that

opens up your whole throat and always makes you think, with about 2% of your mind, hey, when did I last laugh like this? Like that. So then I thought maybe we were seriously on the same wavelength.

I mean, the thought of Suzy losing forty pounds was crazy. Suzy does not need to lose forty pounds. Or ten pounds. She is five foot seven and it was my educated guess that if she lost forty pounds she would be the best part of halfway to weighing nothing.

My guess was educated by then because we had fucked standing up earlier that day and I frankly doubted whether I could have done all that all the way with someone much more than one hundred twenty pounds, whatever adrenaline was doing to my heart+lungs

Now, I say Fucked advisedly, not just so as to open the F-word stakes again. It is a good old word, and my in-house solicitors (Honesty & Enlightenment, purveyors of Legal Advice to the Relatively Privileged Classes) forbid me to say we Made Love because that is something else.

Fucking on its own does not equal love any more than tenderness on its own does: the world is full of people fucking and people calling each other piggywig and babykitten, and good luck to them all, but they have to remember they could all be doing the same to someone else tomorrow, because all that sort of thing is no one, it is anyone, you can buy T-shirts saying Love You Kittenface and stuff, which proves it, and we should not lie about that. It is not love.

Look, how can I say Making Love? I mean Christ, we hardly knew each other, really, till last night.

I'm taking you back now, to then, to last night. This is not in order to confuse you, it is just to explain, so you know what was when and we know where we stand. OK then:

Last night. Friday Night, this is:

OK so I had met Suzy, of course, with Chicho's sister Pilar, which was how I knew she could do different accents to make people laugh, I suppose I had bumped into her here and there about three or four times since Pilar and I split up, I knew how she was called The Black Widow because she always wore black, head to toe, and because when she tried out being a junkie for a couple of months, two half-pushers/half-junkies both ended up killing themselves rather than go on living without being able to fuck her or be called junky-wunky by her or whatever it was they wanted her to do that she wouldn't. They thought they were in love with her, I suppose.

That kind of thing can get a girl a name, and it had.

And I knew about her driving, of course.

But first I had to check out if she was really off smack, because you can never really trust a junkie because one-third of their brain is thinking about scoring, whatever else they are doing. They are nearly as bad as winos.

So anyway, we met in Filthy MacNasty's Whisky Joint, and first we had to get our social orientation going, which meant we had to talk about the common link between us, which was (like I said) Chicho's sister Pilar.

—Pili was really bad for a bit, when you two broke up.

—Yeah, I know. I was really sorry.

—So why did you do it?

—Jesus, I don't know, you know, every time she mentioned Where Was This Thing Going and stuff, I knew she was talking marriage, that was what she meant, and I told her how could I get married, I knew she meant kids as well, I live in a fucking shed for Christ's sake, I don't have a job, but when I told her all that she just said OK, OK, like I was actually lying, like I could actually turn round if I Really Loved Her, you know, and say Hey Pili, guess what, surprise surprise I've got this great job and a nice flat, we can get hitched and have rug rats, I was just kidding. You know? So the longer it went on the worse it would have been, that's all.

—Has it ever happened to you, the other way?

—What, me been blown away?

—Yeah.

—Course. About fifty-fifty I suppose.

—Good.

—How about you?

—Oh, well, everyone knows about me, she said all tough.

—The Black Widow, I said.

—Those two evened things up a bit.

—Two dead to even things up? You must have been a long way behind.

—Quite a long way, she said.—But I think I must be just about fifty-fifty too, by now.

—Who was it?

—Someone.

—Someone I know?

—Just someone.

So that was the end of that conversation, Suzy was pondering something two inches below the surface of her beer, and I was thoroughly wobbled by the unexpected heaviness which had descended. So since we had got onto the stuff about her dead junkies, I got us talking about smack to see was she off it.

Which is what really broke the ice.

Ah, Romance!

But seriously, smack is actually a wonderful topic to talk about with someone if you want to know how this person really feels, I mean really feels, about being alive and everything. Smack is not dangerous because it is so addictive, it is not that addictive really, it's dangerous because it is so good at what it is, and what it is, is:

Heaven To Go.

Smack is powdered harps and wings, it is Buddha under the Tree and Siddhartha watching the river run down to the sea, you just squeeze away and the pale warm light fires up the veins in the side of your head at the count of three, it rolls you gently up and backwards, after ten seconds you are back on earth softly, you can talk and drive and work and whatever, the only thing that has gone is the fear and the stress and the horrors. You are you as you knew you were always meant to be. Good? Smack is God's Own Stash, the drug of drugs.

Which is why doctors keep it in their black bags to give you if they find you with your spine ripped out on the highway and the morphine is not strong enough to stop you screaming while you die. Smack is the last of the last things, it is Your Friend Death, that is all.

So if deep inside you, you actually want it all to stop, if you want out, if really and truly your life is just a heavy rucksack, and it feels like your sentence is to carry it as long as you can stand it, if you look at the calendar stretching ahead of you and you can see no signposts, no lights, no tracks, and your first and most honest thought is: God help me, how the fuck am I going to get through all that time, all those long evenings, all those wasted days, all those empty Sunday afternoons, then smack is your only man.

Which makes it a pretty good litmus test, said Suzy.

I agreed.

That was the first important thing we definitely agreed on, and so it was a very big moment for us. I will always be grateful to smack for that.

So then we swapped smack flashbacks:

I told her about how I mainlined it every other day for two weeks (I wasn't sick the first time, that is just bullshit, likewise that crap about tying things round your arm, if you've got decent young veins you just pump your arm a few times and there it is). I stopped after I did a speedball (you know, coke and smack mixed and shot in, the job they say killed River Phoenix, I think it nearly gave me a blowout in the brain too), but it was no big plan, I just stopped because I was out of town doing something else in some smack-free rural placelet, after about a week I had one wild dream, just one, in supertechnicolor digital nicam stereo dolby surround-sound, I dreamed the needle was already in, my thumb was whitening on the syringe, my brain was tuned up and waiting for the fire to roll on in, I woke up shouting and clawing the sheets up because it wasn't real, I wanted to chew the veins out of my arms and suck them down whole like spag bol, but by the morning that was it, it was gone, and it didn't come knocking again because I never called back.

So then Suzy told me how she chased the dragon for nearly a month, every day, and coming off was just like having a heavy flu, except (aha! aha! except!): imagine, if you can, as you can, having the mother of all flus and then someone (—Who? I said.—Just someone, she said) comes along and offers you the stuff that you know will (a) make you stop feeling like sun-dried shit and also will (b) make you feel like you have a Special Relationship with God again in four seconds flat. I mean, come on: imagine if TheraFlu could deliver that! No government health warning would keep people off it.

Suzy said:

—People are so grateful to feel nothing, they think they are having a great time, but it's just relief at feeling nothing.

We agreed that actual junkies are simply fucked-up people who would have done something else if there was no smack. If you think that sounds like shit, bad luck. You try drinking a bottle of vodka every day for two weeks, just a little bottle, just two short weeks, and you will find that your own personalized place on ye olde park bench can be booked a lot quicker than you thought: the offer is always open, and no one checks your credit rating, it just depends if you want it or not. Hard but fair.

I never did crack, nor did she, that is a very young scene and very hard-core what with the bad odds on meeting guns and stuff, I stopped doing anything hard-core a couple of years ago, I only do the odd line or finger-dip of coke when I happen upon it, these days. They say crack is serious stuff. Maybe. Maybe it is serious because it is very good at what it does. I do not know so I will not say. But then, whisky is serious if you want to take enough badly enough, Christ, even swilly old beer can fuck you up eventually, take a look round Sheps Bush at closing time, when they are all trying to stand to patriotic attention for The Soldier's Song and see what the black stuff and the barley can do this side of the law.

(I once heard this Dublin drughead say, at the end of a very long party:—Hey, man, I gotta go score some sleep, ya know?)

Anyway, Suzy was off smack, so that was all right, you can always tell when someone is off it by the way they are into talking about how great it is, people who are not really off it do not dare admit how much they liked it. The only way to treat smack is make it part of your happy past, which is following your determination into your even happier future. If you want to forget it, forget it: you never will.

So we had a great chat, letting our smacky past out to play and sigh for a while in the dark romantic sun, and by the end of that chat I not only knew Suzy was fine to drive for us.

I also knew that I wanted to fuck with her very badly.

I do not know how anyone gets to bed with anyone without fags. They are such handy little gifts! All that delicate potential for bridging silences, confirming tastes, offering and accepting, exchanges, confessions of needs, touchings, longings and ambitions! And fags are now the perfect way to tell who among a gang of people is worth meeting: if you want to filter out the people who believe in Eternal Life Assurance, then smoking is your thing, be it workplace, plane, train or party: it is the surest statistical indicator that whoever it is belongs to the blessed tribe of the slightly fucked up. This is especially true of Americans: if ever you meet an educated Yank who smokes and does not appear to be completely MAF (Mad As Fuck), shift into Friendship-Offering Mode without delay, it is almost sure to be worth it.

So anyway, the fourth time we swapped cigarettes, I couldn't resist asking her if she wanted to get some air.

I could, of course, justify this move in terms of the Plan, because rumor had it that Suzy had another boyfriend who was still alive, some man who was seriously fixated on her and who was said to be something of a MAF knife-man and who (they said) she could never really break off from either, I wondered if this was this Someone she mentioned, so I wanted to see if she was really tied up with this asshole or not, since it sounded like he could be trouble.

I could also say to myself that fuckability or lack of it is the first thing you have to sort out if you are going to work with someone, and the sooner the better.

But that was all bullshit.

The reason was simple: I was worried.

I mean, I had to know if I was crazy.

You know when the deep sonar radar says, alert alert alert, something is on here? And your daylight AWACS says, hey, come on, Mr. Bollockbrain, not again, are you some kind of sex maniac or something, are you really incapable of talking to anyone face to face for ten minutes without thinking about fucking with them?

Well, when that happens, you just have to find out.

So I asked her outside (weird how that phrase means To try and get a kiss or To have a fight, depending) to find out if I was just a normal homo sapiens with functioning socio-sexual radar or a sad, sex-obsessed weirdo. So as to avoid any possible misunderstanding, I asked about the fresh air with a big look in my eye, almost a wink.

—OK, says she, and gets up just like that.

So that was that.

It comes easy or it doesn't come at all.

It hadn't come to me for a while.

It turned out our mouths fitted beautifully.

Disappointing, is it not, to kiss someone and find they have a mouth that is too little or too dry, or lips that are too hard and tight-assed or too floppy and sentimental, or maybe they just don't know how to kiss, maybe they just kind of nip at you annoyingly, or else lick away like some walnut-brained labrador?

Not Suzy.

I was shocked, I had nearly forgotten what good foreplay just kissing can be. I had nearly forgotten what kissing WAS. Except that we were not just kissing long: because quite soon I felt something flat and hard, like a book, shoving on purpose against my jeans-crotch.

Suzy's tummy.

At the time it was something of a surprise, but I know now that she was doing this because she is almost (but not quite) excessively proud of her very hard flat tummy.

This pride is because (she explained later) she has only just got it back. She did a lot of dance training and choreographing when she was at College and afterwards. (Her backside was too big for her to be a proper dancer and her legs were too short and her ankles were too fat, she said. I don't think she was being objective about this, but who is?) Then she stopped for a year, what with trying out being a junkie and everything, and lost her stomach muscles, she said, but in the last three months she had been working away like mad at them, and here they were again.

Now she has got this fabulous tummy back, she can hardly believe that it is actually part of her. She feels it almost like some piece of incredibly horny dressing-up gear that she has saved up to buy and slipped on to hype herself up, she wanted me to know right away that it was there and just how superb it was so she could feel my erection starting up helplessly at the feel of it, so she would then know that I knew that she was excited by this remarkable new piece of herself, and that I would agree it was fabulous and gobsmacking and unbelievably sexy, which would convince her it was, so she would then feel hornier herself, because it was part of her.

Or something like that: one of those things where Cause and Effect just melt together.

I know all this because she told me it all herself, later, when I post-coitally mentioned about her tummy being amazingly flat, which turned out to be the luckiest piece of verbal footwork I ever did.

It really is flat flat. When she lies on her back the line of her goes down from her ribs and along almost dead straight and then just gently curves up where her pubes start.

She was not so proud of her breasts, she does not really get off on them being kissed or licked or squeezed or bitten, in fact, I think she downright does not like it. Strange, I mean, they are perfectly fine.

I did not ask her about this at the time, at the time I thought it was maybe because they are about average size, which is about far too big for being a ballet dancer and maybe she blames them for her not being Barcy D'Arcy D'Avignon or whoever at Covent Garden or maybe she got fed up with men looking at them and not her eyes. Or her stomach.

Much later, I found out all about this.

But honestly, I liked her eyes best of all.

She went to the lav and they were green, she came back and they were blue.

I only just realized it was colored contacts, Jesus, I thought either I was going crazy or else I was drinking with some kind of magical sex goddess, which comes to the same thing.

And (the brain being the biggest sex organ) the best thing about her is that she is just fucked up enough to be interesting.

I love that.

I hate totally fucked-up people because they are boring in bed and out, they are all fixated, and nothing is as boring as fixation, in bed or out: it is like watching some film about some MAF person, once they are actually and definitely MAF they get boring very quickly, a Primal Scream, every Harvey Keitel doing his Primal Whimper, can only raise your hackles for thirty seconds, then it just gets boring, because it says nothing, it cannot say anything you can understand, except maybe goodbye goodbye goodbye.

On the other hand, totally unfucked-up people are also boring. They do not know the meaning of danger, but everything that is exciting is somehow dangerous (not the other way around, by the way). They think that the world is by and large and broadly arranged for their benefit, their ambitions are so modest that they are almost bound to be fulfilled, they can buy bungalows beside dioxin plants and snore the pelmeted sleep of the terminally content.

No, give me people who are slightly fucked up any day, people who are just fucked up enough to show they can see all the crap about, but not so fucked up that they are stuck in it, like rabbits in headlights. Give me real people.

Anyway, talking of real people and real things, Suzy is proud of her arms too, not because they are wonderful arms (though I think they might be, I love the way they are covered in that sort of hair you can only see in a certain light) but because they are entirely free of needle marks, since she never used needles.

She only pointed this out AFTER we had fucked the first time without me saying anything. That was a very important trust thing for her, she said afterwards, and she meant: that I would think her smart and straight enough to know if she was HIV, or likely to be, and tell me, so we could go safe. Actually, I had just never thought about it (sorry, but do you?)

But it WAS weird that SHE didn't ask ME, since I had told her about mainlining. I mean, I knew I was OK because I tested a year or so ago, but how did she know?

It turned out she had heard all about how I had only ever used totally fresh works that I picked up in Europe, where you can just go in and say, Guten Tag, gib mir zwanzig Nadeln 0.3mm bitte (which you can work out for yourself), I snapped them out new from plastic bubbles, myself, every time. Apparently, this was regarded as so bizarre at that time (this being nearly ten years ago, way back before people were educated) that it was still remembered, like I was some kind of evil bastard who had known more than other people but had said nothing. Actually, I had just done it because of hepatitis and general sanity. The junkies that squatted those abandoned, asbestos-infested flats over the Westway because what the hell did they care about asbestosis, had laughed at me and called me Mr. Clean and John Denver. They would say stuff like:

—Fuck off John-boy, if you don't need it bad enough to share works you don't need it bad enough, Mr. fucking Clean, take it or leave it, and they would shove this shared needle over, with blood in it and the end lying in the spoon. I swear to God, it was like they were actually proud of being hard-core junkies or something, like they were in some big club that just had to be good because the membership was so expensive. And I would make to go and then they would sell it to me anyway, even though they hated me, like I knew they would, they hated me even more because I would never buy anything unless I saw them cooking up from the same bag themselves first. They hated this, they were used to people who were desperate, they could not handle someone who they knew could walk away, and they would have sold me something bad if they could, just to fuck me up. Once or twice I really thought maybe they hated me so much they would actually grab me and try to force me to use one of these shit-filled needles, so I always carried a big carving knife when I went to score, and made sure they could see the handle.

These junkies were like Daily Mail readers dying of mortgage repayments, who hate gypsies because the bastards keep reminding them that you don't actually NEED to crucify yourself like that.

And now they are mostly dead, and I have (as I now discovered) this weird reputation among the few dying survivors, that I am some heartless scumbag, like I should be dead too.

What did I tell you?

I have no marks on my arms either, now.

So Suzy and I compared our faultless arms, and exulted in our survival, in our own not wanting to die, in our own smackless pleasure in being just alive.

As far as pleasure goes, I could tell you about her legs, which (the dance training again, I suppose) are like a small footballer's legs except not hairy and not shaved either, but covered in the same hair as her arms, except a bit longer, a soft, light-brown hair you can only really feel when you stroke it up the wrong way, or with your cheek. She has that on her upper lip too. I think it is great. She has hairy armpits too, which I likewise like.

If you like hairy armpits, go to Germany.

If you don't, don't, and stop listening quick.

I don't mean there are lots of hairy armpits to come, this is not a hair-raising tale of armpit fixation, but the thing is that there are lots of things to come which kind of go together with liking hairy armpits, in a way, as you may already have guessed.

My best (actually, my only) Armpit Story is about when I was taking American 18-year-olds around Europe. What a scam! The whole of Europe lying in wait, slavering to rip them off, you would not believe the ways there are to make money out of American 18-year-olds if you work hand-in-Euroglove with glass blowers in Venice and diamond cutters in Amsterdam and watch men in Lucerne and gondoliers in Venice and Bateau-Mouche guys in Paris and all the other hucksters and hustlers of the Olde World! Christ, even their own teachers are on commission. Anyway, this one girl, she was kind of a cheerleader type, one of those seriously weird, David Lynchy, American phenomena: they train their young girls to dress and dance as pros like it is just some fresh-smile social skill, nothing to do with sex. I got several beers out of businessmen in the Hofbrauhaus in Munich in return for not stopping her doing her ra-ra dancing and rotating her ass in front of their zoom lenses to The Chicken Song, I tried to cool her down at first, but the Yank teachers thought I was crazy, Why was I being a party pooper? Was this the cheerful+enthusiastic service they had been promised? So I gave up and took the beers from the businessmen. Anyway, this cheerleaderette developed a drop-dead 18-year-old crush on me, just because I was The All-Powerful Tour Guide and 26 and looked like John Denver. This was most inconvenient, since I was at that time into making vats of dollars out of helping various Europeans rip off her and her friends (we were talking Daddy's Gold Card here) and while in principle I would have been keen enough to fuck her, I really do not feel comfortable with the idea of fucking someone I am rip-ping off financially, sorry, I just don't, and at that time I needed the money more than the fucking, so I showed her and her girl-friends a picture of my then girlfriend, Kattrin, who was Polish and very dark, and they all said:

—Aw gee, she's sooooo beautiful, and made those Can-I-Join-The-Harem? eyes that young girls often make when they start to think about fucking, and I said:

—Yep, girls, ho ho, she suuuurely is purty, and do you know the best thing about her? She doesn't shave her armpits, I looove that!

After that they looked at me like I was The Thing From Planet Gross, so that was OK, I could rip them off with a clear conscience. When I came back, Kattrin the Pole and I fucked on a bed entirely covered in dollar bills, which was fun for me and, I recall, nearly drove her crazy with lust: a couple of thousand dollars in one-dollar bills just looks like so much more than it really is, it looks like all the money in the world, especially if you are Polish, I suppose. Our foreplay was her counting them out in the pub, one by one, and then she led me home by my dick and we laid the greenbacks carefully and slowly on my bed-on-stilts in my shed, like tarot cards, and fucked ourselves stupid on a shrine to George Washington's face, an altar of the pursuit of happiness. When I woke up she had taken exactly half of the bills (strange but true) and was gone. She left a note saying she could not stand my shed any more, it reminded her of Poland too much. I sometimes miss Kattrin the Pole because she was even more unique than most people, she had this amazing patch on her back that was just like a monkey's skin, or a coconut mat, a sort of dark birthmark, as big as my hand, covered in short hard black animal hair, she used to scare people shitless, she would unstrap one shoulder in the pub and say go on, stroke it, and these guys would say, Can I really, are you sure, wow, amazing, never seen anything like it, and she would say Sure, go on, it feels nice, and then when some eejit plucked up the courage to actually touch it she would suddenly jump up in the air and scream like a wild chimp. Brilliant.

Anyway, all this worshiping armpits and eyes and stuff is water off a duck's back to Suzy, she knows the easy secrets of making any man die of lust at thirty paces.

—All you need is leather, henna, SOTs . ...

—SOTs?

—Strap-On Tits. A wonderbra to you.

—Oh, right. And?

—And a snot-nosed look like you have voting shares in the world.

—Nice.

No, all Suzy desires from her man is that he worship her flat tummy.

So what the hell.

So outside the pub she made sure I liked her flat tummy against my dick through my jeans before she knew how to spell my name. I knew she had short hard pubic hairs before I knew her address. And this alarming suddenness, this entire lack of consideration for our common Individuality, for that fantasy of individual Soul and Salvation which is the basis of Western Civilization, did not (surprise surprise surprise) stop her being wet in about thirty seconds, I could smell her (I warned you, when we were talking about armpits), and it did not stop me suddenly having to take my hand away from where I was stroking her cunt bone through her jeans and think:

—No please, I do not believe this, I absolutely, Jesus, AB-SOLUTELY refuse to come in my jeans after all these years! Oh fuck, why do I wear trousers that trap your half-erect dick down the inside of your thigh, and rub dangerously? Answers on a postcard please, the correct answer being:

I do not know how much longer I will be able to get away with wearing 32-inch-waisted 501s before I become quite clearly MDL (Mutton Dressed as Lamb). So I am bloody well going to wear them while I can.

I can still close my top button without it knifing into my belly, I can sit without my balls imploding. I have a year or so of quality Levi time left, I can break the 30 barrier and survive, I am sure of it. Of course, all other MDLs think the same. But I am sure I am different. Of course. Anyway, fuck it, I think I can still get away with it, I am not REALLY balding yet and anyway, OK, hey, if we want to get down to it, did you ever see a tummy as flat as Suzy's? No you did not. Did you ever see someone drive better or drive a bargain better or make better jokes or be straighter or more perfectly balanced on the eternal tightrope of slight fucked-upness? Na. And, ahem, who is fucking her? Sorry, again please?

Pretty sad, eh?

But then, remember, this is nothing if not a brief trip into the Bullshit Free Zone (can we breathe that thin air?) and bits of me are just that, sad.

I admit it, yes, it pleases me that someone who is only just sniffing 25 on the wind, never mind 30, does not consider me MDL, and thinks it a pleasure to push her strong, flat tummy against my denim-covered dick.

I stand revealed and condemned.

It gets worse.

There is a nasty little voice which I hate more than anything, which whispers in my ear, the last year or so, when I know I am going to fuck with someone interesting+attractive, thank God the last time wasn't The Last Time.

That is soooo very sad.

I hate the bit of me that says that. I hate these intimations of mortality. But I get them, I get them a little worse each month, and I have this certain feeling they can only get worse, because Time (as they say) is a one-way trip and we all die on board and the next Station Stop will be 30.

If we are not changing, age means just decay.

Which is why I need to save my life.

But for now, set up the foaming drinking skulls, gather around, and let us go back to armpits and suchlike, to the little pleasures we had bloody well better enjoy while Time's Wingéd Chariot is still a mere dot in the rear-view mirror.

All in all, all the above faffing+footling+foreplay was very nice and I was feeling great having just disengaged from our first embrace in time to avoid coming, and when I nearly came again just undoing her black 501s, button, button, button, button, no knickers, ah, so that's why I could smell her so quickly, mmmmm, she sitting astride my chest, it all felt wonderful, like I was 16 all over again, like I had cast off all the ballast of control weights you gather up over the years.

But it was not love. I make that clear.

This was in Suzy's flat by now.

One strange thing about the world is that girls and gay lads know how to make horrible walk-ups look like Home, whereas single straight laddos managed to make whole flats look like horrible walk-ups. I know this bloke who reckoned he never got girls because he lived in a shit-hole walk-up, so eventually he got a bent mortgage through his brother and bought himself a house with six rooms in Acton, and rented the three up-stairs rooms out to pay the mortgage, so now he had three rooms downstairs all for himself, but it did no good because his three rooms always just looked like three walk-ups tacked together and any woman that saw them made sure she only saw them once.

You have to avoid begging for salvation TOO clearly.

That is why I take such care to make my shed look like a place lived in by something vaguely human. You even start to believe it yourself after a while, and after all: belief is all you need. Which is handy if it is all you have.

Suzy's flat was Home, you could tell.

More about Suzy's flat later.

More about Suzy now.

So like I said, she sat on my chest and I downloaded all the buttons on her black jeans (button, button, button, button) and she stood up high above me and grinned, a woman knickerless and superior, and shook the denims down to her ankles, and did a kind of bump-and-grind hip wiggle for a few seconds so she could watch me starting to die for her cunt, and then came on down, and slipped me inside her, smooth smooth smooth, and we found I could kiss her nipples with us like that, so well did we fit together, and we could both admire her flat stomach comfortably for a while until I had to come out so as not to come, and then we found that with me kneeling above her head and nearly dying happy of deep-throat sucking, I could comfortably reach around and stroke her clitoris (having patted her flat stomach appreciatively first of course).

These are all very nice things, very very nice indeed, the more people did of them the happier the world would be, and if that was all there was in life, then perhaps that really would not be much of a tragedy; but they do not mean love. I repeat that.

So we ended up (as I already hinted, but hey, if it's worth doing it has to be worth more than hinting about, as Achilles maybe said to Homer) bouncing around the room standing up, me leaning back a little to keep our balance and she leaning back a lot for ease of mutual thrusting and so she could see what was going on down below.

—That looks so good, said she.

(I wasn't sure if she meant her tummy again or my dick and her cunt, or what, I mean I was concentrating too hard on not falling over or slipping out of her, partly, and partly I was roaring away like crazy, and it just felt too bloody good to worry about what the hell it LOOKED like, so I just took her word for it.)

Then she stopped saying anything and started digging her nails into my shoulders and I opened my eyes and saw her eyes kind of clouding over, or maybe she was just going cross-eyed because we were nose to nose, we were eyelash-locked, all I could see of her now was one big eye, our foreheads were pressed together hard, she was clawing at my shoulders to hang on through the sweat, my hands kept sliding off her ass, and then she started to shiver, and she made that so-nice-it-hurts noise, and I moved my head to get some air and take a look at the so-nice-it-hurts face she was making, and she looked at my so-nice-it-hurts face too, and then we were reflecting each other's faces without knowing who was leading and who was following, we were snarling and pouting and leering and frowning into each other's eyes and it was just too good, I was going to come, I just wanted to wait for her too, I tried to hold myself back by thinking crap profound thoughts like (cue Mr. Hauer again):

—On the verge of satiety, desire still seems endless—but it was no good, all I could do was lick her face and let my body go turbo, I could hear myself yelling and gasping and see the room spinning, I was trying to find a wall in her room to shove her up against, but there was no wall without these fucking clothes hangers and clothes hanging everywhere.

Yes, Suzy's walls are all covered in her clothes.

More of these later too.

I was staggering, I knocked into her standard lamp and the ballet tutu fell off of it and landed in between our faces just as we were tonsil-locking again, and nearly choked us.

Yes, ballet tutu.

So I shook this fucking tutu out of the way with my teeth, and while I was shaking it off I smacked my head on a wooden beam and I shouted and swore and laughed and nearly lost her but caught her again and caught her eye again, and my laughing turned into growling and she leaned back and looked down with her tongue out and her lips curled up and her face going like some All-Black war dance, and then just when I thought the heart attack was coming, she did instead, she shouted YES, like she had just hit a big topspin winner at tennis, and then OOOOOOOHO-HO-HO, her voice went straight through me like an ice cube up the ass and I came too, screaming, and staggered and tripped over this big old bear she had on the floor, and I almost fell forward with my knees going liquid and managed to rearrange us at the last minute so we fell flat-back onto the bed, she still atop me, me still inside her, and then just we two, still, holding each other, miles away from anything like irony, just still, still, still.

It was ten minutes, it must have been, though it was probably really only two minutes, before I recovered motor control enough to reach over for a cigarette and thus restore what I suppose pass for my cardiovascular functions.

All this was so nice it was far more than nice and I would love to tell you about it all over again, but don't worry, I won't. But it is not, not love.

Before I quite fell asleep, just when the ground was falling away underneath me and the sweet dreams were coming out of the trees across the river, I looked at her and I thought without thinking: now Suzy is in, the Plan is real, with her aboard, it cannot fail, it is all just look-down/shoot-down, locked on and running. And the last thing I thought of, in that post-sex half-dream way when the weirdest fragments of the world suddenly fit together unexpectedly but without surprise, was the last piece of the Plan.

It just came to me: the one thing I could bribe Fred the Security Chief with, I laughed at how stupid I had been.

—What are you laughing at? said Suzy, half asleep.

—Jimmy's Will, I said, and explained to her.

—Nice, she said, already halfway gone.

So that was OK, I could sort Jimmy's Will out with Dai Substantial, so now the few megabytes of my brain that had been taken up with this for days reformatted themselves into clean, clean, virtual space, I smiled and stretched, and the next thing I knew, I was waking up beside Suzy and it was this morning, Saturday morning.

This morning we discovered that we fitted like spoons or dogs or even missionaries even better without the drink, and wanted to even more, which is very nice, and perhaps a little surprising, but not love. There is a pathology of the night, which everyone has after a few drinks, and that is all very well; but there is a pathology of the daylight too, and when you start getting into that, when the sun is shining and Radio 4 is trundling out its post-Pathé reassurances, and you are neither drunk nor hung over and you still want to die in each other's arms again, then things are getting out of hand. But still not love, not necessarily.

In the shower, where we both got in together without thinking about it, we found ourselves immediately on blackhead-squeezing terms, which is very nice indeed, and really quite surprising on the first morning, I even let her put shampoo on my thinning hair without flinching much, which was nearly amazing, and then we kind of got interrupted halfway through drying each other down, by the prospect of fucking rearwards standing up, which we had somehow omitted to try earlier, so we ended up still sweaty and smelly after all after the shower, which was not the plan, but which was all very, very nice indeed. But not love.

And then I saw her driving her mini and dealing with Mr. Supaservice and generally walking and talking and eating prawns and stuff, it was getting better and better and then, well, then she went and said that thing about going to India and losing forty pounds and talking shit, which I liked so much I have gone and told you about it again already, and why not?

For all of the above fucking could be done and has been done by everyone, it is nothing, we have Most Favored Species status in Nature, we are all into fucking all the time and with almost anyone, the difference is what makes you want to do all that, with the same person, again and again, and that is where the stuff about laughing open-throated with someone comes in. In short+to conclude:

by Friday at 10 p.m. Suzy and I knew we shared some experiences and judgments on important points of end-of-millennium urban living, she had shown that her driving was better than ever and she could still do that UC accent perfectly, so she was perfect for the Plan;

by Friday at 11 p.m. we knew we wanted to fuck each other;

by Saturday morning we knew it worked, drunk or sober;

and now, at 11 o'clock Saturday night (as the song goes) we had gone thieving together, we had started to make a Team, the ante was got, the wheels were sorted, we had taken the first step towards Moscow and now I was laughing my throat open at her deadpan jokes.

I mean, come on.

OK, OK, fair enough: it was still possible that I was wrong. Maybe she secretly liked free improvisation jazz or Prince Charles's Ideal Village, maybe she had not really noticed I was going bald yet, love may be blind, but lust can be pretty short-sighted. Who knew? But as far I could see, it was all there:

We were on the same mental plane.
And the seat-belt lights were off and Christ
knew where we were headed.
Except that wherever it was, we were going
via Michael Winner's private bank.

4

ALIENS FROM THE PLANET GOLD

I only found out about Michael Winner's private bank last Wednesday.

(It is not Michael Winner's bank really, of course, I am sure he does not own it and I am not sure he even ever goes there at all, but now I have gone and called it that to impress Brady [it's OK officer, I have a clean Poetic License] I can only think of it like that myself. I am stuck with my own story.)

So anyway, on Wednesday I had go to Michael Winner's private bank and deposit a check for £500,000 in it.

You heard right.

Have you ever seen a real, live, loaded check for £500,000? Try to, just once. Or at least imagine it, now.

OK?

Nice.

But ownership is all, and it was not (tragedy!) my money, I was just the slave dropping it off.

It happened like this.

Last week I was temping for Baron Films in Wardour Street. The first two days were quite normal for temping, I was franking letters with the franking machine, going out for sandwiches for the girls in the photocopying room, taking maybe-location snaps to the developing place around the corner, telling the receptionettes they should not put up with sexual pestering from the Suits, delivering publicity stuff to the Baron Premier in Chinatown and films to the cinema at Paddington and stuff like that.

My life: at nearly 30 years of age (No! Not yet for Christ's sake, I am not even 29 yet!) with a degree in History from an almost half-respected third-level institution that has since even become a University. Very successful I must say.

At least with temping you get to see all sorts of nooks and corners of London and people you would never see. Like, I worked for the National Anti-Vivisection League and when I asked how come so much of the mail I was franking was going to South Africa, they said this was because S. Africa had a wonderful record on animal rights. This was in 1989.

(The day N. Mandela became president, I happened to take a bottle of S. African plonk up to Bob's for dinner. Bob [1] dropped dead with horror, [2] realized that it was now not only OK to drink it but positively virtuous, and then [3] choked on it when I pointed out it was three years old.)

Other temping weirdnesses: I worked for a hotel chain re-shelving seven years of tax returns, and Brady and I (I got him taken on too) spent the whole time mountaineering about on this huge roomful of cardboard filing boxes, like they use for stunt-men, because the supervisor was a sad loony who wanted us to be his friends. He had been in Army Intelligence in N. Ireland, dis-guised as a Queen's University student, but he fled when he got a letter addressed to his real name saying WE KNOW WHO YOU ARE, LOVE FROM THE IRA. Understandable. Once he went up to Alexei Sayle when we saw him in a pub off the Edgeware Rd. up behind the cinema at Marble Arch, and said he had all Alexei Sayle's albums, to which Alexei Sayle replied that this did not mean they had a relationship, whereupon Mr. Sad said:

—I'm doing this for you Alexei,

broke his glass, and cut his own hand open with it. If you do not believe me, ask Mr. Sayle. Or we dragged big sacks of tax returns through the foyers of hotels, saying in loud voices in front of jet-lagged Americans that they were dropping like flies this year, what with the Legionnaires' Disease and the Bovine Spongiform Encephalitis. Crap like that. Or:

I worked for IBM with this extremely UC-sounding black bloke called Barrington-Charrington or something who wore the most beautiful suits I had ever seen and the whitest shirts and (he was shocked that he had to tell me what it was) a Guards tie. They had taken him off TelesalesForce and put him in Mail-Shot Research (which is what I was temping at) because he sounded so UC that he was putting off all the Prospective Clients from Watford and places: they were so ashamed of their own accents over the phone when they were talking to Barrington-Charrington that they started hating IBM for reminding them how LMC they really were despite their huge mortgages and BMWs.

Barrington-Charrington had been an NCO in the Guards, he applied to be an officer and they kept him waiting and (as he realized later) hoped he would forget about it, but he didn't, The Regiment was His Life, and it is hard to forget your Life, so at last they let him go to Sandhurst and he passed all the tests three times instead of once, and was always the first over the assault course, and beat the crap out of anyone who tried to do initiations and other repressed weirdnesses on him, so they had to let him through in the end, and he went back to his Regiment, to his Family, and he naturally thought he would now become an officer in it, but his CO, who was supposed to be like his Father, said— not, Barrington-Charrington admitted, without some real embarrassment—that Barrington-Charrington was splendid officer material, but that The Men would simply not stand for a colored officer. For the good of the Regiment, said the CO, he was suggesting that Barrington-Charrington accept a commission in another branch of the service, and Barrington-Charrington asked what regiment and the CO said REME.

—What's REME? I asked.

—Quite, quite, old boy: not a regiment. They drive things about, I believe, said Barrington-Charrington, and sniffed.

—So what did you do? I asked.

—What do you bloody well think I did, old boy? I joined in the bloody Brixton Riots of course. I tell you old chap, all we needed was a bit more discipline, and the willingness to take a few casualties of course, and by God, that second evening we would have chased the bloody Met clean into the river!

(I thought of Barrington-Charrington straight away when I first thought that the Plan might involve machine-gunning a few aristocrats, but I could not work out how he could fit into the actual Plan, and in any case I have no idea where he is now. Somewhere in London, I suppose. There is something very troubling about the idea that you can get to know someone quite well, and then one day you realize you have lost touch, you have no line, no track to them at all, they still live in the same city, but you will never see them again. Recently, I started keeping an address book properly for the first time, I spent a whole day fishing out bits of paper and old beer mats and stuff from around the place and writing names and numbers in a real little address book; a back-up file for my life.)

Temping is tempting because you do not know where you will be next month, except you know it will not be here: moving about lets you kid yourself you are moving on.

Until you wake up one day and realize you are not, but the world is, and it is about to go without you. Which is when you decide you need to save your life pretty soon.

Anyway, so I was in my third day at Baron, so this was last Wednesday, I was mainly having sad, time-killing private competitions to see which of the mail-shot letters I was franking would fly the furthest out of the franking machine. (Oh, yes, and a fine effort from MR. A. CHARLESWORTH of STEPNEY there, but it's still MS. P. PRITCHARD from CLAPHAM with just an elegant nose in front) when suddenly in came a Suit and said I had to tidy up the bloody mail and then go with Fred the Security Chief, and next thing I knew I was in the back of this limo with Fred driving, and an envelope in my hand. The envelope was unsealed, so I looked inside and found an extra-large-size, pen-written, unendorsed check for £500,000 signed by Herr Dr. Siegberth R. Mittelmaier.

There was definitely a lighting change in the world at that moment.

The same happened on Thursday as well.

I have no idea why they chose me. I suppose they didn't want to trust any permanent employees with the secret of Michael Winner's bank, and they supposed that no one could use that kind of information in two weeks, which was all I was down for (little do they know). And anyway, even if I did a runner, would any bank clear a check from Herr Dr. S. Mittelmaier for half a million, made out to (and naturally signed on the back by

Baron Filmsworthy

or

Mr. B. Aron Filmschmann III?

No the bastards would not.

It was terrible, because I was temping under a false name anyway, for doling purposes, so they had no idea of my real name or real address, I just picked up my unendorsed, cashable checks from the temp office each week. The temp office—it is one of the big chains—is sort of halfway into the black economy and they know it. They never asked for any proof of identity or anything, they knew damn well that everyone was signing on because they knew no one could afford to live in London on what they paid without signing on as well. The government were subsidizing their huge 60% cut.

So I could have just disappeared.

But no one would cash the check.

On the other hand, the third time I made the trip, i.e. yesterday (Friday), another Suit gave me a bag with £37,000 in cash to deposit as well as a check for £247,560. I could not believe it. It was just an ordinary canvas bag with a string, full of money, like in some cartoon. And this time they called a cab, they were going to send me alone, alone with £37,000 in a cab! I sat there, waiting for the cab, trying to control the sweat and the sphincter muscles, wondering if I had the balls to do it. But at the last moment the Suit drifted back and said:

—Oh God, I suppose we'd better send Fred with you, in case you get mugged or something.

So I now had TWO reasons for not trying to make off with the money:

(a) £37,000 is not enough to save your life and the whole point is to do ONE big job, one job while you have no criminal record at all, because that is how they always get everyone they get, if you have no record you will simply not get caught. And if you don't buy a white Merc with fins. Most criminals either (i) have a record or (ii) will get one because they cannot resist buying a white Merc with fins. This is because they are mostly UnderC or Lower WC and know instinctively that it is all worthless if they cannot display it, if they cannot show it off to the Tribe. It was the same in the eighteenth century, highwaymen got captured because they drove around Shoreditch or wherever throwing golden guineas to everybody: what else were they supposed to do with it? Get a mortgage? Pay for College? So nowadays they have big parties and they buy the Merc every time, with fins a compulsive option, and the Metropolitan Police just watch out cunningly for people driving up to big parties in Essex in white Mercs with fins, and get their man. Easy.

But I will not buy one. I learned at College that white Mercs with fins are uncool (I really wanted one when I was 17), the same way I learned that my Mum's nice clean net curtains were uncool. You get a degree in the secrets of MC Heaven, whatever you get a degree in. I know exactly what to do with money, I am one of the millions of LMC people kicking about Europe and America and the Pacific Rim who would know exactly what they would do with the money, we who have been selected and educated specially so that we could mutate into proper MC people.

I know that my ass is the perfect height to lean against the rail of an Aga, I just can't afford one.

No, if I get the money, they will wait outside big parties in vain for my white Merc with fins. I will just melt away into MC heaven, I will be invisible. Not above suspicion, just invisible to it.

But I need more than £37,000.

And then there is the other reason for not robbing Baron Films without due care+attention, which is:

(b) Fred.

Fred is Baron Films' head bodyguard/chauffeur. Each time he drives Michael Winner or whoever to the airport, Michael Winner or whoever gives him a gold lighter or whatever. He will be able to open a nice scrap precious metal business when he retires, says Fred. I was in the foyer once when Michael Winner (it really was him, this time) came strolling in off Wardour St., and suddenly all these minor Suits extruded themselves out of doors and woodwork and godknowswhere in order to surround and worship him, but Fred just got up all sort of chest-heavy and slow and shoved his way through them and held out his paw and said:

—Wotcher Guvnor

and you could see that THIS was what Michael Winner really liked to happen best.

Fred has the archetypal skinhead-squad-leader look. He is not even as tall as me, let alone Brady, he used to work for the Krays, so he must be 50-odd at least, he looks like an ad for the theory of evolution, his arms hang loose under the weight of his big hands, his head is shaved and runs straight down at the back, he has a little mustache, like a gay clone, and he still wears docs and tight Wranglers rolled up, and a black nylon bomber jacket with A MORDECAI GOLEM FILM: THE BETA FORCE on the back, and under it a white T-shirt.

Fred's bomber jacket is vacuum-packed full of muscles. I once bumped into him by mistake when we were moving furniture, it was like hitting a walking sack of spuds, I just bounced off. Fred has slow, transparent brown eyes and that unnerving weight around the neck and shoulders that you have to be born with.

I would back Fred against Brady any day, any money, even at 50-odd. Personally, I would not go down a dark alley after Fred with anything less than a flame-thrower and full SWAT back-up team.

The only thing was, I could not work out why Michael Winner would want a skinhead Nazi bodyguard, it just seemed too bizarre.

I had about put it down to the uncharted abysses of human psychopathology, when one day I found Fred in a very good mood, due to just having heard that his fifth grandchild had been born, so I dared to mention some skinhead march that was in the news, just to see his reaction. I was ready to dive for the door.

Fred was sitting on the receptionettes' desk (they all loved

Fred like an uncle) and swinging his 16-eye Doc Marten steelies backwards and forwards and he said:

—Oh yeah, right, I've often had to smack those Nazi bastards myself, me being half Jewish and half Irish. I hate that lot. I'd stiff the lot of them if it was up to me, a nice little rocket-propelled grenade through the window of the pub, whoosh! And a tommy gun for the survivors when they come running out. Don't think I haven't thought about it. Good riddance to bad rubbish, mate, you stay away from that crowd, scum they are.

So there you go.

Fred also told me lots of useful things to do when (not if, when) I went to prison, like getting someone to park a vanload of explosives outside the wall and then going to the Governor and saying you couldn't face the thought of innocent people being killed, and thus getting remission even though your friends had never intended to detonate the bomb anyway. Or making someone who owed you a favor drop their kid into the Thames so you could jump in and save it while you were on bail.

On Thursday when we came back from the pub at lunchtime, we came upon a big lanky traffic warden with pebble lenses, in the very act of taking the number of a horrible old B-Reg Jag, and Fred just went up and said:

—Take your scummy mitts off my fucking car, and he took the book off the warden, tore it into little pieces and dropped the little pieces carefully down the drain and then smacked the guy, though quite gently. As we left, I said:

—Jesus, Fred, but you'll never get away with that, every copper in Soho will be waiting for you when you come back to get the motor.

—Ain't my car, said Fred. —I hate the bloke what's car that is.

So all in all, Fred was a very good extra reason not to try to jump out of a taxi with £37,000 of his boss's money.

He would have torn me up like a pickled herring.

Fred was thus the one big problem in the Plan, because (i) he is so hard and (ii) I knew it was going to be very difficult to succeed without doing Fred in some way or another, because Fred's one unattractive character trait is an apparently absolute loyalty to his multimillionaire employers.

I spent days trying to work out what Fred's weakness might be, he just had to have one, everyone has something somewhere, we each have a quiet shed where we keep the secret, gyroscopic fetishes of our lives.

Some people's lives rotate in serious orbits, they would shrivel up and die if you stopped them doing cutting-edge research into cancer or whatever, but other people would get instant brain tumors if you taped over the mileage counter on their speedo, or banned collecting air miles, or forbade them to make model airplanes, or criminalized wine snobbery and weather predicting. People do not go to their sheds because they have a sane desire to, but because they have to, because their world would stop if they did not: find a man's shed, and you have the man.

What was in Fred's shed came to me when my brain relaxed after sex with Suzy, as described already. I knew I could offer him something he would simply not be able to resist. The Plan was saved.

Oh yes, the Plan. That still needs explaining.
OK.

The Plan is the way it is because Michael Winner's Private
Bank is the way it is. It would not work anywhere else, not even
the idea would work anywhere else, the Plan is no cheap old off-
the-peg thing, it is a figure-hugging made-to-measure number
for this one bank, it all depends on this bank's nature. Its private
nature.

Now, with your average bank the way to rob it is very simple, and demands one quite specific skill, which I do not have,
which is being able to radiate violence: you just have to walk in
and convince everybody, customers and staff, straight away, that
you definitely will hurt them very badly or maybe even kill them,
without blinking, if they do not obey you in all things, then you
collect the money from them and get out before the police come.
Naturally there are variations, such as waiting for the workers
when they come to open the doors in the morning, or kidnapping
the manager's children and threatening to burn them alive or
whatever, but essentially the favored mode remains the classic
one, because in your average bank, physically getting in and out is
not the problem: your high-street bank is designed to positively
invite people in through the doors, if people feel threatened or
questioned as they go in, they might go elsewhere. That is the
free market for you. So all the bank owners can do is take every
precaution to make sure (a) that it is as physically difficult to get
at the staff, and thus the money, as possible and (b) that the police
come as quickly as possible.

Not so with Michael Winner's bank.

It is private.

It does not have to, or want to, entice the plebs (us).

It pretends not to be a bank at all.

It pretends, indeed, not to exist.

You would never know it is a bank from the outside, there is no plaque or shield, let alone a big logo, just a nice polished number, No. 6 Crown Court WC2, a big brass knocker shaped like a lion's head, like any old big Georgian townhouse, not even a TV camera, like on many of them.

But this is not any old house: it is one of the secret troughs of London, where the office slaves go by, insanely convinced they are MC now because they have negative equity on their maisonettes in Walthamstow, loyal, Tory and unaware that a few feet from them as they pass, munching their prawn+mayo sandwiches in malted bread, lie riches that no career incentives, no attractive salary packages, no share options or career moves or bonus deals could ever make theirs, wealth that may not be beyond the fantasy of their Hello-reading hours or their lottery dreams, but is quite certainly beyond any rational possibility of attainment.

It is one of the vaults of the people who own the world.

There are dozens like it in London, no doubt, since London is one of the places the Owners Of The World like to hang out, but you do not know and I do not know where they are, and we never will, which is all as per their deep plan.

Except now Fate had shown me where this one was.

But so what?

Because since it is a private bank, it is very easy indeed for the owner to stop burglars coming in, even if they do find out where it is, because the door does not have to stay open. It hardly ever does open, in fact.

When it does, it is only because Michael Winner or Siggy Mittelmaier (as he is known) or some other friend of the owners has told Janey Herzberg at Baron Films (she is a sort of super personal aide) to call the bank on the secret number which you will never find in any phone book. Like all the best security, it is all personal: the Ladies in the bank (just coming to them) know Janey H. from lunches and parties and maybe from midnight feasts at school for all I know, so they know it is her when she phones and says that so and so (likewise known by name/family/face) will be around in so and so many minutes to deposit or pick up so and so many hundred thousand pounds.

When this happens—I watched it from inside, so I know— a security guard called Joe waits beside the interior door and watches through a sort of periscopeish thing that can see through a little lens above the door, until the correct forecast person arrives. What happens then is what happened the first day Fred and I arrived outside the bank, he a blasé old hand, I a mere lad again, full of mystery and wonderment.

—Here we are, said Fred, and stopped the limo.

—Is this a bank? I asked.

—Not your ordinary S&L, is it, he chuckled, with that incomprehensible, oriental, enraging capacity of those who have nothing to gain by surveying the power of their cloudy masters.

We got out and went to the door and instead of ringing or knocking or speaking or whatever, Fred just stood there without moving, looking up at the top of the door for no apparent reason.

Then I saw the little black eye, and thought it must be a TV camera watching us.

—No, said Fred. —It's just Joe. No cameras here, mate. I mean, think about it for a sec. What do you want a private bank for, eh? To be private of course. Don't want no one taping you, do you? This ain't the Natwest!

There was no electronic buzz, no voice check or anything like that, just a soft clunk from the big Georgian door with its brass numbers, and suddenly it swung spookily open, inwards. We walked forward (I could not resist looking to make sure there was no one behind the door) and entered a small room, grayly lit with hidden neon and constructed entirely out of black mirror glass, undoubtedly surveyable from the other side. The outer door shut itself behind us with no sound on impact and then we heard the soft clunk of the lock again. For maybe three seconds we were left there, then a vague extra darkening was just visible beyond one glass wall—the one to our left, not the one dead ahead,—and another door was opened, this time by hand, by a large man in a blue shirt and black trousers, but carrying no guns, truncheons or suchlike, just a little black designer box on his belt that had a bleeping red light and a button. A radio alarm.

—Hello, Fred, he said.

—Hello, Joe, said Fred. He did not bother to introduce me, I was some boot-boy figure now, beneath the notice of these Major-domos, just a gofer carrying £537,000 none of us would ever touch. I wondered why Fred was not given it to carry himself, maybe it was below his dignity, maybe he only handled cars and gold lighters, I did not know and I still do not.

We emerged into a hallway, nothing particularly special,

company carpets, fire extinguishers on the paneled wall, stairs going up away to the left, and all we had to do was take a turn to the
right, not even down a corridor, just about six feet, and we were
in the actual bank proper.

It is more like a dream than anywhere I have been when I
was awake, I have been there three times and every time, as soon
as I leave, I almost stop believing in it.

All it is is a windowless room about thirty-five foot square,
with a ceiling of ordinary height and with a modest plaster rose
as its center, dangling a modest enough crystal chandelier, as I
suppose crystal chandeliers go, and walls of quiet ochre rag-
rubbed paintwork, with oil paintings of hunting scenes, just ordinary repro tricky-Vicky genre paintings. Nothing that special at
all, I had seen this stuff in any number of offices while temping,
though the 30-by-30 Arabian rug must be several dozen thousands' worth.

But when you come in the doorless doorway, which is in one
corner, you gasp and shake your head, because the only, absolutely the only thing in this entire room is three big simple
Georgian desks, one in each of the remaining corners, each one
womanned by someone out of a Vogue spread, three flawless UC
beauties who all look up at once and (in my case) do not appear to
see you at all.

They saw Fred, though, and all said:

—Ay Hellay, Fred, and he stood happily in the middle of the
room and said:

—Wotcher your Ladyships. Then he turns to me and says:

—Go on then, give Lady Caroline the money.

This made me suspect that they sent me in order to make
Fred feel good by letting him boss a nice young MC-sounding

man around like he was a piece of shit in front of these women. I didn't blame Fred for this, though.

Lady Caroline (I do not know if she is really called that, I suppose Fred would not dare take the piss out of his betters, so she must be) does not even see me walk up. Why should she?

I am infinitely poorer than her.

I am older than her.

I am going bald.

Suddenly, temping did not seem such fun. This was Reality.

I had never consciously come into contact with The Ruling Classes before (it's easy to miss them, after all, since there are not very many of them and you will not see them if they see you first) with the exception of a few fucked-up old queens who, being fucked up, are human and so do not really count.

I was horrified at how ignorant I had been.

I mean, of course I have friends from school and stuff who are much richer than me, because they work as lawyers and tax accountants and stuff, that is quite comprehensible and fair, one of them even has a gold Ferrari with JEZ95 for its license plate because '95 was when Jeremy Frankel made his first 100 biggies doing ads for BogleBogartBuggery or whoever, but that is OK, I have not worked at it like them, maybe I would if I could have my time again, but I can't, and I didn't, so that is all OK and even fair+square. But this is different. This is another planet, for fuck's sake. I could stand here with my cheap clothes and my bag of their money and whistle a piano concerto while simultaneously farting Keats out of my ass and knocking up counterfeit Van Goghs with my dick, and these women would not think it at all strange, because for all they know the WCs do that kind of thing all day long, why not? What do they know, why on earth should they care?

They are not human like you and I are human, they are aliens from the planet Gold.

So anyway, Lady Snottina von Gold takes her check and her bag of money from The Invisible Scum (me) before her, and opens her desk to pop in the half-million quid.

I have never seen anywhere near so much money in my life.

The whole full-length drawer of this big, Georgian desk is stuffed with money stacked edge-up, I get only a glimpse, but a good foot and a half of it is fifty-quid notes and there are at least three rows. Most of the rest looks like Swiss Francs and Deutschmarks. Big denominations, I can see a serious amount of noughts.

Oh for a Kalashnikov!

But then the drawer slides quietly shut and Lady Caroline pulls out a receipt on paper that looks like the paper my degree certificate was trying to look like, rag-laid, watermarked paper with an embossed crest but no name, just the phone and fax, she swirls a lovely UC signature over it with her gold fountain pen and shoves it over to me, I have to pick it up myself, then she immediately looks straight through me and says to one of the other girls, thirty feet away:

—I don't know, I was going to give absolutely everyone home-made-oid chutney this year, but I simply must get some of those nice french-oid sealing jars with rubber lid things first, you know the ones they put jell-oid pheasant and things in, I mean old Nescafé jars would be a bit grott-oid, wouldn't they?

This (it appears) is the sign for Fred to say:

—See you tomorrow, your Ladyships, and then they all look up again as if they are surprised we are still here and say:

—Oh, goodbye Fred. And then Fred says:

—See you tomorrow, Joe.

—See you tomorrow, Fred.

And then we are allowed back into the black airlock, the door behind us shuts and once again we are in limbo for a couple of seconds, and then we hear the soft clunk in front of us again and the outer door swings inwards on its own and we take three steps forward, the door shuts behind us and there we are again, out in the sun again, incredibly, in London, in what I thought till now was the real world again.

I look back in disbelief, then I look round at all the people milling about in utter ignorance. I feel they should be all looking at me in amazement, like I have just stepped out from the Realms of Gold.

—Not the Midland, is it? says Fred.

He is delighted that I am gobsmacked, as if it is all his. As he opens the car door I look at him and wonder what it is like to be Fred.

Happy, is what.

Not me.

I spent Wednesday afternoon dreaming blackly of revolutions as I franked the mail, thinking: the breath of the UC is the death rattle of freedom!, stuff like that.

On Thursday we went back again and everything was exactly the same except this time I took the money to Lady Catherine, and found out several interesting facts, which were:

(a) that she and her pals were actually not that beautiful at all, and I could not work out why I had thought they were the day before. (Later on, as you now know, Suzy told me the secret, which is the shiny hair and the snooty look, but I didn't know that then, I was still a fool) and

(b) that Lady Catherine's cash desk was as full as if not fuller than Lady Caroline's and

(c) that Jamie wanted to take her to Singapore, but he was getting a bit bore-oid recently.

—Sling the Singapore bore! whinnied Lady Caroline.

—Well, his family-oid place is near Shrewsbury, so I usually call him the Severn Bore, actually.

How we laughed!

How I looked at the money!

That was when I discovered

(d) that Lady Cat's desk (like the others, no doubt) has a little button beside the right-hand drawer, with a little red light flashing away most un-Georgian-like and, last but not at all least

(e) that the receipt I got had their secret phone number on it.

I can only describe what I felt as a sudden bowel-dropping veinful of adrenaline. The first door had just opened.

On Friday (i.e. yesterday) we went back again, trudge trudge, trundle trundle, yawn yawn, soft clunk, hello Joe hello

Fred, morning your ladyships, another half-million poured into the bottomless vaults, dearie me, just another day in Olde London Town, and everything went the same except this time I had to give the money to Miss Buck-ffrench, the poor fat, horsefaced, untitled cow. And her desk was about as full of money as the other two, and she was worried about whether she ought to try having a prole-oid boyfriend for once:

—Oh God no, darling, said Lady Cat.—Don't do that whatever you do, I had a prole-oid boyfriend once and he ended up dragging me to the Gorbals or somewhere vile to see his aged mother, it was all quite ghast-oid, she asked me if I wanted to eat a Piece.

—A piece?

—Mmmm.

—A piece of what, darling?

—Well, exactly.

I was starting to calculate yardage of fifty-pound notes by now. It doesn't take as much as you think:

A shrink-wrapped yard of new £50 notes is over £600,000.

Even if they are used, a foot of £50 notes is about £70,000.

Some of theirs were shrink-wrapped new ones.

I could feel my mouth desiccating and my face tightening up round my temples as I looked.

(Fred explained afterwards why they had so much cash washing about: I would be surprised, said he, at some of the things that went on in the Film World, there was a lot of funny money about, one way or another, you always got that when there was all this cash coming in all the time, from the cinemas, just like with the dogs or football clubs. And this particular company was funnier than most, said Fred, he was sure he'd had Mossad agents and ex-Stasi men and suchlike in the car at one time or another, and anyway, these men like cash. Say Michael Winner comes in and wants a quarter-million just like that, to go to Monte Carlo or something, then half an hour later two mates of Siggy's come in and want to go and do some deal in Russia, they don't take plastic in Russia, do they? I mean, that's the whole point of a Private Bank, innit, if they had to get on the blower and book up and wait till Tuesday tea time to get their million quid, they might as well go to the local Co-Op bank, mightn't they?

—Oh yeah, I said faintly.—Stands to reason.)

As I took my receipt and looked again at the phone number on it, to make sure I had memorized it correctly, I thought what a pathetic bastard I was to bother memorizing it since I would never have the chance to use it. I was just thinking this when Fred pushed me gently against the wall. I looked up and he hissed to me:

—Look smart, customer's here.

At this, he assumed a position sort of halfway like a military stand-at-ease, with his hands behind his back, and his feet apart and his eyes looking straight ahead at something about twenty feet away and eight feet up. He nudged me and I did something sort of similar.

The inner door opened and a huge, fat, gray-haired man in a world-class suit entered. You know the way all suits look more or less the same at a hundred yards, but when you get closer you can tell straight away which are from Marks&Spencer or Top Man (purveyors of livery to the slaves of money) and which are from the weeny quiet places without prices in the windows. Something to do with the way the shoulders sit. This was one of those. And in case no one noticed, there marched behind Graf von Gold, or whoever he was, a tall but square-built and blazered bodyguard. Graf von Gold passed us by without a flicker except to nod to himself when Fred and Joe said, together,

—Morning, Sir.

The bodyguard nodded to Fred as they passed, and glowered at me suspiciously, which was pretty sound judgment on his part, because I was at that moment wondering if I should re-join the Revolutionary Communist Association after all, and plan for millennial vengeance.

When they had passed, Fred nudged me again, and we went to leave as invisibly as possible, so as not to be there when Graf von Gold (actually, Fred told me afterwards it was the Count de Giglio) was doing his business.

Fred whispered to Joe:

—See you Tuesday, Joe.

—Not Monday, Fred?

—Nah, Monday's bank holiday in New York or something. Double dose on Tuesday. About two.

—Right you are, Fred. I dare say you'll find me here.

—I dare say, Joe. Have a good weekend then.

—And you, Fred.

TUESDAY AT TWO O'CLOCK!!!!
TUESDAY AT TWO O'CLOCK!!!!
TUESDAY AT TWO O'CLOCK!!!!

And the agency had told me on Thursday that Baron Films wanted me again next week!

As soon as I knew this I knew I had to make a Plan. I spent most of the afternoon either really on the lav with the hammer-heart squits, or pretending to be on the lav so I could think in peace.

I had the number.

I had the time.

I would be in there myself.

My brain ached with the battle.

But the final revelation came only when I was grabbed by a Suit and told to get over to Kwik Pix to collect some prints for a friend of Mr. Golem's.

The sign at Kwik Pix (it is just by Soho Market) says Unconditional Confidentiality, but when I went in and gave them the receipt for this particular film, a strange thing happened: even these hardened Soho professional film developers, who one supposes have seen a thing or two over the years in ye olde red glare of the developing light, looked at me like I was something you would expect to find sticking to the end of a sink plunger, not walking into a shop. After that, I could naturally not resist taking a look at the prints.

The most appalling thing about them was not the milk bottles up people's asses and the donkey being wanked off over someone's face, but the fact that these were very very cheap polaroid-looking shots, it was almost impossible to see what was going on anyway, it was just blubbery lumps of flesh whiting-out in flashgun bursts, out of focus and wobbly-handed. It made you wonder what the hell kind of low-life Mr. Golem's friend was, I mean, this was serious slumming for a multimillionaire, even the shots had to be cheap, never mind the tricks.

I showed them to Fred and the receptionettes.

—But he looked like such a nice man!

—Yeah, like my grandad, said Fred. —You know, it was that bloke with long white ringlets and a big beard that come in from Tel Aviv this morning.

—Coo, I said.

Then I took the pictures upstairs to Janey Herzberg, that super personal assistant I mentioned, to hand them over, while Fred and the receptionettes sat down to drink tea and agree that well, you just never can tell.

Janey H. was on the phone, I heard her voice halfway down the empty corridor, it was even more bellowy and UC, never mind UMC, than the Girls at the bank, it was like someone taking the piss out of that kind of voice, she was saying:

—But I AM still sort of socialist-oid, darling, I just think that the country really HAS gone a bit pleb-oid. Well exACTly. Yobb-oid. But I DO still believe in fair shares for all, it's just that I don't like social climbers, Socialists really oughtn't to be snob-boid, don't you think, so why on earth do they CARE about how much money one has? But of course the climb-oids are the worst little snobs of all. One should be far above all that nonsense if one is going to be at all left-oid. Well quite.

The funny thing was, her voice reminded me of something, of someone I knew, so strongly that I almost went away again without dropping off the photos so as to be able to think about it and try to rewind my memory banks.

I dropped the photos off and five minutes later I was sitting downstairs again, still prodding away at my synapses with a mental toothpick, trying to work out who it was that she reminded me of, slurping my tea with Fred and the receptionettes, when Mr. Golem's friend from Tel Aviv came down the stairs in person.

He looked just as nice as they had said, the Rabbi Father Christmas or something, and everyone looked away in embarrassment. Really, it is not good to pull back the curtain on the depravity of mankind. I mean, OK, each to his own when the lights go out, and let's just leave it at that.

—I just wanted to tip whoever fetched my snaps, said he.

That was me, of course.

Shit.

They all pointed to me halfheartedly, and looked away again, grateful it had not been them. He came up to me and gave me a fiver and watched me go red and then looked around the room and said:

—I guess you all saw the pictures?

—Well, yes, we all nodded.

—You like them? he asked me.

—Um, well, the focus wasn't too great, you know . . .

—Yes, yes, you're right, they did not come out very well at all. It's all very curious, because my camera is really quite a good one, and the film was of some people having dinner by a lake in Switzerland and these pictures . . . (he looked at them again, and frowned slightly). —Maybe I need my glasses, do you see any mountains?

On the way back with the real pictures (you should have seen them squirm at Kwik Pix when I told them who they were for!), I suddenly had to stop and lean on a wall: while I had been forced to give my conscious brain a rest from planning, thinking about the pictures for the last two minutes, the Plan had revealed itself to my Id or whatever you call those other, unknown folds of the veiny graystuff.

It was all there. Just there.

Suzy the Black Widow doing funny UC voices!

That was who Janey Herzberg reminded me of. And Suzy could drive!

So that is how and why on Friday night I called Brady and Chicho together and we went and got Suzy and she and I hit it off and got it off (as described) and we all sat down on Saturday to discuss the Plan and Suzy and I went robbing and we got the car sorted out with Mr. Supaservice, which is about where I started, if I remember correctly, so it looks like we have got back to the beginning at last.

Sorry about all that.

But at least you know the how and the why of it all, which I think is important. So now we can move on all together, all hand in hand in Real time. OK then: the Plan.

5

LOCATION
LOCATION
LOCATION

The real reason for the Plan being as it is is very simple: to get the money while avoiding guns and hence killing people.

I want to make one thing clear: I could get a gun if I wanted to.

Life is full of little shadowy places. Who hasn't pulled on a joint or kept quiet to the taxman or had a camera conveniently pinched on an insured holiday or fiddled their expenses? Come on come on come on, who has not done SOMETHING that would lose them their job or their spouse or their license or their freedom, if THEY ever found out? It is just that the shadows are closer when you live on the jam roll in a shed: one day you sign on illegally, because everyone does, and after a few months you don't even think about it, it stops being Crime and becomes

Nature. You buy pot outside some pub you heard of, so what, any sane person agrees that toking does far less harm than swilling, except that because it is banned, after a few times, when you get to know that scene, someone else who doesn't know it so well asks you to get some for them, and you take a good shave out of their lump because that is what happens, it is accepted, and then suddenly you wake up one day and realize you have become a small-time dealer without meaning to. Or you buy a hot car because it is cheap and then someone asks you how you got such a good price and you introduce them to Mr. Supaservice or whoever and he asks via you exactly what kind of car they might like if he happened to suddenly find he was offered one, and now you are a little party to thieving cars. And maybe around and about all this, someone you know has hit the Hard Times and needs money right away and they offer you their checkbook and car and while they pretend to be looking for it and canceling it you are out cashing checks to split with them 60/40, and so what is the big difference?

(I knew this man, one of Augustus John's illegitimate grandsons, a serious UMC background, he has a housing trust house and he rents out another house he owns and doesn't tell the housing trust or the taxman or the mortgage people. And when a girl who lived in his house and paid him her rent once wanted to sign on and claim housing benefit because her little jewelry-making stall on Portobello Rd. wasn't bringing in enough to live on, and asked for a kosher rent book, Mr. Augustus John Jr. was horrified: But that's FRAUD, squeaked he. I asked him the difference, and he said that it was OK not to tell the taxman+housing trust because that was HIS money, he was not stealing from the state like SHE would be doing. I offered to get Brady to break his arms, but she was too nice to say yes, she just ate bread'n'water and kept paying the rent. Good old LMC morality: lucky old UMC.)

So why the hell, I hear you ask, if I can get one, not just stick a gun in the belt of my trousers, walk in with Fred on Tuesday, like always, and hold them all up?

Believe me, I am really not scared of five or six years in prison, which is the max I would do if I got caught first offense with an unloaded real gun.

You see, armed bank robbery is the Aristocracy of Crime. I will start ahead of the game. I am not in the least pretty, I only learned the College-boy stuff after I was eighteen, it is no built-in part of me, it can vanish without a trace anytime, and I have drunk often enough with men with tattoos to know exactly how they behave. And Fred has given me the best tip of all, which I suggest you take down just in case you ever end up visiting one of Her Majesty's big houses.

The first time anyone in your prison tries anything on, when they try to rob you or bugger you or bully you or publicly humiliate you or make you their servant or whatever (which they will eventually, even if you are in for sexy Armed Robbing), the very first time, you have to say No. Not Go Fuck Yourself or anything stupid and flash, just No, slow and sure, like you have tattoos. This will mean you have called them, and then they will certainly try (because they will have to) to make sure you do whatever it is they want, which means physically and publicly, and in the way of public physical violence the world over they will first see what happens if just one of them spills your dinner or slaps you in the face or hits you in the guts once or something: the cheaper it comes, the bigger the victory, the smaller YOU are. When this happens—you must wait for it to actually happen, you must not on any account act first—you have to hit whoever carries out the physical intimidation, straight away, as hard as you can, not kick them in the balls or anything flash, just hit them in the face as hard as you can, make sure you mark them, no matter how slightly, no matter how big they are or how much backup they clearly have. You will now get seven shades of shit kicked out of you, no question of that, you will be slaughtered, you will be in bits for weeks and probably need private dental treatment now and then for life, but they will not kill you or cripple you for good, and so long as you are alive and walking, the rest is simply a question of degrees, so that doesn't matter. You will recover. And when you have, and are walking about again without too much pain, they will come to you and try it on again, in public again, and that will be the hardest time, because you will have to do it all over again, just the same, just when you know how much it really hurts. You will have to say No again and hit them back again and make them do you again, though usually (says Fred) not half so bad as the first time, unless they have some particular reason to hate or despise you. But then it is almost certain that they will leave you alone for good, and pick on someone easier, they will have granted you your first Respect, which is your life-support system in prison. Nasty but simple.

And then when I have recovered, and everyone knows I am not going to knuckle under, I will be able to reboot my proto-MC College-boy training with nice Guardian-reading social workers (I often read the Guardian too, we shall have such a lot to talk about!) who will intervene for me. They will ask me to write a book about how a nice MC-sounding graduate came to be in prison for armed robbery. I will write it and tell everyone how sensitive and yet hard I am.

Don't get me wrong, I do not want to go to prison and I do not make light of how foul it will be. But I do not make light of the prospects ahead of me, either. Let us rationally consider the choice:

(i) you end up at 35 still in your shed with your adoring nephews having turned into teenagers with terminal acne who now think Uncle is a sad old toss and why can't they have the shed to wank in privately, or else

(ii) you have a crack at saving your life, and either (a) get your nice flat with the garden, or else (b) walk out of the prison at 35 with a few scars, big muscles from all the bodybuilding you did to kill time and defend yourself, a load of mad tales to tell, a book to write, hundreds of nice MC women wanting to fuck you because you are so unusual, and having reached the point which must be reached and which we are all so bloody terrified of, which is the point of no return.

I smell smoldering boats.

So you see, it is not fear of being caught with an unloaded gun that stops me getting one.

The problem here is that an unloaded gun is just no good for Michael Winner's private bank. Worse than no good. There are two reasons for this:

(a) Location location location and

(b) Fred again.

The location location location problem is that Michael Winner's private bank is located in Crown Court WC2 (as you already know) which is (as maybe you do not know) a small little tiny lane of a court with bollards at each end, which doglegs between Russell St. and Bow St.

These bollards are cunningly and accurately placed so that a car, even a car driven by Suzy, can only creep out of the Court at about 5 mph. I do not know if this was actually done to put the kibosh on speedy getaways, quite possibly, or if it is just to stop peds getting squashed, but there it is. So getting away quickly from this bank is very difficult, and you would have to get away quickly because being in Covent Garden, it is a long way from anything like a clear road, let alone a freeway. If you could not make it past Trafalgar Square before the call went out for you, you would have virtually no chance of getting away.

But what do you think Fred is going to be doing while you are trying to get out of the Court at 5 mph?

Tearing the doors off your car, is what.

OK, so you have to scare Fred with a gun, even Fred is not as hard as a bullet.

But think about it: this means you are going to have to prove it is real and loaded, because if Fred does not think it is, which he will not unless shown otherwise, Fred is bound to have a go, and if the gun turns out to be unreal or unloaded, he will just pop your head off like a champagne cork.

OK, so say you shoot a bullet into a desk or something to show it is real? So what? Fred will be watching for any chance as soon as your back is turned, like when you are getting into the car, or driving off, you blink and you will find a fire extinguisher up your ass or Fred coming for you head first through the windshield, or chewing off your tires or something. Even Suzy in an automatic Merc would have virtually no chance of getting us out past the bollards with Fred unleashed.

So we would have to shoot him.

But by then it would be too late anyway, because what about Joe and the three Aliens? What are you going to do about them? How are you going to stop them from tripping their alarm buttons? Forget that, did we? Cover them and tie them up? Sure, sure, OK: How many of you, did you say? All with guns? Who ties Fred, and who covers him meantime and who stops one of the three Aliens, one in each corner of this big room, remember, from quickly pressing their button, please? And Joe? Uh-huh? How many did you say we would need? And how are we going to get that many into the bank?

No, no, no. I can get three of us in, I think, but not quickly, not together, and with only three of us, the logic is very simple:

We would have to shoot them all before they could hit the buttons. Just walk in with an Uzi in my belt and shoot the lot of them. As Brady would put it in his direct+straightforward way: Budabudabudabudabuda, end of story.

I mean, fuck, why not?

Anyone can always do that, you could walk up and shoot the Prime Minister if you didn't care what happened to you, that is why the Muslim terrorists are so much more dangerous than the IRA, they really don't care if they get killed too. If you really and truly don't give a fuck you can get anyone and rob anywhere.

But I do give a fuck.

Lots.

Yes, I probably could get me an Uzi or a Carl Gustav or a

Heckler'n'Koch or something similarly small+fast, it would cost, but I could probably get it, maybe even by Tuesday, maybe even with a silencer, and walk in with Fred as usual, with this gun in a sling under my jacket, like your man in Crime and Punishment, and then just blow them all away (Fred first, of course). Budabudabudabudabuda. I have had that idea too, of course I have, and as soon as I realized I had even thought of it idly, it made me want to drop the whole thing and go and get therapy and run away to become an accountant.

Look, I am trying to save my life, for Christ's sake, I am not some chortling little doggie gun fetishist, I do not think the world is full of slow-mo blood splatters. I have no intention of walking into the bank and doing something that will condemn me to nights of fear and trembling that will go on until one day I wake up at 3 a.m. with the tape running wild in my head and realize that today is just the right kind of day to step off the platform in front of the early train.

No, no, if I took a gun it would have to be unloaded, and so here we go again, we know all this, there is not really much point in an unloaded gun when you have someone like Fred about, so a gun is no good to me either way.

So no guns.

Thank God, because the other thing about guns is that you have to go to Good Old Villains to get them, but Good Old Villains are actually twisted horrible people, they are mostly abused and abusers and cowards who dream of bungalows in Essex, it is better than 50/50 they would tip the police off about you as soon as you took the gun anyway, because you are not one of their nasty tribe and it would be no skin off their nose to chuck you the Met's way just to keep things sweet there. Or else they

would think you were a nark and then what would these nice traditional Villains do to you? Trash-bag you, is what.

So all in all it is lucky we do not need a gun.

Lucky we have the Plan.

The Plan is very simple, and very dangerous.

It will not be dangerous on the day, because we will have no
guns and there will be no connections between us, so even if it
goes wrong none of us will get done for long (as described). That
is the whole beauty of the Plan. Anyway, even if I have not
thought of something, even if we do get caught inside the bank
somehow, we will have used no weapons, they will not be able to
connect us with the rest of the Plan, we would only serve about
three years tops for a first, unarmed, MC-style robbery attempt,
so (as I said) that is not what scares me.

It is making the Plan itself that scares me.

Because the only Plan I have, the only Plan I could work out
between Friday and today that could work by Tuesday and not
involve guns, means I have to go nuclear, it means I have to go
and try to do a deal with some very very heavy people indeed.

Which scares the shit out of me, because these people are not
men you pick cherries with. If I get to see them (which I think I
can) and it goes wrong (which it might) then I could well end up
being found in several different trash bags in Hackney Marshes,
having died very slowly and horribly.

I feel sick.

My emotions are taking me over, they are saying: Get out of
this, get the hell out of here.

So I have to think very, very hard about the alternative,

which is me getting old in my shed, and how it will not be a picture of me as an old toss, but a real me, me, me with a real bald
head to bang on a real brick wall.

And so it is mere logic that strengthens me, and makes me
sit the Gang down on Saturday night (Brady already has his
Reservoir Dog suit on, for Christ's sake) after Suzy and I have
sorted things out with Mr. Supaservice (as described) and tell
them what I propose to do to save our lives.

I do not want to scare them off, so I remind them of the ster-
ling qualities of the Plan first, how we are going to get into the
bank and how we are all covered until the last minute and so on,
before I introduce the real bad subject slowly and in a balanced
fashion. As I do so I watch them carefully: they are all trying to
look like they are really concentrating, but I feel what I have felt
before, which worries me that none of them really believes, I
mean believes like they believe Tuesday follows Monday, that we
are going to do this. Brady is chewing gum (he never chews gum,
the eejit); Chicho is scratching his armpits thoughtfully; Suzy is
looking up at me carefully as she rolls a cigarette. But then I come
to the point, I actually describe the whole Plan.

And for the first time in my life I see the reality behind saying something that Makes People Sit Up.

They do.

They actually sit up.

They stop chewing, scratching and rolling.

Brady doesn't like it.

Chicho doesn't like it.

Suzy doesn't like it.

—I don't like it either, I say.—What has liking got to do

with it? We have two days, two days to plan a bank job, that is nothing, we don't have the big gang and the four cars and the back-up, and we are not having guns (Brady shifts his big ass on the chair, I stick my finger so close to his face that if he tries to get up he will poke his left eye out on it), I said we are not having guns!

—So what are we getting? asks Suzy, rationally.

—Nothing anyone can prove, that's what's so good. There will be no links if it goes wrong. I mean, the police might guess, but they won't be able to prove. No fingerprints, no chemical traces, no fibers, no video pictures . . .

—Get on with it, said Suzy.

—Yeah, so what the fuck are we hiring then?

—You making my head gyrate.

So I told them exactly what we were hiring, and from whom.

And now the full glory of the Plan unfolded before them, and lo! they were gobsmacked.

And so, by a unanimous vote of three (I did not vote, since it was my proposal) it was agreed that I should call Sammy.

6

THE
WHITE
NOISE

Sammy is a slightly fucked-up journalist, she is an old friend of mine, she is about 38, she has big pre-raphaelite hair, she dresses UMC-MDL and can still just about get away with it, and if it were not for my ex-guru Fergal F. Fitzpatrick, she would be a lost, moth-eyed soul drifting about London, sleeping around aimlessly, because if it is true that we are all here to learn one lesson again and again while Eternity itself turns ye olde barrel organ, then Sammy's lesson would be: not to mistake the brief unconditionality of men's gridlocked testosterone for true solidity.

When I knew her (in the Biblical sense) all anyone had to do was glare at her for a few hours across a pub table, and ignore everyone else, and generally behave like Heathcliff in the rutting season, so that she would feel like she was the center of their universe (which she was, of course, but only for the evening and only for one thing), and she would be ready to be thrown onto the nearest bed or bed substitute.

Sammy is one of those people who, by some tragedy of nature or nurture, seem to have never got beyond that 17-year-old stage where you half stop existing when you are on your own. She has no Story for her own life and so she has to borrow someone else's, anyone else's. This means, of course, that on the sliding scale of S and M she is right up there at the serious end of M.

The particular story which Sammy has seized upon to provide the backdrop for her existence is the Oppression of Ireland and how the whole Edifice of British Imperialism, and even World Capitalism, would collapse if Ireland were A Nation Once Again, and how the IRA (or whichever splinter group of the IRA or INLA or whatever she decides is the current Real Thing) is actually a liberal, socialist movement dedicated to peace and justice and niceness-in-the-end. When the IRA or whoever go on about the eternal soul of the Gaelic folk being rooted in the sacred blood and soil and ancient language of Ireland and stuff, which they sometimes do even in the London versions of their papers, never mind the Belfast+Boston versions, Sammy says not to worry, this is OK At This Point In The Struggle because they are a Small Nation, and Authentic Representatives of Small and Threatened Nations are allowed to spout this kind of crap (except if it is Israel, of course).

Sammy once followed her story so far as to go and live amongst and write about the brave nationalist people of Newry, and in her letters back she referred to The Britz and went on about Sisterhood and Rough Warmth and Solidarity at some considerable length. She went on demonstrations calling for the violent overthrow of the Fascist Military Junta in Ulster and was outraged when the Fascist Military Junta arrested her and kept her in overnight. She sued them for false arrest because they had forgotten to caution her, and won £3000. This was all heroic stuff, but unfortunately she took with her to Newry not only her longing for Rough Solidarity, but also her consequent taste in men, and after about three months, all the local IRA men's mothers got together and told her she had better feck off back to London with her English morals or else.

She was in pieces upon her return, and I tried as gently as I could to explain to her (I having meanwhile advanced to the sage-like age of 21 winters and being as clever as clever) that she might consider whether it was the hard men+tattoos she was interested in, not the politics. After all, think how much easier this would make life for her! She could easily find some boy who would be happy to knock her about, right here in homely Sheps Bush.

She smashed me round the face and walked out of the pub.

She was right.

I was stupid.

It was not Hard Men she was after, it was Meaning.

The hard stuff was the price she was prepared to pay, not the goods itself.

I should have known this, because after all, she only believes in Irish Freedom because of F. F. Fitzpatrick, which is my fault for introducing them, and I could not have introduced them if I did not know him anyway, and I only knew him because I too once believed that stuff.

I did.

And no wonder.

I mean, come on, consider the Set Special Menu: first, take the watertight jesuitisms of Leninism, that handily allow you to be a democrat and an elitist at the same time; add the only decent English-language rebel songs and permission to wallow in dubious folkish emotions wisely forbidden to White Yanks, Englishmen, Germans and suchlike (no wonder Yanks and Germans are so into the Irish); whisk in an atmosphere of guinnessy subculture, David'n'Goliath plotting and street-fashion cred; garnish with lochs and rural idylls; finish with a dose of redhead revolutionary sexuality and serve piping hot to any impatient 20-year-old in Channel 4 accents. What a Story! The only thing that surprises me is why everyone isn't in the Revolutionary Communist Association when they are 20.

You know those meetings in Red Lion Square or whenever, where they treat it like it's a big secret society, and tell everyone to watch out for Special Branch men, and then put the bucket around for The Party and the guy on the platform points to the back of the hall where some cadre is putting a Twenty into the bucket and shouts:

—Plenty more of those, comrades, let's see plenty more of those, like Billy Graham or someone?

Well, I too used to think this was a set-up, I thought it must be The Party Twenty-Quid Note that this person had been given specially to put in the bucket. That was before I realized that people really do give 10% of their money (well, say 7%, actually, because most of them cheat a bit) to The Party and all that.

And what a bargain.

Because for your pathetic little 7% tithe, the Party gives you 100% back: it gives you a whole, brand-new life.

One minute you are a rootless pile on the ass of the world,

not knowing who or why you are, and the next minute, bang! The Party not only tells you what to think in any given situation (helpful), it even makes you get up in the mornings (very helpful) to go sell newspapers and (most helpful of all) it gives you a regular date in the pub, where you can sit and nod and know what everyone is going to say, just like it was a bunch of football supporters, except you can think you are Conspiring too. When you are really really in, you are allowed to stay in the room when A Comrade from Derry is going to appear through the back door. You should see the MC Comrades swell when this day comes for them, they know that they have just won 1,000,000 kilopoints on the Sexy geiger-counter: as they stick around toughly while the poor crappy ordinary Comrades straggle out wistfully, they can hear the twang of knicker-elastic, male and female, far and wide.

I loved it.

Fergal F. Fitzp. was my chief mentor in the Revolutionary Communist Association (who are very good at assigning mentors), he was 30 and I 20, for a month or two I adored him with all the power of unfocused teeny sexuality. I wanted to be him. I mean not just walk and talk and dress like him, but actually BE him. I was open to him in a way that was miles beyond anything like physical penetration, I watched him and listened to him and copied him like some method actor on amyl nitrate.

F. F. F. is not the kind of man to deny adoration. He is the kind of man who must have been very loved by his mother or whatever, because he is so sure he is the very navel of the universe that all he needs is someone to listen to him and nod and talk like him back to him, which I did, it would never occur to FX3 that there is anything weird about someone who acts like a mirror to you, because to him, being a clone of Fergal Fintan

Fitzpatrick just means being the only way anyone can be: the more like Fergal F. Fitzpatrick you are, the more normal he thinks everything is. So between my youthful need to find the Way and his inbuilt certainty that he knew it, we got on like a gas station on fire.

I adored unconditionally, he accepted wholeheartedly: very soon, I was being tipped for swift entrance into the inner core of the RCA, I had the quickest get-in to the Comrade from Derry anyone could remember. (Unfortunately, it was not a good evening for the RCA because the Comrade from Derry in question had already scored over lunch with a nice UMC girl, and was half pissed already, and proceeded to inform the respectful comrades that the IPLO or whoever it was did not want a load of Communists embarrassing them and frightening decent Catholics, OK, so they were to keep their shagging support secret, OK?)

However, I had been in, and seen a Comrade from Derry in the flesh, and this confirmed my status, which was why Sammy fancied me when she turned up to her first meeting, having deserted from the SWP to the RCA.

Fergal F. F. was away somewhere else, so I was being him for the night at the Thursday pub meeting. I could already be Fergal so well that even I hardly missed the real him. People talked to me like I was him, they even bought me the drink he drank. Sammy sat and watched, her pre-raph hair caught my eye and my eye caught hers, and soon her fine-tuned radar panels had picked up the signs of certainty about me, not realizing it was borrowed, she saw that the others were following MY mouth and followed MY words with their eyes; so she followed me home.

After three days, Sammy's need for certainties had wiped out my own convictions. As she learned the Party Line off by heart, it was like it was being siphoned out of me into her. Her need for The Story was so blatant, she was so undisguised in her longing that after a bit I could hardly avoid wondering if I was like that too. I saw her eyes fill up, and her pupils grow big with this new Truth, and saw myself reflected in them, spouting Fergal's bullshit in Fergal's voice, like in a dream. Now I was the one being adored and copied, and I found it first boring then embarrassing then ridiculous. Suddenly, I was getting these helicopter shots of myself as Mr. Ultimate Sad Case, I got the Galloping Doubts, after three days with Sammy I discovered that I would just never, physically never, be able to stand about again with a stack of papers, shouting

RevoLUTionary Communist

RevoLUTionary Communist

De-FEND the workers

SELF-determinationfortheIrishpeoplenow

never mind hand over 7% of my hard-earned to people no one ever voted for.

Really, if the white noise in your head is that bad, you might as well join the Krishnas or the Young Tories.

But before I deserted the Cause, I introduced Sammy to Fergal. By the time I got back from the bar with the first pints on the night of their first meeting, it was evident that they had already clocked on, they had locked their invisible whiskers, they knew that he was the real thing, the big spiritual S to her big spiritual M.

Unlike most of the Irishmen Sammy had previously gone

with, Fergal did not have scars and tattoos. On the contrary, he had a long sad pale face, like a young tortured priest (except he grinned a lot), and short, side-parted black hair. He was basically time-locked in the Punk Summer and the Hunger Strikes and stuff, he played bass in a seriously crappy MDL grunge band called Partyline. But he had conviction. And when he listened to anyone, he did it very well at first, he would stop grinning and kind of lower his forehead just a little bit and drop his jaw and raise his eyebrows and make his eyes go all sort of popped out, like he was opening up his entire face to you, and just sit head-on, nodding encouragingly, yeah, yeah, yeah, and then suddenly he would take over halfway through what you were saying, and start to talk instead.

He had this way of talking, he would wave his arms and his big white hands in long circles as he spoke, he always had a pint of lager (he hated Guinness) in one hand, but somehow it self-leveled the whole time. When he was trying to get going, his arms made me think of those old films where someone is trying to start a biplane by hand, they jerked and stopped and jerked again in time to his words and then he would catch his rhythm and he would be flying, and his arms would start making these big smooth circles and figures of eight and the pint of lager would be making strafing runs around everyone's heads, you had to duck the whole time when Fergal F. Fitzpatrick was talking on cam, and yet he never spilled a drop, and the speech would go something like this:

—Yeah, no, hold on, you're right, I mean no, yeah, we all know that, sure yeah, in a way, but surely any revolutionary strategy which excludes the possibility of individual agency is self-contradictory, since the very purpose of revolution, the very revolutionary nature of revolution itself is to enable individuality, you copy? Struggle can only be individual in the sense of individual responses agglomerated into the mass reaction, of course that's true. But we have to distinguish, don't we, surely, of course we do, between individual activity as defined by the bourgeoisie and that other individuality, that true individuality of socialist action, we have to call it a meta-individuality for now, because as Trotsky says, we have no notion, we cannot yet have a bull's notion, so we cannot have a word, for how that true individuality will appear, how it will function, under the conditions of revolutionary struggle in its mass phase. Yeah?

I mean, Christ, no one talks like that. Not many people even write like that. But Fergal Fitzpatrick could do it, he could talk like that clean off the cuff, he could deliver this 100-proof, triple-distilled bullshit, so pure tasting it HAD to be more than bullshit, on demand. And all that it all meant, very simply, was: if you want The Answer, stick close.

Which was just what they wanted to hear.

Sammy most of all.

She just ate it up, she loved it, she listened to it without hearing the words, it was like a big aria to her, she sat beside Fergal and nodded time and twiddled with one finger in her big red hair, and murmured Mmmmmmm to encourage him, it was like she was half desperate to fuck him then and there and half a mother proud of her son doing something she did not quite understand, she watched the secret patterns his hands were drawing for her from the corner of her eyes and listened to the waves of his voice breaking, that was all, like she was following a long, curving melody, the tune of that pure self-belief that she longed to hold in

her mind, but knew from experience that she would never remember once the singer had stopped, so she had better keep the
singer himself instead.

Which (a) shows that there really is someone made for
everyone if you are honest and admit what you are like and stop
looking for the kind of people you think the kind of person you
would like to be like would like, instead of the kind of people
YOU really like, and (b) means that, although I have not been to
any of their meetings or whatever for about five years, I can get
in touch anytime, since Fergal and Sammy are now a fixture as the
happiest, steadiest, sortedest couple on the radical left/Provo
groupie scene, and all thanks to clever matchmaking me.

I still run into that crowd now+then. The weirdest time was
when I ended up drinking back at Fergal'n'Sammy's and was introduced to the widow of an IRA man who had just been shot by
the SAS. The first words she addressed to me were to declare that
Only A Brit Could Walk And Look Like That, and the next were
much later, when we were the only two left up smoking and
drinking, and they were: So you think I'm just going to let some
Bastard Brit hop in between my legs just like that, do you?

I am not much into game-play fucking, because usually this
means you are entering the Fixation Zone, and all fixated people
are full of banality and boredom, they have this laughable seri-
ousness about their pathetic fetishes, like they say, Yeah, well, I
first got into the adult-baby cross-dressing nappy scene in 1984,
no was it 1985? But this was clearly no game: the words were
coming straight up through her eyes from out of her guts, unplanned but there and solid, because of what had happened to her,
it was the authentic voice of her sudden fucked-upness, and thus
interesting. Still, I entered the room after her somewhat doubtful

about exactly what a Bastard Brit was supposed to do. So I left it up to her and it turned out that he (I) was supposed to inflict the depraved horror of cunnilingual orgasm on a decent Catholic girl, after which (she said, with catseyes) she supposed he would make her do the same for him, but he (I mean, I) was suddenly unbottled by the idea that she might not quite be able to see the border between reality (hers) and role play (mine), I mean, what if she suddenly found the bagpipes and bodhrans going in her newly widowed head at the same time as she found my dick between her teeth? Potentially un-nice. So I feigned alcoholic collapse instead, and after a few brief but cutting lines on the pathetic nancified weakness of the anglo-saxon male, she cried a lot and then went to sleep still holding tight on to me, I had to keep myself awake for ages with telling myself how heroic I was until I was sure I could turn around and sleep without waking her up. I ran pretty quick next day, I knew there was not enough of me left over from coping with me to cope with that kind of thing. And when I really woke+sobered up and really realized who I had been sleeping with, I nearly died of bowel rot.

Anyway, that is all by the way, the most important thing is that because of all this, even now I could go to an ordinary phone booth on an ordinary London street at twelve o'clock on Saturday night and phone Sammy and Fergal and expect that by doing so I would be able to arrange a meeting with the IRA.

There.

Said it.

The people I needed to get hold of for the Plan were the IRA.

Well, whatever splinter group of a cell of the extreme IRA

or INLA or IPLO or Republican SF or whatever that Fergal is now linked with. Let's just call them IRA, since I really do not know anymore. And I do not care either.

I don't care about calling the IRA?

Of course I fucking do.

It terrifies me. Why do you think it took me so long to come clean?

The thought of it curls me up and gives me instant amebic dysentery, do you think I am stupid or something?

It appalls me. It makes me unable to swallow, it pulls back my skin around my eyes, it shrivels my foreskin and drags in my balls, it makes my tongue stick to the top of my mouth and my teeth knock, it breeds a big lump of ice in my gut, on the way to the phone booth I keep inexplicably forgetting how to walk, despite 27 years' practice I keep having to prop myself up on bus stops and walls, I am forced to just stop and stand still and put my hands up to my brow, I have to talk to myself like an idiot to stop myself throwing up.

What else can I say? This is the worst thing I have ever done. This is goodbye.

So how come I am still aiming for the phone booth? Why don't I just stop, turn around and go home. It would be such a relief.

Simple: when I close my eyes I also see my possible future:

I see the bald man in the walk-up, waiting for me.

I can smell model airplane paint and dead socks, I can see the corners of pre-owned porn mags peeping from under the bed, I can hear the orange curtains sagging open and I can feel him looking at me from his greasy armchair on the day I finally have to leave my shed, and it will be Sunday alone forever. I have been there when I was 20, and I am not going back there when I am 30, for good, for bad.

I feel sick and I feel scared and I feel balder than ever, and all I want to do is roll up in a tight heap and cry myself to sleep Mummymummymummymamamia how the hell did it come to this, this was not what was meant to be, this is not Nature, this is a class-one fuck-up, I was raised and trained for MC Heaven, not this, this is someone else's life, give me back my own.

Our Father that art in MC Heaven:

I just want to sleep for a week and wake up in clean linen sheets in a nice flat with tall windows and a garden, and find out that all my blood has been changed and my liver transplanted from out of a 16-year-old teetotal virgin and my hair grown back and my clothes washed+ironed and it is Monday, and I have got The Job, and a fully powered-up legit mastercard in my own real name, in my pocket, in the bag, and in the evening I have a date with this wonderful, nice, normal MC girl, and everything, everything is all right, all right?

I just want to be like everyone else!
I just want to be what I was supposed to be!
I want another chance!

But no one was listening, of course. That is the bad news about being an adult. So eventually I remove my forehead from the brickwork it has been resting on, and take deep breaths, two, three, four, and tell myself that this is why I am here, trying to hit back, trying to save my life.

So I stand up again and I put my shoulders straight again, and I sniff a bit and snarl a bit and growl quietly and spit, and now I have this hard, cold, metal air in my nostrils: in my virtual world I raise the Uzi and splatter the secret Guardian Reader in my head, budabudabuda, I waste that hidden little jerk with a jerking knee that still responds to certain buttons, like IRA TOR-TURED HERO ARMY CAPTAIN, however much cleverer we think we are than Daily Mail readers.

If you are going to save your life, the first thing to do is cancel your subscription to The Guardian.

I look at the phone booth that is going to be my door to where I've been heading a long time without meaning to, the other world, and in my mind I see shreds of The Guardian blowing over a loch somewhere. Someone bumps into me as they leave the office, a skinheadish type (I keep forgetting I have that kind of haircut too), he just bounces off me, and looks up as if he is in for a battering, and is glad to leave. I am surprised, for this is not at all normal, I look at my reflection in a shut-up shop window, and I see this man staring out at me, a man who looks seriously MAF, like he has just stepped out of a wind tunnel: me.

And I think clear and straight:

I do not give a flying fuck about the IRA blowing up Paras, I have got drunk with several Paras and they all had unhouse-trainable hair-trigger control-freak psycho tendencies, I mean for fuck's sake, the Paras were invented to be used+lost jumping out of planes onto SS men, whatever nutter decided to try them on semi-armed demonstrators and joyriders should have his brain lanced.

On the other hand, I would not care if every IRA man was taken out and shot one fine night, because knocking off Paras is not what the IRA really do for a living, their day job is heroically bombing pubs and chip shops, shooting retired cops off their tractors, and extorting money with menaces.

Look: I am not a Para groupie, but I am not a Provo groupie either. I would buy what I want from the Villains if I could trust them (which I can't) and if they could deliver it (which they couldn't). You see, we need something bigger than a handgun, bigger than an Uzi, an AK47 or even a GPMG for the Plan: the name of the game is deterrence, we need something so big+scary, so completely macho, that we can get into the bank and get what we want and get out again without actually having to kill anyone. I would get something from the Paras if I could, but the Paras are not into Private Enterprise violence (they don't need to be, they have a fucking great State Subsidy) and so there is only one lot in London who can deliver, and that is the IRA.

The IRA are my monopoly supplier.

And by the flukes of history I do have an old, tiny track record of already once knowing some of the IRA's very smallest, least important Trade Secrets, so there is, weirdly enough, more chance that the IRA will deal with me than the Villains will.

If anyone ever tells you there is no crossover from the super-hard public Left to The Boys, you can tell them bullshit from me. Once, Sammy had to cancel her hols in Ireland, she was going to stay in this woman she knew's caravan, but the woman Sammy knew got shot by the SAS in Gibraltar. It happens. The hardcore Left is where postgrad theories of rebellion meet hardmen with guns. The postgrads provide the theories, the hardmen provide the guns, the postgrads love having guns to back up their theories at last and the hardmen love having theories to back up their guns at last, and ding! voilà: Baader-Meinhof, Red Brigades, IRA or whatever. Just like there is a crossover from the super-hard Tory Right to your actual fascists: I have personally overheard rich Young Tories discussing their rank in the Honor Guard of the National Front.

So this was it.

Crossover time.

Goodbye MC Heaven.

I walked into the phone booth and looked at the phone like it was some small but dangerous animal that might fly in my face any second, and I looked out again at the normal traffic rumbling by, and I thought:

It happens, like it happens that some people end up on park benches or making plastic airplanes in the night, and it happens more easily than you think. It happens in earshot of Radio 4 and just round the corner from people shammying their cars. You just hang out with the wrongish people and one day you wake up and realize you have just blown your last chance and you are heading for the walk-up and the orange curtains, or you remember that this woman beside you is a gunman's widow, or you agree to give someone you don't know a bed for the night or whatever and there you are. The door to the other side is closer than you think, you do not get there because of why you do the things you do, WHY you do things does not matter, WHY you do things is a game for internet philosophy nerds, all that matters is WHAT you do and who you do it with, and you can stroll on through the door before you even know it is there.

And here I was.

Desperate, with desperate friends waiting for me to do it, and I was hesitating?

I was so full of shit it made me want to throw up. I punched

the metal of the phone booth to make myself feel myself, to remind myself it was all real.

So we might be giving the IRA money to make a bomb that
might kill innocent people? So what? So if I bought guns from
Villains instead they might shoot some granny on their next raid.
So we pay our taxes to keep the Paras liquid. And meanwhile the
tin mines of Bolivia and the sweatshops of Taiwan are full of 12-
year-olds slaving away under armed guard to keep the pension
funds nicely topped up so we can all be sure we will be able to buy
enough patio furniture and golf sweaters when we are old.

Call it statistics fatigue, or just call it the grateful distance
from the cockpit of Enola Gay to Hiroshima ground zero, I do
not know, I can only be honest with you: it was just too far away
for me to really care.

See what I mean about the armpits and sucklike?

Did you think I was joking or lying? Did you think it was all
merry bullshit? Did you think I am not really that scared of becoming the bald man in the walk-up?

I am, oh, I assure you I am.

And that was the picture I held framed in my brain as I
stretched out my hand and picked up the phone and dropped in
the coin. Then I punched the buttons fast, without thinking about
anything, without even having to think about the number: my
brain had already found+locked it.

It is a very strange feeling, when something you do ten times
a day, like pressing the little buttons to make a phone call, is
something that seals your fate. It makes it seem very unreal, it
seems impossible that something so normal could be so spooky. I
suppose that is why when people think it is time for them to evac-
uate from Spaceship Earth they do things that they do every day:

the despairing commuter starts his car like every morning (he just leaves the garage locked), the career girl who has woken up one day and realized she is 40 takes the sleeping pills like every night (she just takes twenty), the bankrupted bachelor farmer walks into the field, in his own footprints from yesterday, and raises his side-by-side again (he just points it backwards). That way, the actual moment that says bye-bye, the turn of the key, the water washing down the pills, the gentle squeeze on the trigger, is so utterly natural. There is no break in the apparent order, and that is what scares us, not the end of us, the end of the world we know: it is easier to end yourself than really change yourself.

So I went for it, I hit the buttons.

And what did I get?

A fucking ansaphone is what.

There was no point leaving a message (Hi Fergal, look, I need to talk to the IRA. Call me back?) so I was about to put the phone down with a deep, shameful, secret feeling of gratitude and relief (well, I TRIED, didn't I?), when I realized what the ansaphone was actually saying. It was saying:

—Hoi, Comrade caller! This is Fergal F. Fitzpatrick, and I may in fact be in because the house is tall and my study is at the top, so I have tried to make this message about the right length for me to race down and get to you in time, in time, in time. But if I have not managed to do so by about right nnnoooooow . . .

—Hoi! said Fergal F. Fitzpatrick.

—Hi, I said.

—Hey, The Man! How's it going?

—Not so bad. Christ, you sound weird. How's Sammy?

—Plain grand. Are you calling from a phone booth.

—Am I stupid? Can I talk?

—Am I devoid of telecommunications know-how? Hence the weird sound effects.

—I have a business proposition to put to you.

—Oh yeah. (Pause) To me?

—To some people I know you know.

—Uh-huh? Well well well. Long time no see, and now such fancy footwork. Listen, no, yeah, you know, I just, yeah, let's get this straight, so you just come to me now out of the wild blue yonder and you have this big proposition and you consider it likely that people you think I know, by which I suppose you mean who I think you mean, would be somehow interested in it? Yeah?

—Yeah.

—Look, you know, I mean, we know each other, yeah, I, you mustn't take this as, you know, an insult, but, hey, it is possible for an individual, in the quiet places of their own imagination, to overrate the importance of what they are pondering, it may well be that when the idea is run up the flagpole, no one salutes it.

—Would they salute a hundred grand, and not a risk in it for them? I thought that kind of money might come in handy, what with all the splitting and regrouping going on.

—Well well. Still got the finger on the pulse, I see.

—I read the papers, I hear the talk.

—Hmmm. Make it quarter of a mil, and I can see a possibility of some general interest, depending of course on what you want.

—A hundred and fifty grand.

—You intrigue me. Don't get me wrong on this, but it is rather unexpected from your good self. I confess I thought you might be an accountant or something by now.

—I still live in my shed, Fergal, and time is getting on. I have one chance.

—Holy God, Mystery of Mysteries! You know you can get a neat shooty-tooter for a fuck's sight less than that elsewhere? Even a biggie-wiggie.

—I know that.

—I thought you might. So what do you want?

So I told him.

—Fuck me, I can't supply that, my man. I am not that close in. I mean, come on, even if I had it, I wouldn't have the authority, know what I mean? We are talking top-of-the-range security clearance here.

—Fergal, I know. That's why I need to meet your friends.

—A hundred and fifty K?

—Is my cash offer.

—It might have to be modified.

—We can talk about that.

—OK, OK, OK: I suggest we meet in the last place we met. Remember?

—Yeah.

—Good man yourself. Monday?

—If they can come ready to deliver on the spot, otherwise it's too late.

—Curiouser and curiouser. Monday at eight?

—OK.

—Just one thing, my man. How shall I put this? I am about to call numbers I do not call often, to talk to people I do not talk to without good reason. So this had fucking better be serious. As friend to friend I tell you: be there, or beware! Byeee!

I was sweaty when I put the phone down.

It had all got suddenly very real.

The Story was taking me over.

Vertigo.

I looked out at all the buses and cars and taxis going by, just like they always did. I thought everyone must be looking at me madly, like they were expecting me to decompose before their eyes or something wild, but of course they were not. Nothing visible had changed, I had walked into the doorway and I was still me and the world was still the same old world.

So I went back to Suzy's house and I told Chicho and Brady and Suzy that it looked as though it might really be on, and they all went all quiet until Suzy said:

—Great. Great. So what happens next?

—Um, I said.

—Yes? said Suzy.

—OK, um, right, tomorrow, I have to see Dai about Jimmy's Will, you have to get this Story started, I suppose, it has to be there and ready on Tuesday in case we fuck up, it's your cover.

—I've got a friend who sells ads on the News Of The Screws, I'll get in touch with her, like it was a real idea.

—Brilliant. Leave lots of ansaphone messages and stuff about it, things you can use as evidence if you need to.

—What do I do? says Brady.

He is unnaturally quiet.

—Well, you have to sort the Doggies out. Make a date for Tuesday. Do you go out with the Doggies on Sundays?

—Hampstead Heath on Sundays.

—Then do it.

—And I? says Chicho.

—What do you do Sundays?

—I am eating with the Pilar and the family of its husband, then I am sleeping, says Chicho.

—OK, so you eat and sleep. And borrow that suit Pili's old man had at the wedding, you know that horrible shiny Armani thing.

—Oh, is very easy for me. Such a nice Sunday. Such a nice plan.

—And we meet up Monday morning, eight, Brady's place, unless you hear anything else.

There was now a long pause, like we were waiting for an anvil to fall out of the sky or something. Suzy was blowing smoke rings and looking at something way back inside her head.

—Christ on a bike! said Brady suddenly, like he had been accidentally holding his breath for much longer than he meant to.— I need a drink.

—Have one, said Suzy.—Have six. Act normal.

—No problem, said Brady. For once, Brady was too gobsmacked to argue, that's how bad it was. Chicho got up to go too.

—Don't go to the same place, said Suzy.—Remember, no links.

We shook and the two of them went. That left just me and Suzy. I lit a fag, I could hardly look at her, but I made myself do it.

—I want to stay. Shit, I know we said no links . . .

—Hey, what's the big deal? So long as you go early tomorrow? Anyone who's seen you come in has seen you come in already. It's done.

—Yeah, you're right. I'm losing perspective. I mean, shit, Suzy, I'm scared.

—I'm not. It's a good plan, it might work. And if it doesn't come off we should still be OK.

—I'm still scared.

—Hey, who's here?

Which is all she said.

Which is how I found that here, in the middle of London, at the end of the twentieth and arguably worst century there was, unbelievably, someone who liked to talk about big things and make deadpan jokes and drive like a speed queen and fuck like crazy, and all with me personally myself, and as if all that was not enough, when I was scared, like I was scared now, about the Plan and about seeing the fucking IRA, God help me, and, for the first time, scared of nothing I could put a name to except going back to my nice shed, I was scared of nothing, like, nothing was waiting for me, nothing was going to get me, NOTHING suddenly had a shadow and claws and bad breath, and then, then she could just come up slowly and put the world to bed for the night, she just had to say that, and just by saying that and being there, she could turn off the white noise.

7

SUZY
ON
PLANET EARTH

I dreamed I had a big old teddy bear, wound all round with white thread, and for some reason I hated it, I was afraid of it, it was voodoo or something, I said to someone I was with—I do not know who—that I had to get rid of it, and the person said: you tried, remember, but it came back, and I was terrified, and then I looked up and saw myself, I was the Milkybar Kid, sailing by on a huge clipper ship with big misshapen yellow sails, and then I was on the ship except it was now unimaginably vast and it was only a giant frame, a steel skeleton of a ship, but still sailing, I could see all the masts and sails miles above, I was clinging to the very lowest part of the back of the frame, by the rudder, and the ship was tearing through a storm, and the sense of that vastness all about and above was crushing me as I clung on screaming.

I woke up next to Suzy.

Well, someone did, it took a second or so for someone to realize they were actually me, and another one or two for me to realize that I was not in my shed, but in Suzy's place.

I love waking up in other people's places, with this weird feeling of an unknown life all around you. I breathed it in.

The sun was coming in the white curtains, they were moving a bit in the air, because we had discovered last night that we both liked to sleep with the window open, another important thing. I looked at her, it was the first time I had ever looked at her asleep when I was properly awake. It was strange; so much of the time, we are reflecting and reacting and acting with other people, it is nearly unnerving to see someone you think you know a bit, asleep, in their own private world which is nothing to do with you, and where you have no idea what is going on.

On the other hand, it is sometimes best not to think too much about what is going on, because if you think too much about anything, it can easily turn into you thinking about yourself, instead of the thing you are supposed to be thinking about, before you realize it: if you look too carefully into the camera eyepiece, all you see is your own eye looking back at you. I think this is the whole point of Suzy's fetishist trap, which now caught my eye as I lay there.

She has this standard lamp with a shade which is actually a ballet tutu on the wire frame that used to belong to the proper shade. This (she explained) is a trap for dancer fetishists.

Apparently, everyone who is anything to do with dancing,

even if they are an untrained dance choreographer who occasionally used to do half-dancing, half-acting parts to save money for the company, even when she has not danced for years, has to be on guard against dancer fetishists, which means men who are actually turned on by thinking about how great it is that they are about to FUCK WITH A DANCER, not how great it is to be about to fuck with you yourself personally, which means you yourself as a dancer, yes, of course, but also as all the other things that you are as well, like someone who will take a taxi so as not to miss their favorite cop show and always dunks their teabag exactly twenty times or whatever other small banalities and normalities and secret sheds you have in your life. The dancer fetishist is really only into looking at himself doing this fantastically exciting thing, like all fetishists he is really only into himself. So the fetishist trap works like this:

Suzy tells every man who comes into the room to Turn that light on, will you? and then she watches in a little Victorian mirror which is cunningly positioned on the opposite wall, to see if you look like you are kind of excessively keen or excessively shy to do so, because turning the lamp on involves putting your hand right up into this pink ballet tutu, and if this turns you on madly or worries you intensely, you fail the test, making it highly unlikely that you and Suzy will ever fuck.

I am relieved to say I did not even notice what it was until she told me, I just thought, Hmmm bizarre lampshade, so I passed the test A1.

I was just gloating smugly about this, when I remembered I had to meet the IRA tomorrow, and felt a distinct shitfulness in the guts, and a twitching sweat, so I made myself think this was not such a big thing really.

Meeting the IRA not such a big thing?

But we have been through that. It was just the only thing to do.

That calmed my colon down, I was not crossing any great new rivers, I was just upping the ante in a game I was already playing. I looked around the room and took deep breaths, two, three, four, and concentrated on seeing things the way they were: look after the details, and the big picture will look after itself.

What I saw, as I looked around, was Suzy's clothes.

Suzy has this particular thing she does with her clothes, she keeps them all out on coat hangers on the walls, and not only jeans and coats and T-shirts and knickers and suchlike, but party gear and costumes and stuff from when she was a dancer, there is every kind of material and color, strokable deep-dark velvets, crackling metallics, floating faded silks, starchy crackle-cottons, squeaky shiny plastics, and of course a fair smattering of clawable black leather perfuming the air like a refined saddlery. Her clothes cover all the walls of the room, the lowest hems brush the floor and the highest coat hangers are on nails right up by the ceiling, they are arranged not in straight lines, but just anyhow they look good.

Suzy told me this was to save space, to stop her needing a wardrobe and keep them from getting crumpled and damp, and it probably was, though I half thought maybe it was also to remind her of her dance-making days, which now seemed to be over. The thing is, her company lived on beans and scratched around for money for three years in Glasgow and each time they put something on, The Scotsman or even The Guardian said it was A Vibrant Evening or whatever, and everybody loved it, and nothing happened. Each time, for three years, they read the reviews and had drinks to celebrate and woke up the next day half waiting for the phone to ring and the Funding to come through.

They did not realize that MC Heaven had ended.

And what LTD in its right mind would sponsor stuff that was radical-fem revolutionary? Actually, loads of individual businessmen would like to watch athletic girls rolling around in heaps or jumping about without much on, frequently in leather jackets (which I suppose was Suzy's idea), and I'm sure they could have ignored the in-your-face politics and looked at the legs instead, but that just goes to show that LTDs are not naive about who they sponsor.

Anyway, two years ago, the Scottish Arts Council wrote a nice letter saying that they thought The Department of Dance (Suzy's group) was very good, but what with limited funds and all, they thought it vital to have a Gaelic-speaking contemporary dance team instead. Think about it. Suzy did. So she decided to come to London, and then found out about the mincing machine, and got into drugs, and so forth, about which you already know as much as I knew then.

I lay and thought about all this, and her, and I felt that she was becoming more real to me each second, but each second she was getting further away, the focus was getting sharper but the lens was zooming out, the more I knew her the more I knew I knew nothing about her, I had opened the encyclopedia at the section headed SUZY, just to check out a few details, just for the Plan, and now I found the entry was going on for pages and pages, it had footnotes and references to things I had never heard of, it was going on out of sight, into forever.

I watched all her clothes on their hangers moving gently in

the breeze, it was like these were all her different possible ways of living, the whole cast of the show called SUZY ON PLANET EARTH, just hanging up and waiting to come alive when she got up and going, all chapters of her I knew nothing about, or maybe had got half-glimpses of them flitting by, and maybe would never have anything to do with, Suzies she could change into and disappear from me at any moment.

Then she kind of snuffled and moved over a bit and flopped her arm over my chest without waking up, and I looked at her again and noticed for the first time how long her eyelashes were, and how pumped full of sleep she looked, and now when I looked around the room again all those clothes on their hangers felt like things that were waiting for me to find out about them, a nice, long story I would learn bit by bit.

I was a big windsock, she could blow me this way and that way just by waving in her dreams.

Next thing I knew I was waking up, so I make the risky guess that I must have fallen asleep again. As I surfaced, I thought I heard the echo of a man's voice saying Goodbye Princess, and I half caught the final clunk of the ansaphone turning off.

Suzy was out of bed and sitting at her table at this museum-piece Amstrad PC, with her hands in her lap, looking at the screen.

—Hi, I said.

—Hi, she said.—This is a big shitty bummer, I can't even think of the title.

—Well it doesn't matter, does it? I said.—It's only cover, it can be a load of unadulterated crap for all we care.

—Oh yeah, I forgot.

I watched her for a while as she looked at the screen, and then I looked over at the ansaphone and saw the MESSAGE light was blinking so I had not been dreaming.

—Looks like there's a message for you, I said.

—Och, never mind that, she said, without looking round.—It's just someone.

—Oh, right, I said, and wondered who this someone was.

Then I watched her starting to write, clitter-clatter went her fingers, and I felt kind of superfluous to requirements. And that made me think: we are not married or anything, I am still at the toothbrush-borrowing stage, for Christ's sake, why should I just hang around here anyway?

Quick: Look like you've got a life! Looking like it is half the battle.

—I've got to go. I've got to get things sorted.

—How very traditional of you, she said and smiled.

—Well.

—Well?

—I don't know.

—Let me know how it goes with Dai?

—Can I ring you?

—From a phone booth.

—Yeah, of course.

—Okeedoke.

I felt like some ameba parting as I went away, like I was leaving a lump of me behind too. I had not felt this for a very long time, it was horrible but wonderful.

And so off I went, to meet my own life again.

It seemed very disposable now.

Except that I had the Plan, thank fuck.

Nice to have a Plan.

The Plan meant I had Things To Do, and what I had to do next was go talk about Jimmy's Will with Dai Substantial.

8

A FAT
WELSH TART
WITH TATTOOS

Dai Substantial is my emotional adviser. He can see through my life like it was a jellyfish, and tell me what is going on inside me, so I intended to combine asking him about Jimmy's Will (the Plan) with telling him about Suzy (my life).

Obviously, no one is born being called Dai Substantial, he was born David J. Evans, but his passport and driving license and bankers' cards, all the things that prove someone exists, say: Dai Substantial. You must not go thinking that this shows he is a pervert who has changed his name to sound more interesting, like someone I know who is really called Albert Scraggs but changed his name to Joey 8. Yes, 8. I award Mr. Joey 8 the Nobel Prize for Sadness, I mean, who is so utterly boring at heart that they even have to try and make the name on their checkbook interesting? This is a good principle in Life: the more wacky the haircut or clothes or politics or whatever, the more boring the person is likely to be once you get used to them.

Dai did not change his name on purpose, what happened was that he is 38 now, so he is just old enough to be in the last generation who got taken on in the Welsh mines, and he started as a trainee engineer underground at Merthyr Mawr, and on his first day everyone was rather taking the piss out of him, since he was the new boy, all these old blue-scarred miners asked what did he want to be called because they could not call him Dai Evans, there were already three Dai Evanses on this shift, they had all been given new names, each according to his most visible characteristic. So everyone demanded on Dai's first day: he would have to be called something as well, what name did he want? And young David J. Evans, being somewhat on his mettle, retorted hastily and (it turned out) foolishly that he did not give a shit what they called him, so long as it was something substantial. So that (of course) was that.

These Valleyites, says Dai, defined as a nancy-boy anyone who was seen in public with a girl, or who did not like sticking his head up a prop-forward's bum. So when Dai discovered that he was actually gay, he thought it might be wise to leave his valleys and come to somewhere a tad more liberal, though far more Tory. But by this time he had been called Dai Substantial for so long that it had become his actual name.

I was 19 and he was 29 when we met, but we had both just escaped from places that would have been at the end of the line if there had been a line left, both of us wanted to mainline the sights+sounds of the big bad metrop, we scurried about Fitzrovia and the West End and Holborn like two labradors in spring, with Dai holding a guidebook and reciting about the historical greatnesses of London in a Welsh preacher voice, and for three months we pickled our friendship solid by living in Dai's patented three-day rhythm, which goes like this:

DAY ONE: remain in coma until about 2 p.m., wallow about racked with pain and remorse until about 3 p.m., from about 4 p.m., decant self into the metaphysical stage of hangover, when Pain has gone but Reality is not yet working. By 7 p.m. approx. begin to feel the miracle of restored health. At approx. 10 p.m. retire to bed with Classic Novel and hot-water bottle if the season demands.

DAY TWO: Awake refreshed to a day of discipline and morality. Stuff self with organic tomatoes and suchlike all day. Get loads of work (whatever kind it is) done due to feeling so healthy and renewed. In the evening watch Frog film on video, go out to theater or whatever, drink mineral water while discussing same with pals. When offered Satan's Buttermilk, refuse, saying: I obey no laws but my own. Sleep at approx. 12 p.m.

DAY THREE: Up too early and work slightly manically all morning. When the Afternoon Blues descend again at about 3 p.m., and life seems to be an empty+pointless slurry pit, a cocktail of equal parts banality and pain remind self that it (you) will definitely be off its (your) head within eight hours. This gives the courage+conviction for another few hours' work before the News, then you can fill the remaining couple of decaying hours with eating, washing hair, shaving and choosing sexy rig for the THIRD NIGHT MADNESS.

DAY FOUR: See Day One.

Eventually I decided I wanted to booze when I felt like it, not when some mad bloody timetable said I could. And Dai replied:

—Each to his own, lad. If I boozed when I wanted I would booze all the time. But then I do not seek secular salvation, and you still do. There lies the difference between us.

So from then on we drank less together, we only met up when his three-day cycle and my desire to drink with him coincided. But before this, Dai introduced me to the Friends of Mrs. King.

Another free tip for success in Life: If you ever find yourself wanting a job at the Opera in Covent Garden or Glyndebourne (it doesn't work at the Coliseum, which is considered non-U by the Friends) or the Bastille, or the Met or Sydney or Toronto even, you must always mention, when applying, that you are a Friend of Mrs. King.

This is a way of declaring that you are

(a) gay

(b) a social insider

which is a potent combination in the world of Opera.

The Friends of Mrs. King are a tribe like any other male tribe except richer and Out, they sit about together in bars and clubs, you stroll up, you sit down and you know exactly what you can talk about, and how, and what is forbidden.

Everyone needs a tribe.

If you do not have a tribe, you are nothing, no one will come to your festivals and your funeral, you will just wear out your life in a spiritual walk-up.

(I once had a walk-up in Acton with orange curtains of course and this old armchair in it. The armchair had a sort of grayish greasy trough at the top of the backrest, which seemed to fit my head exactly, as if it had been made to measure especially for me. Spooky. When I was on my own in the evenings, wondering what to do with myself, I kept thinking someone was going to come in and say:

—Well, as you can see, we have everything prepared just for you, even a made-to-measure chair, so welcome to your life.

That was when I decided to ask Big Sis if I could build a shed in her yard. I made it sound like a Merry Plan, but actually I was pretty desperate, I thought if I sat in that chair again I might just melt away into the clammy stain, like some crap horror film: If You Want To Stay Alive, Stay Away From THE GREASY CHAIR).

There is a great pleasure in learning tribal secrets and codes. I mean, who knows, maybe there is a tribe around for us, somewhere, and we will not find it if we do not look, so we just have to wander about and keep on inventing ourselves by adding bits on here and there, like we were some model kit human being:

Locate and cement FERGAL'S GRIN (part 362) to DAI'S VIEW OF THE WORLD (part 157) and attach the result to SENSE OF HUMOR ASSEMBLY (parts 127–144). Your personality is now complete and ready for painting.

Anyway, with most tribes, the actual secrets are pretty feeble when you discover them, but the Friends of Mrs. King did have some secrets about people you had actually heard of. I knew years before everyone else about Pat of Eastenders, I learned why hamsters in Hollywood are called Richard's Gear, I gasped to hear who Ian McKellen had been seen with last week, and laughed at how they all fancied Peter Lilley and Michael Portillo (the Friends of Mrs. King all vote Tory). I lapped it all up as the layered washes of green lasers bounced off white singlets and drug-induced muscles or the transsexual queens held court, the same as I liked it when Barrington-Charrington told me how to spot the secret death announcements of SAS men in the Torygraph.

I liked hearing the gossip from On High, it all made me feel like some nice Stewardess had mysteriously decided to upgrade me to the big wide seats at the front of the world.

But soon, of course, the question of my fuckability arose.

You cannot get the benefits of the tribe without applying for full membership eventually, you cannot expect to get security but keep freedom, no tribe will make that deal with you.

Now, like all men and women with power over male or female actors, singers, dancers and the like, the Friends were used to some pretty hardnosed dealing when it came to fucking, underneath all the culture-vulture fluttering and high-church campery. You can't blame them: what, after all, is the difference between an actor and a whore?

Actors kiss.

So anyway, one evening I was at a table outside Halfway to Heaven, lightly doped up, admiring Trafalgar Sq. with (by now) a proprietorial eye and scoffing lager gently, when Jeremy of the Corps de Ballet suggested with almost mathematical clarity that a full-time temporary assistant stage-manager's job for me = regular sex with him. I was flattered, since the normal rear-entry-level deal for Young Lads is a part-time box-office summer vacation job, but this seemed the right time to say that actually I had not been holding out for a good offer, I just wasn't gay. To which Jeremy replied, Really? How did I know?, not at all put off (because of course, me saying that was the ultimate pricing strategy, it was like saying I was a virgin being head-hunted) and I answered that I had tried two days ago, that's how.

Well, I thought I should.

The great thing in Life is to work out the difference between what you want and what you think you ought to want, especially with something like Gayness, which is one of the boom-time thangs of our day. In twenty years people will ask you: What? You were free+twenty-something in the nineties and YOU NEVER EVEN TRIED BEING GAY!, like you had been twenty in the seventies (when AIDS meant Marital and Free meant girls thinking they ought to fuck anyone who was friendly) and somehow missed out on sex. Well: the only way to be sure about whether you are into something is to suck it and see.

I put this to the person who I suspected was the most handsome+sexy of my friends (I was not sure, I was new to the idea) and he thought it might be sensible to try too, times being what they were and this not being a rehearsal and all, so we did.

The excitement was the exciting thing, if you see what I mean, it was like Being Sixteen (reprise), slipping in between the sheets and another person's arms without having any real idea what was about to happen to your body+mind.

Not much, sad to say.

The hairiness was fine by me, like I said, I like hairy armpits and stuff. The scratchy face was bizarre, but not a problem. The first problem was the bones, there are just too many bones in a man. But the big problem was, just where the other person's belly should smooth around down into a beautiful cunt, all you find is a boring old dick just like yours. I mean, wow, thrilling. Give me a chorizo any day.

And if sucking that doesn't turn you on (dick, not chorizo) then tick the box and take the next bus back to Straight City, because dick-worship is the main thing about being gay. I mean, of course there are assholes too, and a nice ticklish vein or something around there, as in the Playground Ditty:

She stuck her finger up my ass.

I came enough to fill a glass

Or, as Chicho's song of Olde Zaragoza has it (cue flamenco-ish guitars), Las putas te tocan al culo, meaning whores stick fingers up asses in order to increase turnover, but that is nothing to do with being gay, it is just to do with having an extra Y-chromosome: assholes are standard procedure wherever women are not about or when men are too drunk, doped or fucked up to come otherwise.

Ask any doctor.

I was once drinking with two of them, two young professionals in the field of human fucked-upness, and I told them about my accountant cousin who went in to work one unexpected Sunday, plotting to knock out the Senior Partner with his zeal+ dedication, only to find Mr. S. Partner tangled up in my cousin's gas-suspended executive chair, legs round his ears and the cleaning lady's hoover-nozzle up his bum with the switch on BLOW. A difficult social/professional moment.

Hey, said the Young Doctors, Surprise us, Tell us news not history: for it turned out that when Mr. Average suddenly gets the loud blood in his ears and finds himself looking wildly around for something to stuff up his ass, a hoover is very often what he hits on to sit on. Dickish shape and motherly associations, maybe? Whatever, your hospital doctor just yawns when the next hoover-up-ass case is wheeled in. One of them had this bloke with a turnip stuck up his ass, it had to be cut up in situ with a scalpel before they could get it out. As the guy was wheeled out again, Young Doc 1 could not resist shouting:

—Next time for Christ's sake leave some foliage on so we can pull it out!

Doc #2 countered that the other day he had had this guy with a bust of Beethoven up the bum.

—Hmm. Life-size? asked Doc 1, sipping his 6% Old Fruity ale with mild, off-call interest.

—No, about one-third life-size, I should say. Very sharp looking around that coat collar, though.

Docs 1&2 agreed the best laugh was whenever some 17-year-old Young Gun came strutting in, cap on backwards, half-proud of his first dose of the clap, saying he had to give a sperm sample, imagining that he was on for a pile of blue mags and a jam jar in a quiet lav somewhere, only to be met by Nurse Alisdair MacLeman, a 250-pound ex-oilworker from Aberdeen, snapping on ye olde lubricated latex handwear and growling, in Caledonian vengeance:

—Knees to the chin and think of England, laddie.

So then I replied with my own Prostate Tale, which is this: I once had this fiber-optic thing the size of a ballpoint slid up my dick because my Doc cocked up and thought I had prostate cancer (nice Doc). I came up from the anaesthetic and out from the hospital, passed A1, cursing the medical profession but praising God, and assured that I would only Experience Mild Discomfort when pissing. I went for a couple of pints to celebrate, with the result that twenty minutes later the poor sod standing unluckily next to me in the lav had by far the worst moment of his life so far, when the happy+humming bloke next to him (me) suddenly sprayed a plume of bright red blood out over the white porcelain and changed into a screaming, agonized loony. In the pub, they heard the yells, turned round and saw (a) Mr. Unlucky running straight out of the pub, doing a fine imitation of a melting-face routine from a splatter movie, and (b) me crawling out, white and sobbing.

But as for prostates, so you come if your prostate is prodded, so what? If you were tied down in an unwankable position for two weeks, you would come without anything, on autopilot. Ask any monk. Just biology.

And all the Queer Lads, being lads, always have their green lights on and blazing away, it is satisfaction guaranteed, Christ, the world would be much happier if all men between the ages of 16 and whenever, when the old hormones are beetling about muttering WHATCANISHAGWHATCANISHAG? were told to leave girls alone and get on with the role models and pecking orders and muscle worshiping and uniform fetishry and saying how smelly each other's feet+farts are and reminding each other how much they drank last time and getting lots of hard, speedy, who-cares-who, fun-time fucking under their belts, and all that sort of testosterone-flavored deal. No wonder so many young thick straight men are so filled with secret jealousy+hatred of Chaps Who Bat For The Other Side: while they are squashing themselves into a fucked-up fantasy world where boys don't cry and girls who say yes to anyone say yes to everyone, they can hardly help seeing that the gay laddos are having a much better time in the here+now.

Myself, I think I was maybe too late starting, I found it rather dull to feel a body just like mine, no imagination involved, no strange, distant, half-guessed feelings. Not unpleasant, horse or jockey, assuming plenty of hi-tech lubrication, but hey, what about the metaphysics?

Look, I was once in some club with Dai and he said he was off to the Dark Room, and I asked him what happened in it and he just gave me his Nero of the Valleys look and said:

—Anything.

Which sounded wild and thrilling. But it was not really going to be ANYTHING, it was going to be whatever can go on between strangers with one dick, one mouth and one asshole apiece, half off their heads, in total darkness, which is quite limited when you think about it, however desperately you mix+match. Everyone was going to go home having come (being male) and having done exactly what they planned when they left home, which sounds about as wild+thrilling as an evening with a Clean and Liberated Couple in Sidcup.

But let he who is not fucked up cast the first judgment.

Dai reckons that what all straight men really want is their mother, 30 years younger and in suspenders.

I am not aware of this in me, but then I wouldn't be, would I, because it would be subconscious, wouldn't it? I mean, my mother does not have a Scottish accent or wear black leather, like Suzy.

My grandmother does (the Scottish accent, I mean).

Who knows, who knows?

It all looks like freedom until you get there and turn around and look back and think: of course!

Each to their own, say I.

So I decided I was Stray not Gay, and just stayed pals with Dai, who is my sexless brother in the great free-masonry of the slightly fucked-up, those people who can see (i) shit for what it is, but (ii) no further than the next party.

And if it's a party you want (and who doesn't?) Dai Substantial stands alone.

Dai is so popular not due to having the body of a miner, the voice of Dylan Thomas and the liver of a polar bear, but because he is the great master of keeping the dream going. In his life, the pose has become the reality, WYSIWYG and what you see+get is (as Dai puts it) a fat Welsh tart with tattoos.

These tattoos are quite famous, they are a tribute to the Grammar School System which, says Dai, gave the world J.P.R. Williams and at least a few WC lads+lassies the chance to get a half-decent imitation of a kosher UMC education: what on earth (Dai asks) is the point of having schools that act like there has been a revolution when there hasn't? Have both, says he, or have neither. Anyway, the tattoos say:

BORN TO BE CHEAP (left shoulder)

ARS NATURAM ORNAT (right buttock)

and ARS LONGA VITA BREVIS (left buttock)

and where you get to see them, if ever, is his unique flat in Camden Town, which seems principally designed as a dope-smoking and coke-sniffing emporium, it is full of big, fat sofas and cushions, it has fashion magazines thrown everywhere, a life-size cardboard cut-out of Maria Callas which I once spent half an hour cadging from the EMI shop in Oxford St. to give to Dai for his birthday when I was totally broke, it has the spring-frame out of an old mattress up on the wall to put glasses and bottles in, window frames just hanging on walls, a huge harness of angel's wings from Wings over Berlin hanging from the ceiling and in the middle of the room there is the altarpiece from a Bayreuth production of Parsifal, a gift from a besotted German, complete with a lidded, costume-jeweled Grail in which Dai keeps his coke and dope and beside which lies a huge Welsh Bible bound in brass.

Also, the room is always full of mallow and larkspur because his mother is German, she met his father in 1945, Dai Evans Senior woke up one morning and found the guards from the POW camp had run away from the approaching Red Army and so he set off due west to find some British or Americans, except the first thing he found was Dai's mother-to-be, Gretchen, sitting crying in a ditch with her entire family all dead around her from an SS mine on the road, and they decided to go on together, both being 19 and lost, and all the way through May 1945, across half Germany, they had no food, but the hedges and roadsides, being free of orderly German peasants that year, were full of mallow and larkspur, and when at last they settled down in Cwmdoom, Wales, to live and have Dai Junior+sibs, that was all they ever grew in their garden, mallow and larkspur.

I do not know if this is true, because you cannot tell with Dai, but it should be, so who cares?

Dai reckons this family history is why he does not care about food but cares about flowers; whatever the reason, it is true that he has never been seen to open anything more foodlike than a carton of milk, never mind actually cook anything, he really lives in cafés and pubs and clubs, this is just where he dresses and sleeps and holds court and fucks. So when he got the flat, he decided to make it a kitchen-free zone, he+me just slung out all the easy-to-clean surfaces and fitted units and everything and knocked the wall through to use the extra space up for his enormous bathroom which has one bath on clawed feet, another sunken one with water jets, and an enormously powerful shower unit which stands freely in the middle of the room, on a chrome stalk. The whole floor slopes gently from the corners towards a big central plughole, Dai says he copied it from Scandinavia, you can use the entire room as a giant shower if you want, which people frequently do.

Apart from this there is only an allegedly well-equipped bedroom which, for obvious reasons, I have never been in, and so anything I said about that would be just guesswork, so I won't, I will leave you to guess for yourself.

The whole gaff was paid for outright by the Friends of Mrs. King, who are all rich and have (of course) no school fees or spouses to worry about. Despite them paying for it, the pad is Dai's alone, no one has a key or comes in unless he wants them to, it is all in his name, lock, stock and freehold, he only takes presents, says he, not payment, and a present with strings is like a violin without them.

Dai never goes anywhere, except to Milton Keynes once a month just to remind himself what Hell looks like, he says. He says that when a queer is tired of London he should get a wife. He hopes his flat will become remembered in Queerstory as the birthplace of post-AIDS art. He thinks that in another five or ten years, if there is no cure, HIV will be like TB was a hundred years ago: people with HIV will write acres of poetry and music, but it will not be about HIV. Chopin and Keats and Kafka knew they were going to die painfully of TB but they didn't write about TB, they wrote about Life, says he. Like then, a lot of people will know they are almost certainly going to die in five or ten years, but will not be crippled by pain or deformity until very late on. It might concentrate people's minds wonderfully, says Dai. He hopes to live to see the first massive novel or great oratorio which is driven by HIV but never mentions it.

He is allowed to talk like that because of course he tested positive two years ago, I was one of the first people he told, I was calling him from a phone booth in Hammersmith, by the Met station, about something else, I can't remember what, and I ended up being in there for an hour and ten minutes talking to him, it was horrible to be so far away, but I think he preferred it because everyone he met was hugging him anyway, it was a change to just talk to a voice for an hour without having to see the other person and let them hug you to make them feel better about it, so I let him let me suffer like that, because it was him that needed to feel better, not me.

When I tested negative about a year later he bought me Krug champagne. (I had to take the test, I was fucking some years ago with a semi-junkie girl who swore she never shared works, she said she fixed like I did, with new needles each time, I was flattered and so I believed her, but then a year ago I happened to be drinking beer with her and a load of other people, and someone said hey, had we heard that Bill the Wop had just died of AIDS, and she went completely white, I had never actually seen anyone go white, I had only read about it, I thought it was just poetic license, but it isn't and she did: all white and boneless, she went. She was negative too, as it turned out, but I naturally finished with her after finding she had lied about that. That was a very very very bad time, waiting. The worst mistake I made was, I flew to Ireland to go drinking for a week, to forget it, because Ireland is the best place to go drinking for a week, but when I landed in Dublin the first thing I saw was the car-park, and in it half the cars had number plates like 567 HIV, which is very common over there. Spooky.)

So that is why I am allowed to talk to Dai like that about HIV and how it is going to change the world.

It is also why I will be allowed to talk about what I want his friend Jimmy, who is dying quite quickly now of AIDS, to do for the Plan.

So anyway, I waited until about 12:30, because Dai is never up till then at the earliest, breakfasted nastily on cancerous fried eggs and bacon, stuffed my brain achingly full of the crap in the Sunday Qualities, and wandered over to the flat in Camden Town, rang the bell, and put my ear down to listen at the intercom above the traffic noise.

But the door lock buzzed first, I pushed it open, and only then did a voice come out of the grille, a voice deep yet deeply camp, sounding as if it came from the unplumbed depths of despair:

—Oh thank God, somebody here at last, I thought I was going to die of sensual deprivation! Come in, come in, whoever you are, and bring the world in with you!

So I get in without saying who I am, which seems a bit crazed to me, I mean, why have an intercom if you just let anyone in? Anyway, I get to the door, which is highly respectable except for a poster in black and white saying

FUCK AGAINST AIDS

and Dai opens it. He is dressed in silver latex trousers and nothing else, he has a fat hairy belly hanging down, but his hairy pecs and big arms look heavily worked-out.

—Thank God, someone straight at last, says Dai, kissing me paradoxically.—I am just bloody sick of Art.

—Art?

—Well, it's easier to say than neurotic coke queens having their breakdowns all over my flat, and over me, come to it, which they mostly did of course thanks to my matchless erotic skills, I suppose it's all part of life's banal dralon, man cannot live by wanking alone, but I do so long for someone with a soft dick and a stiff upper lip to visit me, I find they go together, don't you, someone nice and repressed for once, I can't stand a bloody moment more of this Californian emoting, so if you've come to emote at me, don't, salvation is off the menu, we are not At Home To Mrs. Despair today. I'm so glad you came, lovely boy, I was dying of boredom.

—Is this Day Three?

—No, only Day Two, and I DID keep off the drink last night, though the cocaine got me when I wasn't looking, but IT'S SUNDAY! Ugh, I couldn't stand Sunday on my own, I'd end up hanging myself because the wallpaper was wrong. And look, half my mallows need changing, they are just TOO bloody bio-degradable, but then, who isn't?

Like a lot of people, the thing that makes Dai such good fun most of the time is also the thing that makes him a pain in the ass some of the time. I mean, I was supposed to be here on Operation Jimmy's Will, but Dai is so into keeping the juggling game going and resisting what he calls the Brute Gravity of Reality, that when you actually need some serious advice from him, you end up talking for three hours about nothing, yarning away, leading him on, helping him keep the ball up, feeding him the right lines, like

—What's so bad about Sunday?

—Got a fag, butt? Mmmmmm, gimmegimmegimme, Nature's Way to healthy bowels. I don't know, I just always think that if I ever decide to take a short cut to the great Cottage in the sky, the last still of my life will show a clock saying three in the afternoon and a calendar saying: This is the day of The LORD. Oh God, I think you're starting to recede! You are!

—Thanks.

—Oh, there's a shame, you used to be quite pretty in a boring sort of way. Baldness doesn't suit you.

—I didn't choose it.

—If you tolerate something, butt, you choose it with every breath. But then I suppose Time is like going to an apprentice evening at Vidal Sassoon: you get whatever cut you're given. At least I never had looks to lose, thank God, I was always just a fat tart, which is fairly easy to keep up. But I WAS the heir of two thousand years of repression and doom. At least we had something to fight against. Now everybody believes in Life Assurance and Shopping. There is only one cure; we have to make everybody think of death all the time.

—Death?

—Death.

—All the time?

—Every day, all day. I long for the day when we all say, with a smile, on any social occasion, And don't forget: you're going to die! Let's try it. Come on.

—How?

—You are a customer in a burger bar, right?

—I am?

—I see it all so plainly as I saw it long ago.

—All right then. A hungry customer.

—And I am the eager burgermaster. Note my spots and greasy hair. Come on, come on.

—Um, right. Hi.

—Hi sir. Are you being helped?

—Not yet, as a matter of fact.

—Then lay it on me, baby.

—Well, I think I rather fancy a hamburger please.

—You've come to the right place, sir.

—With some cheese.

—A fine original touch, sir. And look! Here it is, fresh-cooked just for you.

—Flame-grilled, I trust?

—Five days ago, sir.

—Well thanks. Here's some virtual money.

—Ta guvnor. Here's your virtual change.

—Thanks. Bye.

—Have a good day—and don't forget: You're going to die!

—Oh, right, thanks, and you too!

—Bye sir. Well? What do you think. I mean, imagine it! Merry Christmas Darling—and don't forget you're going to die!

—Pretty depressing.

—On the contrary, you rancid wanking pervert, it would make people stop being banal and boring and thinking it's all going to be all right if you keep the payments up, because it isn't going to be all right, this is the only chance you get and I am sick—sick to death!—of seeing people wandering around the world with glazed eyes as if they were sure of getting a second shot of life. That's all for this evening, the next national news is at 9 o'clock so goodbye until then and don't forget: you're all going to die! Much better. Dear God, they seem to have thought of nothing except dying in medieval days, but they still planned cathedrals that would take a hundred years to build! I long for the day when the school trip of kiddies going round Tintern Abbey will stop for a solemn moment to watch some poor old lad being given the injection because he has decided that he would like to die now, looking at the Abbey surrounded by his friends, and not in some senility ward with Peter bloody Frampton playing on Radio 2 in eighteen months' time. And the children will look gravely on with their big eyes and the teacher will say, with great care and feeling: This is where he wanted to die. One day you are going to die too, children, you will be able to choose this place too, if you want. And now let us all go and have a delicious ice cream, and enjoy the sunshine dappling the leaves. And down with shopping! Well, that's quite exhausted me, lovelyboy, though it has cheered me up a bit. Nice to have a butty to talk to about the tragic basis of existence, like, isn't it? But come along now, you didn't come here to talk about Sunday, go on, then, do your worst, tell poor Dai your woes, I feel just about strong enough again now.

—I'm totally fucked up, I said.

—Oh good. Come on come on come on, we are all sitting comfortably, tell us something exciting.

So then I told him about Suzy, which I think took quite a long time.

It certainly took a lot of cigarettes.

—Well, said he, when I had finished.—I must say I like the sound of this tummy of hers. Is it really that flat?

—Yeah, I said wistfully.

—Like a boy's tummy?

—No, I said definitely.

—Just testing. Yes, well, after all, it is about time you settled down, you know.

—Is it?

—We all have to leave the party sometime, lovelyboy, and no one ever wants to, but who wants to be the oldest swinger in town? Scrag End Dressed as Lamb. Economy Mince Dressed as Lamb. If you go at the right time, people will wave a nice good-bye and say after you have gone how nice you were, and even mean it. It's all a very delicate balance, isn't it? You can't just go off home with the first person who finds your G-spot, what about all the other people you might have liked? But on the other hand what if you go on looking for too long, so you get used to the looking, not the being with the people? They say Get it out of your system, love, but I wonder if you do? What if you get it into your system? I myself have considered recently the possible advantages of settling down with a nice homecounties homeowning homo before the champagne goes quite flat and the gray morning comes. So my own advice would be to go for it, lovelyboy, but then it always is, isn't it, and look where it's got me, merely used and abused by neurosing maniacs like your good self, no milk to offer a suffering friend the life-restoring NCOT—Nice Cup Of Tea—and no fags left either, I see. Dearie me, was it for this Socrates drank the hemlock?

—Sorry, I've smoked them all. I'll get some more, and some milk.

—Cigarettes and Milk and Wild Wild Women.

It was mad, I mean, I actually got to the door before I remembered about the Plan and why I had really come, that (like I said) is the trouble with talking to Dai. I stopped and leaned on the wall and looked at him.

—There's something else, I said.

—What, something else than love? Come come.

—It's serious, Dai.

—It all is, dear, it's known in the trade as Life. All the more virtue in making light of it, mmm?

—It's got to do with Jimmy, Dai.

Dai looked at me, and his eyes never wobbled at all, they just kind of got deeper.

—Yes? Well? Really, I never put you down as someone who would confuse ponderousness with profundity, lovelyboy, so don't disappoint me, please. What business have you with our poor Jimmy?

—Is he still doing money laundering with his Will?
—He is, said Dai.

Let me explain.

Jimmy is Dai's long-time part-time partner, who has now got full-blown AIDS and no money. This is not a pleasant combination. There are too many people with AIDS now, it is hard to find someone to pay Jimmy's bills to keep him in a nice private hospital with a view and books and flowers and exciting food and stuff. The only person who would pay for him if he could would be Dai, but Jimmy will not take money from Dai even when Dai has it, because Jimmy has spent his short life largely in cadging money from people he did not really like by pretending to like them, and he is terrified in case he starts to think of Dai as a money machine too, and thus loses his only true love just when that is the only thing he has left and the only thing he needs.

So Dai hit upon this scheme that means Jimmy can live off the fact he is dying.

In the last three months, Jimmy has become the world's first pre-posthumous money launderer.

What happens is this:

You go to Dai and, like anyone wanting to launder funds, you tell him that you are getting paid, or paying, so-and-so for something-or-other, but you do not want anyone ever to know who paid you or vice versa, or when or even that anyone ever paid you for anything at all anyway and so on. So first, Dai checks you are happy to wait for six months to a year to get your clean money, which people are, all money laundering takes time, and then you go and give your money to Jimmy, and he puts you (or whoever you want) down for that much in his Last Will and Testament, minus 10% for his services in dying. The Will is all legit and clear, no one will contest it, Jimmy is fixed for kosher death duties and everything, so the Inland Revenue will have no reason to take a second look. And even if they did, even if the police ever heard of the Will, even if they tried to prove a link between you and whoever it is via Jimmy, they will have a hard time because Jimmy (who is already way beyond all threats) will soon be just plain beyond. The link will be cut by Death, the blade that breaks all links.

You are quite safe in your investment, because it is all done through Dai, and Jimmy would never go to his death knowing he had left Dai stitched up, what possible gain would it be for Jimmy to end his life in lies and guilt? Of course, people often go psychotic in the final stages of AIDS, but Jimmy and Dai know this, and they know that Dai will just refuse to alter Jimmy's Will if he goes mad, on the grounds that he is mad. You get to see the Will, if you want, Dai keeps it for him, it is re-witnessed every week in case anyone is worried, you can see your bequest to whoever written in for you. Jimmy's rates compare (I am told) very favorably with other forms of money laundering, even taking death duties into consideration.

Apart from the monumental hospital bills, Jimmy gets Dai to spend most of the money on flowers for his room. It was Dai who got him hooked on flowers, I went to the flower market once with Dai, at five in the morning, nicely half-high on coke and with body loose from dancing, to buy a carful of mallow and larkspur for Jimmy, Dai spent hours choosing them, I just sat and buzzed away gently to myself and watched Dai choosing flowers while the night changed into the day. I think it was maybe the best piece of happiness I ever saw anyone having.

—OK, said Dai, when I described what I needed Jimmy to do for the Plan, though I didn't tell him why.—In your case I will make Jimmy make an exception, you will be written in now and pay later. Write the lady's name down, lovelyboy. Very well, leave it to me. I'll drop a copy of the Will round to your place tomorrow. Will you be At Home?

—I'm working.

—How very unwise of you. Come for a Day Three drink tomorrow night?

—I can't, I've got to meet someone.

—How very frightening you make it sound.

—It is.

—Dear God, what is the point of being madly in love if it doesn't turn you on?

—I'm not madly in love, it's just . . .

—Yes, oh transparent lying bastard?

—I'm not on about Suzy. I'm meeting someone else.

—Two-timing fart.

—It's a man.

—I always knew it!

—For Christ's sake! Look, there's something going on, I can't tell you about it now, but I will one day, I promise. I'm sort of . . . trying to save my life.

—Still? Silly boy. Life isn't for saving, it's for spending, before the big taxman with the scythe comes to claw it back. Spend spend spend, lovelyboy. Off you go then, I must retreat to my bed, I sense an attack of the vapors coming on, I feel no longer fit for human consumption. Farewell. Close the door on the way out, butt.

So that was that. I said goodbye and went to go. When I got to the door, I asked him what the point was of having an intercom if he let any old person up.

—I mean, you never know, it could have been anyone, someone horrible.

He looked at me from his bedroom door and leered:

—Well come on, they couldn't be more horrible than me, could they, lovelyboy? Farewell.

I watched him stagger off to his bedroom. I stood for a moment in his living room, and found I was looking around at it as if for the first time, but then Dai always has that effect on everyone: when he goes, the world sort of gets less 3–D.

When he dies, it will be like someone has bitten a chunk out of me.

I shut the door and walked down and out into the world again. Dai says the trouble with being in love, or being best friends, is that one of you will have to watch the other one being buried.

I want the world to be happy.

I want no one to die.

If only God read The Guardian.

Sugar and sunshine, MC Heaven.

While I was thinking this I found I had gone over the road to the nearest phone booth, and I could not work out why. I circled it and looked at it, and eventually sat down in a little café where I could observe it from the window, as if it was the only one in London and it might dissolve away if I stopped looking at it.

Then I realized I was about to phone Suzy.

9

A
DISTANT
CAMPFIRE
BURNING

My brain was ticking over too fast.

I was thinking:

Christ, this is crazy, this is so heavy, this is getting ser-i-ous, you are going to scare her off, play it cool, Mr. Brainhurt, Jesus, it's only a couple of hours since I saw her anyway, she's probably still in bed, I mean, what would I think if someone did that to me, if someone was that desperate?

Run run run runaway?

Look, if she likes me that much, if I like her that much, there's no need to rush, is there? And if we don't, then there's no point. Obvious, I mean she's not going to stop liking me just because she hasn't seen me for a couple of hours, if I phoned now, that would show I'd been thinking about her a lot and stuff, very heavy.

No one wants that, you have to sort yourself out before you get into these things, that's the point, it's just no longer possible to kind of just BE or whatever, we haven't got that anymore, maybe we never had, that's what the Garden of Eden was all about for Christ's sake, we know who we are, we think about what we do, we can't help it and we can't get rid of it even if we wanted to, and that way lies smack, so we'd better get on with it, we just have to think more and more and more until we work it out, like Global Warming and stuff, you can't stop the machine, you have to go with it and make it better, a bunch of hippies can't cure what scientists have fucked up, only a different kind of scientist can do that.

I mean Jesus Christ, all that crap about The Old Wisdom and stuff, you know, The Ancient Rhythms of Life and the Earth Mother Gaia, don't the DOS (Dog on String) kids at Glastonbury Tor realize the main thing about Ancient Wisdom is that it was all pure crap? For Jesus' sake, they thought if you cut off someone's balls and sprinkled the fields with the blood, the sun would come back. Very wise. Nothing mystical, just wrong, just crap. So we can't go back or else we end up with torchlight parades and stuff before we know it.

And the same goes for sex+love, you can't be instinctive, we are not instinctive, we stopped being instinctive when we started being Homo Sapiens, that's what being human MEANS, being not-instinctive, coming down from the trees was a one-way ticket, we have to get less and less instinctive and go with what we are, which is thinking out, weighing up, working through, planning ahead, that's what we're good at, that's what we have to do, that's what I have to do now, just sit and work it through, like the Plan.

And that has to happen alone, I mean, we need to be alone sometimes, surely, it's good for you to be alone now and again, maybe if everyone was made to do a week's solitary once a year, or live for a week on an island somewhere, we would all be better people, the Red Indians used to make people go away and live in the forest for forty nights or whatever, you have to show you can live alone before you get to join the tribe as an adult, being able to be alone is part of being a full-powered human.

Isn't it?

How can you be free if you can't stand being alone, and isn't freedom what we want, isn't that what people stand up in front of tanks and bare their chests for? Freedom always means being on your own, in one way or another, surely, loneliness is the price you have to pay, it's worth it.

OK. That's clear then. Right. I will just head home and sit in my shed and try to work it all out, on my own, the way it should be.

Except I don't know what I think because I don't know what she's thinking and I am not just me anymore!

But I have to work it out before I can find out what she thinks. You have to sort it first, you have to come to someone with something to offer, you have to come, kind of, full-handed, not empty-handed, empty-handed and . . . and needy! Ugh! Needy!

What a word.

Needy.

Rhymes with weedy.

And seedy.

Or speedy, as in young and stupid and.

Greedy? Greedy as in egoistical, because so needy and pathetic?

Pleady—does that exist?

Ready, ready for anything, always got the green light on, because he's so desperate? Shit, that doesn't rhyme anyway, I'm going crackers.

V.D.?

From fucking anyone he can because he's such a weedy seedy greedy pleady needy baldy sad case?

No! No! No!

I am not needy!

I will not be needy!

I have my own life. I have my shed in Shepherd's Bush and London is full of people I know, my life works perfectly, it has a long MOT despite the higher-than-average mileage for the year, it is not In Need!

As I was thinking all this, I sat there and stirred the tea and looked at the phone booth and then I took out my little address book and just started flicking through the pages, thinking of all the people I could ring up, here and now, instead of Suzy, if I really wanted to ring someone up, this was my back-up file, my tribe, a list of all the people I had spent time drinking or chatting or fucking with in the last five or six years. I could phone any of them, all these dozens of people, and any of them, if they were in+free, would go for a drink with me tonight if I wanted, say just for example if Suzy finished with me today and I needed someone to drink with, or else they would arrange to meet up soon if they were busy. If I left ansaphone messages, Hi, remember me, just calling to see how you are, call me back sometime, they would all call back within a day or two. Several of them would probably fuck with me too, if that turned out to be what I really wanted.

This was all supposed to make me feel better and less spooked and mad about phoning Suzy up when I had only left her a few hours ago and was going to see her tomorrow anyway.

Only it didn't.

The more I thought about all my friends the more depressed I got. It is horrible when you have this big list of people you could call, except you aren't going to, not because you don't WANT to see them, I mean if any one of them walked in now, you would be happy to introduce them to whoever you were with, if you were with anyone, and you would sit and have cups of tea and fags and review the news and arrange a binge or plan catching a film or whatever, but you would, you will, never call them, not because you don't WANT to see them but because there is just no point in seeing them, suddenly they have become part of an old story, and if you did call them and meet them, it would just show up your memories of them for what they are: just memories, old pictures cut off from you by a see-through wall called Now, and if you try to get too close, all you will have to say will be nothing to speak of, all you will do is leave sticky hand prints on the glass.

But what is the point of friends you will never call? If you can't remember someone's number, or the number of someone who will know theirs, it means the net has got too thin, the parachute has been packed away too long and the moths have been at it, the story has dried out.

So I stepped out of the café and took out my lighter and set fire to the address book and watched it burn.

Bye bye me.

And there I was now, in the phone booth, I was dialing her number already.

All I got was a short+unsweet ansaphone, just There's no one here now, so leave a message if you'd like.

After the beep I just said Hi Suzy, it's me, and expected her to pick it up after all, I knew she was working next to the phone, when she realized it was nice me, not boring someone, she would pick it up.

But she didn't. So I left a long message of nothing because I could not think what to say. I was horrified.

I had phoned and she had simply refused to pick it up.

She was working away at her prehistoric PC and just did not want to talk. To me. I had just blown it utterly. Our equality was gone forever. The scales were tilting.

Unless she was out.

That was possible. She would still get a message, she would still know I had called, which was uncool, but at least she would not have turned me down, I could still recover from that.

But how could I know?

How can anyone ever know, you just have to assume.

OK so I will assume. I will assume Suzy is out.

OK so Suzy is out.

OK so where?

With someone?

That someone who left a message on her ansaphone?

Who the fuck was someone?

I put the phone down and put my hand up to my brow. This was crazy, I was manufacturing Virtual Suzies in my head, but there was only one real one, and she did not live in my head, she lived out there, on Earth. So I tried to imagine Suzy, the real Suzy, doing something without me being there. I tried to imagine her just innocently going for a stroll to think about this false alibi-story thing about how she was trying to get into Michael Winner's private bank as a journalist. I tried to imagine her looking at a tree.

I managed.

Except that only made it worse.

I mean, fine, I had reminded myself that she was a real person, OK, I could enter myself for the Nobel Prize for New Men, I could tell the difference between the world in between my ears and the World, but all that meant was: I now knew that Suzy was really real and REALLY NOT WITH ME, and really breathing and eating and thinking and stuff WITHOUT ME. And she was really not answering the phone, or really somewhere else. Maybe with someone, maybe really.

Who the fuck was someone?

Being without Suzy suddenly felt like being alone.

I sagged down to Camden Town tube and waited for a train, but standing on the platform, I was suddenly years and miles away, back when I was 18 and once I was coming out of a wood at night, on the way back across country from a pub, it was dark like it is only dark in the country, I was with two friends (Christ, where are they now?) and we had got lost for a couple of hours and we were getting hung over and cold and pissed off with each other for getting us all lost, and now suddenly as we shoved and staggered out of the thick summer trees, we could see a distant campfire burning, where we were all camped, on a hill inside a ruined castle, it must have been two miles away still, but even at that range we could see the shadows of our friends moving about in front of the flames, in the middle of the big dark sky. We flew those two miles, laughing and joking and coming home.

It was OK for the Red fucking Indians.

The Red Indians could go out into the forest for their forty nights and they knew, they knew for certain, like you know Tuesday comes after Monday, that when they came back the Tribe would still be there, camped on the plain beside the river by the ancestral burial grounds where everyone knew they were going someday, they would be there to welcome you back and take you in and listen to your stories about what you did and what secrets you learned out there, like the para-military prisoners in Ulster know when they've done their time, the Tribe will be waiting and the campfires will still be there for them.

We haven't got that, we have to make up our own tribe as we go, we are free to do that, that is good, that freedom is wonderful, it is what everyone wants as soon as they are given the choice, as soon as the Great Leaders die we go for freedom, but being free means you have no safety net either.

Now, if we go out into the forest, we could come back and

find everyone has moved on and the tracks are dry, we could just end up sitting by the river all alone and telling our wonderful news to ourselves alone and stirring the cold ashes where the campfires were, and listening to the lost ghosts crying.

It happens.

It happens every day, it leads to the park bench, it leads to people so lost they will do anything to join a tribe, they will shoot up with needles they know are full of poisoned blood just to be allowed to sit around a campfire somewhere with people they know and hate, they will believe that a few thousand old, lost Jews who the SS somehow missed are actually running countries of 30,000,000 people, they will shout God Loves You As You Are, or Eng-a-land Eng-a-land, or Allah Akhbar, or SOcialist-revolutionarygroup, they will grab any crap cheap story they are thrown, just so long as it half hangs together, just so long as they are allowed to sit by some fireside somewhere in the cold, wandering world and nod to the tribal passwords and say: We, We, We.

An unnerving fact about tube travel: a mental nurse once told me that 10% of all loonies in London first reveal their MAFness by trying to fling people indiscriminately under tube trains. Too many people too close, and none of them calling you We, I suppose, they all turn into Them, so what do we do? Easy—fling the bastards!

As the wind from the approaching train started to swirl the litter on the platform, I looked up and down: who was the Flinger here today?

The doors closed behind me, and I sat opposite eight of

THEM, eight people who did not want to catch my eye and did not give a fuck and why should they, I was not from their tribe, I was THEM too.

We cannot be Red Indians. The world is bigger, but thinner for us, we can see further, but on the other hand we might fall through. A hard life, trying to make up your own tribe, hovering between freedom and security, trying to feel should I stay or should I go.

And then I got home, I walked down my own street like I was walking to my execution, I had to bite my lip to stop myself groaning.

Jesus, come on, so what? A few hours alone in my shed. In my nice shed with my own life.

It wasn't working.

LBS (Life Before Suzy), I mean.

My world was creaking at the seams, I looked in the window of my shed, there was light coming in through the cracks, and that light coming in made me suddenly think how dark my shed really was, and how much dust was floating about my life. My shed felt like a song by Leonard Cohen for fuck's sake. I felt balder than I had ever felt.

I wondered who the fuck this someone was, who had phoned Suzy this morning. And where was she now?

I looked out of the window: the man across the way in the walk-up was painting a big model of a German bomber today, he was nearly finished with this one, was Mr. Bald, he was holding it up to the light to put on some little touches that no one else would ever see, with a tiny paintbrush. He had his tongue between his teeth, he was concentrating on this piece of work that meant fuck all to no one, like he was a nuclear technician trying to rearrange some dodgy Ukrainian control rods.

I wondered what he would do if he dropped it. Shut the curtains, probably.

I felt sick.

I felt like I had lost the model airplane instructions to my life, ME was a collection of little bits that did not fit anymore. I walked round to the door of the shed, and I felt my steps were beating out a horrible rhythm that just said:

Here's the good news: Monday will be monumental.

Here's the bad news: Sunday never ends.

I told myself for the last time to stop being a sad eejit and calm down. I took deep breaths, two three four.

I patted where my beer gut will one day be, to make sure I still didn't have one, I patted where my hairline will one day have been, to make sure I still did.

I felt myself starting to break up like a smoke ring.

Then I noticed the note pinned to my shed, from Big Sis, and the note said:

GRL PHND. MSG: DO U WNT 2 GO RND 2 NITE. SAID U WLD NO.

I thought for the last time that this was really not very cool and I could at least wait for an hour or two, I mean, shit, you have to keep something in reserve.

But by the time I was thinking that, I was halfway up the Goldhawk Road, bullfighting the traffic, screaming at passing cabs.

10

OYSTER
MONDAY

On Monday, the world starts again, the saved-for pleasures and unsettling empty spaces of the weekend are gone, the
boyfriends and girlfriends and weekend fiancées, all the cheap-
rate lovers have gone back to their lives, having done their job,
which was to cover for Friday night, Saturday night and Sunday
afternoon, they are no longer needed, because the machine has
started again and the belts are running, on we go, up we get, the
story is on again, and hey! before we know it it will be Friday
night.

If only.

That was what I was thinking, that was what I was trying not
to think, as I looked at Brady and Chicho and Suzy.

We were gathered furtively together in Brady's horrible flat and we were sucking away at coffee and biscuits while I went through the penultimate day of the Plan, the Plan Minus 1, and tried not to think what the fuck am I doing this for, if only Friday was going to be the same, but by Friday I will probably be in prison or worse.

Once, I was engaged to a girl who said whenever I lied my eyes wobbled.

Wobbled?

When we broke up, I looked in the mirror quite a few times to see if it was true, to see if my eyes really did wobble, but this is difficult: how do you lie to yourself? How big is the gap between the truth in your head and the liar in the mirror? Anyway, I gave up lying after that, since I clearly could not do it very well: the world is a tough nut and one must play to one's strengths. But there is a difference between not lying to people and treating them like some confessional, so I decided I should not inflict my doubts+uncertainties upon everyone else.

I had inflicted them on Suzy already, of course, I mean, not by droning on about them, just by thinking them and letting them get into my voice and stuff, she knew all about them all right, and she had done a great job of whipping them away last night by being mega-appreciative while we were fucking, to make me feel good, I did not have to find this out, it was no secret, she said (this was while she raised her bum slightly so I could slip inside her flat-doggy style, so she was saying it partly into the pillow, naturally):

—I want you to feel good. Does that feel good?

—That feels great, I feel great, you look great.

(Which she did, with her hands up by her face and her face on one side on, or in, the pillow, I slipped my hand round and in between her flat tummy and the hard bed, and curved it up through her hairs onto her clitoris, and nibbled her ears and all I could see now was her hair in front of my eyes, and everything felt great, especially me, so I was all right, almost as soon as we were set up properly like that, she started humming through her nose and wriggling, so she was all right too, soon she started bucking and grabbing my ass with her nails dug in, so I bit the back of her neck and growled from somewhere in the bottom of my throat, I could feel my pelvis thumping against the bones of her bum, and I could feel the end of my dick touching something deep up inside her at the end of each shove, a sort of little muscle or something, but that was about all I could feel, the rest was just warm oil, and then she came and so naturally I did too, and that was all very right.)

So I slept the sleep of triumph, not of neurosis, and I only part woke up because she was licking my balls, and or rather someone was licking someone's balls, I was three-quarters still asleep, in that strange jungly state when your brain is still unsure whether it belongs to a higher primate, with limbs and skin and bones and all in complicated architectural harmony, or whether it has rolled over and slid back into the primeval soup while it was sleeping, and is now an ameba's brain, in charge of some shape-less glob of nerve endings and pulses, like when you get into im-possible positions in your dreams. I had no idea who I was fucking with, or rather: I knew it was Suzy, like, say you are in a dream and you somehow know you are in St. Pancras Station, ex-cept it is nothing like St. Pancras really is, that was what it was like, this shapeless person with me was called Suzy and I was shouting Suzy but I do not know who it was, it was Suzy before she was called Suzy, it was her and it was no one at the same time, and I was me but no one too. It was not our egos fucking, not things with names and histories and plans, just our bodies and the strange, flickering, deep-sea bioluminescent drifters of our inner space, the trailers of our lives, our ids.

(I have one id story. When I was temping for IBM with Barrington-Charrington, we had these fotocards to get into the HQ on the South Bank, and there was this thick-as-shit security guard on the door, Mr. Ex-Army Uniform Fetishist, and he thought it showed you were pretty cool and sharp if you pronounced ID like it was a word, so every morning he used to stop us and say:

—OK lads, show us your ids please.)

Anyway, REM-sleep fucking is great, it is just yee-hah, here we are, who am I, who's this I anyway, here is me, here is you, me want Suzy, here we go, and then you just cling on in there and let your widescreen dreams swallow you whole.

Like an instant holiday.

And then the alarm clock goes, of course, because bed is no insulated realm, and although this wonderful id-fucking made me feel great as I left Suzy's house (I left before she did, just in case of Gestapo neighbors) and although I sat on the tube thinking ho ho if only all these people knew what we were going to do tomorrow and stuff like that, by the time I had got to Brady's horrible flat in Acton, all the noise and the smoke and the shit in the streets had got back to me, the whole Plan was hovering over my head, marking time and beating its wings, so I failed to radiate confidence+conviction to Chicho and Brady, they were looking at me and waiting to hear the Story, but I had forgotten it, it was only when Suzy arrived that I felt at all like saying what I was saying, which was:

—OK everyone, what do we have to do today?

Chicho answers first:

—Get these such nice Armani clothes, I get them from my sister Pili houseband, is easy for me today.

—OK.

Then I ask Brady. I try to ignore the fact that he is looking like a collapsed trash bag in a Reservoir Dog Suit, filling the room with doom+gloom. He answers:

—Make sure a load of people see me in my Dog Suit.

—OK.

—No it's not.

(Pause)

—What do you mean, it's not OK?

—No one else can make it today.

—We don't need them today, we need them tomorrow. Today you can just ride about on your own, get seen, set up your alibi, so if everything goes wrong you can prove you're just a sad nutter.

—Is easy for you, says Chicho.

—Fuck off, says Brady.

—Hey, come on. So you just ride around a bit.

—That's the whole fucking point. I can't.

—You can't?

—OK, I fucking won't. It's not the fucking same. It's OK

when there's six of you, that's nice, but you can't do it on your fucking own. You feel . . . fucking stupid!

Shit and onions!

Much as I like Brady's shame, much as I think (as I said) that it is the only good thing about the big gobshit, this is not, NOT the right time for him to realize once and for all that his hobby is about as unsad as trainspotting. Not today, please God, not today.

—But you look great, says Suzy.

—Is easy for you, agrees Chicho.

—It doesn't matter what I fucking look like on my fucking own. You don't understand. I could be Harvey fucking Keitel and I would still look like a shagging wanker riding around dressed like fucking this ON MY FUCKING OWN!

This is definitely serious, I can see his point, it is not just making trouble, I should have thought of this. He cannot do it without the tribe, I can understand this. But I can't go with him, Chicho can't go with him, Suzy can't go with him . . .

—I'll go with you, says Suzy.

—Yeah? says Brady.

—You can't! I yell.—You've got to be in Wardour Street at ten to one to meet Janey Herzberg.

—So I'll be there at ten to one, says Suzy.

—No, no, no, I shout.—You can't be seen together today.

—He's right, says Brady, gloomily.

—Is easy for Suzy, says Chicho.

—Are you crazy? I scream.

—No, I am no crazy, you are crazy, is easy for her. You see

girl in dogsuit, with sunshineglassies and all this things, you give her this hairs on the face, this beard and must-atch, is no Suzy people see, is girl in man clothes.

—You could be Mr. Pink! shouts Brady.—He's got long hair.

—Yes, this one with long hairs, si, is easy for Suzy.

—Oh Christ, I say.

—OK, says Suzy to Brady, you go down to that black people's hair-extension shop in the market and get me a beard and mustache, have you got any money?

—No, sorry, says Brady.

She gives him a fiver and he goes, just like that.

—Chicho, go and get me some black spray-on hair dye from the drugstore on Goldhawk Road.

She offers him a fiver too, but he slow-motion fly-swats it away.

—Is easy for me, says he, and goes too.

That leaves Suzy and me and the first argument of our thing together:

—Well, I say.

—What's the problem?

—Nothing, it's just . . .

—I know, I know. It's your Plan. I'm sorry. But it won't make any trouble and Brady needs it.

—You're supposed to be sorting out the car.

—I can do that this afternoon. We get what he gives us, I can't change that. Does my driving need practicing?

—No.

—Well don't sulk then.

—I'm not.

There was a pause then. Not a nice pause. This pause said: our first fight. Which often really means: the start of the last fight.

I could see that Suzy was thinking this too, but then her eyes went all wise and she said:

—It's nothing that can't be helped.

And she smiled, kind of serious but nice, like it was serious but so what? so what isn't serious? and so I accepted the smile and that was the end of our first fight because I said:

—You're right, I'm sorry, which is a rare thing for me to say and took some effort.

And Suzy said:

—Anyway, I quite fancy myself in a Reservoir Dog outfit.

—Can you get one?

—I've got a man's black suit. Just wait till you see me, in it, you ARE going to come in your jeans this time.

—What do you mean you ARE this time?

—Well, it was pretty close the first night.

—I didn't know you noticed.

—I was trying to make you. Testing my own powers. You must have been in agony.

—It was terrible, I said.—Tight jeans are bad news, and I started to undo her buttons.

Undo undo undo.

But she stops me.

—We haven't got time, so don't you get me started, I'm not spending all day with my hand between my legs.

And she starts to undo my buttons instead, with her teeth, because now she is kneeling in front of me. When she has two of them undone she licks my dick between them and sucks it out. She hooks her fingers into my belt loops and says to my dick:

—If he moves one muscle, except you, I'm going to bite you off like a bratwurst, OK?

—OK, I say, shutting my eyes and preparing for pleasure. After a few seconds my knees already start to jiggle, but Suzy stops, so I open my eyes and see her looking up at me, which looks very nice, it makes her eyes go all almond-shaped, I suppose that means my eyes look all thin and slitty and nasty to her, but there you are, and she says:

—I think I must have mediterranean blood after all.

—Why? (I gulped.)

—Because I suddenly felt this pathetic surge of feel-good hormones at being the main man's girl. (She took me in her mouth again, then stopped again.) That's you, by the way.

—Oh yeah, I said, and that was the last thing I said until I shouted out AAAAH SUZYSUZYSUZY and forgot what she said about not moving and grabbed her hair and fucked her mouth until I came, and then collapsed on the floor and she cleared her throat and kissed me a kiss full of my spunk, and then she rolled it around her mouth and swallowed it.

—Like a raw oyster, she said.

—Suzy, I said . . .

—Work, she said.

—Yeah, I said, yeah . . . Suzy, look: who's this someone that phones you up and stuff?

—Just someone. Someone who is something to do with me but nothing to do with you and me. OK?

—OK.

—Hey: Try and act normal today.

—What, you mean, shout SUZYSUZYSUZY in the middle of Wardour Street? (I was buttoning up my jeans now.)

—Yes, that sounds good, I like that. That's what I call normal. Now get out or you'll be late. I'll be outside at ten to one, but I don't want to see you.

So I kissed her and went out.

I walked to the Central Line, bumping into people and nearly getting run over all the way, and then sat on the train and realized after a few moments that I had not even grabbed a drink, I could still taste my own spunk in my mouth.

So that's what oysters taste like, I always wondered.

11

A
BEAUTIFUL
SCALE MODEL
OF LIFE

Fred was sitting on the receptionettes' desk, kicking his heels.

(I never realized before that this phrase is just a description of what people really do, he really was kicking his heels. Once, I saw a young laddo hanging about outside a big hotel in Piccadilly, he had a very nice suit on, but he looked nervy, I could not work out what was wrong about him until I saw that he was down at heel, I mean, his shoes were old and cheap and worn right away at the heel, you knew that no one who could afford this hotel would ever let that happen to their shoes, so Mr. Cheap Shoes had to be a rent boy or something. I wonder who says things like Down At Heel first, and gets them signed up into the Eng. Lang.? Someone like Dai, maybe.)

Anyway, so now it was Monday at 10 o'clock in the foyer of Baron Films and Fred was sitting on the receptionettes' desk and kicking his heels, one after the other, staring ahead of himself in absolute repose, his eyes completely chimped-out, and I was sitting on a chrome-and-corduroy chair, reading Fred's Daily Mirror.

(Brady was once in a shoe factory in Coventry, where they had a very Modern Flexible Workforce, said the manager, and when it came to the lunch break on the first day he worked there, they all got out their sandwiches and newspapers, including Brady, about three hundred of them, and every one of them, these three hundred Flexible Workers, had the Sun, except Brady, who had the Mirror, and as soon as he got his paper out this big South Midlands groan went up and a voice said:

—Here mate, yow ain't . . . POLITICAL, am yow?)

I was concentrating on being normal.

This is actually quite hard, try it and see, I mean because as soon as you have to think about it, it isn't, is it, normal, I mean? Normal means something you don't have to think about, the norm, so the more you think about being normal the less normal you are. And you can't escape by saying to yourself OK, I will just NOT think about being normal, because deliberately not thinking about it, so you are still not being normal: normal means having no gap between thinking something and doing it.

As I read the paper I was thinking:

Do I always read Fred's paper?

Do I always sit here?

Am I always this quiet?

Do I always sit here thinking about being normal?

It was all very stressful.

But then Fred slid off the desk and came and sat next to me, which was a relief, and he frowned and furrowed his face and then I discovered what he had been thinking about for the last half-hour, and I was amazed to find that it was me.

—You ain't trying to be one of the Suits, are you? he began, just to make sure.

—No, I said, no way.

—Even if you could, I mean?

—No.

—So what you doing this for? You got A-levels and everything.

—Well yes, I said, blushing at my lies.

(I had had to tell the agency I had no degree, the day I signed up I had tried three agencies already and they all said I was overqualified for everything, so when I went to the fourth one I was a struggling actor with two very crappy A-levels, and they immediately gave me as much work as I wanted.

It was quite spooky, the way everything I had done back then now seemed perfectly calculated to help me be invisible to the police after the robbery, until I remembered not to be mad, not to mistake cause and effect: I was already a criminal according to the letter of the law the day I used a false name to work under, everything else just followed from that, I was only going to rob Michael Winner's bank because I knew I was invisible, not the other way around.

People often confuse Cause and Effect like that: one of my college friends once told me it was OK for me to go around living in sheds and drinking and fucking and stuff, he had done His Fair Share of that! But he couldn't do that anymore, because now he had to concentrate on his accountancy training. Actually, it was the other way around, he should have said SO not BECAUSE.)

So anyway, Fred was telling me I had A-levels, he was impressed with that, but he would not have been impressed with a degree, A-levels were good, sharp WC lads got A-levels now and then, it meant you could work in offices, not in some job that deafened you, covered you in carcinogenic pus and took fingers and lumps off you every now and then, which most real WC jobs still do, unknown to The Guardian. A-levels were good.

—So why the hell are you doing this eh? Me now, that's different, I was never any cop at school, I've only ever been good with these (he waved his fists around a bit), I'm handy in a dark cellar, that's all, but why don't you get something decent?

—I'm looking about, Fred, but it's not that easy:

—Balls, don't give me that, I didn't put you down as one of them whinging bastards, you know as well as I do you could find a good screw tomorrow if you was to really try. Hell's bells and buckets of blood, this is London, not bloody Jarrow. I'm starting to think you're a lazy sod, mate, that's the truth, no offense.

This was getting dangerous. If Fred decided he didn't like me, he might decide that someone else should go to the bank tomorrow. I didn't know if Fred chose who it was, but it was possible. But even if he still took me, it was going to be much more difficult if he didn't like me anymore, because the whole Plan depended on him trusting me.

—Tell you what Fred, I said.—You're right and I have got something planned. Honestly. I'm going to try and make this the last temp job I ever do. After tomorrow things will change. Promise. You'll see. You'll be the first to know.

—That's more like it! God, if I had half the brains you got, Reggie and Ronnie would've been working for me, not me working for them!

He roared with laughter at the thought, and walked rollingly over to the receptionette.

—What d'you reckon, Liz, me the big boss, eh? As I walk along the Bois de Boulogne with an independent air . . .

—Hark at him. How's the new grandson, Fred?

She leaned forward and rested her hand in her chin, her eyes looked up and scanned all over his face, she was clearly thinking he would be a nice grandad. Or dad, even.

—Smashing little chap.

—I'd like to have kids.

—It ain't no joke, Liz, you should see the stuff she has to lay in for the four of them already, never mind this one. Criminal. Well, with her old man inside, he never was any good, I got that boy Simon Leefe out of more trouble than Houdini, Liz, but he never learned to work with good people, see, on proper jobs, he's just born small-time stuff, him and this mate of his went to pinch the big copper coils from an old meat-packing factory down behind the Smithfield, right, oh, he reckoned they was worth thousands, you should've heard him, Thousands, Fred, he said, like it was millions, pathetic, and him and this mate, Skanky they called him, they cut the power to this factory and there they are inside and this bloke Skanky's just stretching out on the coils to get at something, I dunno what, and of course the Electric comes back on, Christ knows how, millions of volts or amps or whatnots for all the machines they used to have there, well, this bloke Skanky is just fried, like a crisp, they said, fried alive. Pathetic. Next morning the watchman finds my Jean's Simon, my son-in-law, still sitting there blubbing, too bloody scared to move, and this bleeding Skanky lying there looking like a shish-kebab on a bad day. Makes me sorry for my Jean, poor kid.

That starts me thinking about the Plan, I am getting jumpy, I remind myself that the first sign of going MAF is when you start to think everything is sort of related by more than coincidence, it is a hard job to stop the thoughts about the Plan hopping around inside me and making me twitch, so I am relieved when the receptionette asks the lowest of the low at Baron Films (me) to go and get sandwiches for them all.

—And you think about what I was saying to you, about jobs and that, says Fred.

—I will, I say honestly, and go out into Soho.

In the street, I catch this bloke's eye as he is about to slide into a porn shop, he is hovering about outside one of those doors that is not a door, just red-and-white strips of plastic shivering in the wind, one of those non-doors designed so the poor fetishists can just drift in without having to admit to themselves that they are DECIDING to go in, deliberately, through the door to their private shed-world. Maybe even just a real door would be enough to make some of them stop and think about what the fuck they are doing.

I can see he feels me passing with every nerve in his body.

Maybe he is a child psychologist with a secret pile of kiddie porn in his shed, or one of the people who end up blowing their lives apart because they get so into Bottom Marks For Naughty Boys or whatever.

Most porn is just like the sad ads in the mag of the Sunday Mirror for STUNNING DIECAST REPLICAS of Ferraris and Bentleys: A Beautiful Scale Model of Life. It is there so people who would like a Ferrari but will never get one, and would love to fuck with Candy Shandy but can't, can ADMIRE THE ASTONISHING DETAIL of a Ferrari, or of Candy Shandy's pubes or whatever it is, and feel less like buckets of shit in walk-ups for five minutes. Just another safety valve to keep the wheels turning, and stop Mr. Sad running about screaming for vengeance and revolution because he has been made to want what he can never have.

So far, so sad.

But what about the little dark paths and codes, whatever they are, that lead from the top shelf at W.H. Smith to secret sheds in Essex where men video children being tortured?

When does Sad turn into Evil?

This is a big problem for nice liberals, because of course all porn barons are turbocharged super-liberals themselves, they think anything should go. So when do the nice liberal people decide nice liberalism has to stop being nice? Same problem as with the skinheads.

No problem for Suzy.

Suzy is not a nice liberal.

Nice, but not liberal.

Suzy reckons that if she got a bunch of tough girls with attitude together they could bankrupt the porn barons by threatening porn fctishists with Outing.

Look, she says, you just get ten of the girls with camcorders and hard friends, and they just walk about all day every day for a week, just filming away round Soho, there is no law against filming Soho, you could even just PRETEND to be filming, the wee Clients would run a mile, just seeing the camera would be enough to send for (fanfare):

Messrs. Fear & Trembling
Solicitors to The Lord.

Of course, it would not be like Outing gay people, because this sort of Outing would mean making people UNhappy with what they are.

Here's the Bad News: Your life is really a heap of offal.

Now the Good News: Well, at least now you know.

I mean, can you imagine Porn Fetishist Pride weeks? No, of course not. But who said it was good to always Be Happy With Yourself? I mean, apart from Californians.

I know this quiet accountant who was unhappy with himself, he got obsessed about how he was too scared about everything, he wanted to be More Decisive, More Bold, More Leaderish, to Go For It more and all that kind of Success Guru stuff, so since he had always been terrified of heights he decided to take up parachuting so as to Confront his Greatest Fear. It was really brave of him, he spent weeks unable to sleep, he lost weight, the practicing reduced him to tears on three separate occasions and made him throw up every time, it nearly killed him before he even went up in the plane, but at last he made his jump, he conquered his timid-

ity, let go the handrail and made his leap into unconditional noth-
ingness. He did it. Now he is a quiet accountant who once made a
parachute jump, and talks about it a lot too often.

But not being satisfied with yourself is always a start.

It shows constructive shame.

Like Brady with his shame about being a Doggy?

He is with Suzy now, they are riding about on the tube with
her dressed like Mr. Pink.

The Plan is brewing.

The tea is stewing.

These were the thoughts that snorkled about in my overheated brain as I sat in the café, trying to look normal and waiting
for the receptionettes' sandwiches.

On the way back past Soho Market with 3T's+3prawn/mayo
sands, I bumped into a pal who was heading Dim Sum—wards
with this beautiful peroxided girl dressed in deliberate-fake leop-
ardskin coat and hat. He is about six foot five and she is about five
foot nothing, she nearly had to reach up to his hand as they
walked along, he introduced us and the first thing she said was, in
a German accent:

—I know what you are thinking! If you love someone it
doesn't matter, OK?

Nice, I like meeting people just like that, it is nice to have
a small world in this big busy one. And so I said I would call
about a drink next week, and off they went to eat snacks from
sizzling pushcarts, and I wandered back up Wardour Street thinking, you know, nice day, nice place, nice new story, here I am,
right in the middle of everything, and tonight I'll see Suzy, mmm,

well, where else would you want to be? Who else? Is everything about as it should be? Yes Lord, I can buy into this world just as it is.

So what the hell's so wrong with it you have to go robbing banks and playing games with the IRfuckingA?

What the hell would have been so bad about just carrying on, what was the point of not being satisfied, I mean, Christ, this is the only chance we get, we'd better enjoy it, there are no pockets in shrouds, and when the Great Accountant in the sky winds us up and draws the Bottom Line, we all break even and no one does any better, never mind how many banks they rob, what am I after, am I just chasing pictures of happiness, like some porn freak, am I just planning away wankingly over a beautiful scale model of life while the Real Thing whispers past me on roller blades?

I was in a bad way.

I had to stop in the middle of the street and lean on a shop, it hit me like when I was waiting for the results of my HIV test, every now and then I would actually forget it, I don't mean put it to the back of the mind, I mean actually forget about it existing for just a few seconds, then it would come back, blam!, like you had walked into a metal pole in thick fog, and you stop and rub your head and feel around you and wonder what this big metal stick is doing in the middle of a park, and then the fog clears a bit, a wind blows it into rags for a moment, and you realize that you are standing next to one piece of one foot of the Eiffel Tower or something, you know that above you in the fog this awful, colossal Thing is rearing up all around you, and you feel the ground leaving your feet.

Guess what I did then.

This is seriously worrying.

I ran, I mean not fucking jogged, ran, all the way back to Shaftesbury Ave. and along to Piccadilly Circus tube station, I bounced down the stairs, shoved hipwise through the barriers behind a fat woman with a fat suitcase, and went down to the Piccadilly Line, and stood and waited to see if Suzy and Brady would come through on a train, or maybe be changing to the Bakerloo Line or something, I mean, they MIGHT have been.

Every time I saw anything at all like a black suit, I jumped, I wanted to run up and grab Suzy and say, look, let's forget it, I don't want to do this, fuck the Plan, it was just a crazy idea, please, let's go to bed now and stay there till Wednesday, hey, Suzy, we could do some smack and . . .

That shocked me.

Smack?

What the fuck was I thinking?

I looked at the tube map and worked out the best way from, say, Earl's Court to Euston to get sane again, and then I went back up to the world, and tried not to think that somewhere in London Suzy was riding around, dressed as Mr. Pink, and I couldn't see her and everyone else was looking at her and as they watched her, which some of them were doing right now somewhere, they would all be wishing it was them fucking her, not Brady.

Did I say Fucking?

Did I say Brady?

Brady fucking Suzy?

It was true, they would all think she was fucking Brady, of course they would, I mean, if you are a girl you do NOT dress up like Mr. Pink and ride around all morning with Mr. Wankface or whoever Brady thinks he is, unless you are fucking them too, do you?

That would be the way the man and woman in the street saw it.

It would be the obvious conclusion.

And Suzy had been quite keen to go with him.

Quite keen?

It was her sodding idea!

This time it was a lamppost that lent me support as my legs lost the power of motion. I mean, suppose they talked about smack too, like we had done? No, that was OK, Brady never really took it, he snorted it once and he reckoned it gave him flu, the big eejit, so he would not have that in common with her. Cars? No, Brady knows less about cars than me, which is less than nothing, he is the worst driver in the world, Brady could get sponsored to drive about with a sign saying AVOID ME GO BY TRAIN, he drives like some old farmer out of a bog, he sits back in the seat with his legs apart and one hand always resting on the gearstick with a fag in between his first and middle fingers.

The big sap.

He has a huge dick.

Really, he is hung like a carthorse, and I have only ever seen it at rest, Christ only knows what it is like erect, Brady has had to finish with a couple of small-built girls because he couldn't get it in properly, he says. I believe it. Size may not be an issue, but Brady is a special case, I myself once suffered the carrot-up-the-blackwell-tunnel syndrome with a six-foot-two stablegirl, so I know it is possible for people to not fit.

Suzy and me fit fine.

But what if Suzy finds out about Brady's giant dick?

Jesus this is ridiculous, she was just being nice to Brady for the good of the Gang.

Yeah.

Yeah AND because she wants me, ME, to see her dressed up like a man, she said that, she wants to make ME come in my trousers.

Like a little boy?

Little!

She was excited herself about the dressing up and stuff, who isn't. Ladies+Gents Relish.

Did she do that with SOMEONE, whoever the fuck that is?

But she isn't with this someone, idiot.

No, she's with bloody Brady.

What if she gets excited now, with Brady, it's a hot day, what if they go for a drink and end up swapping fags, what if he asks her would she like a breath of fresh air? Would she press her flat tummy up to his dick that quickly? Would she want to see what happens to his huge dick when she does that?

Ridiculous. She doesn't even know he's got a huge dick yet, so how could she want to do that?

But what if it just happens? Say, Suzy just decides to go for a snog with him and does that thing with her tummy because she likes it anyway and then she realizes the size of his dick, when it begins to get erect.

Would it?

Of course it shagging would, it's a dick, any dick would get erect having Suzy's tummy rubbed up against it.

Hold on, hold on, I had to ask her outside, remember, she didn't make the move, I did.

Will Brady?

Does Brady fancy her?

Of course the bastard does. He was angling for that, he wanted her to go with him this morning, that was why he was pretending to make all that fucking fuss, he was jealous of me, he wants to fuck her just because she is fucking me, that's what, Jesus, I swear to God I will fucking debollock that big two-faced . . .

I tried to fight down a vision of Suzy kneeling in front of Brady and taking his huge dick in her mouth.

I never realized that people actually gnashed their teeth, but they do.

I did, anyway.

(IAN PAISLEY: And on that day will be much wailing and gnashing of teeth.

ELDERLY MAN: Please sir, Dr. Paisley, but I have no teeth.

IAN PAISLEY: Teeth will be provided!)

That's it, then, Suzy will be in bed with Brady right now.

Those that live by sleeping around . . .

At this point I almost got squashed by a horrible old Y-Reg Fiesta (a fitting death?) and woke up and realized (a) that I was just about outside Baron Films and (b) that I must be cracking up. So I decided to go and stick my head in a bowlful of cold water, before it exploded.

I had just come up from the water in the gents' lav and was feeling a bit better, when I realized that this might be classed as very weird behavior. When I came out, however, Fred said:

—You on the buckets of cold water again? I never seen a bloke like you for getting overheated.

So it turned out that I was just being normal.

That worried me.

Was I always this weird?

Maybe being weird was my way of being normal?

Fred came to the rescue again, though, because he brought out the Standard and made me go through the Jobs Vacant with him, looking at all the things I could do if I stopped messing around and used my head. As he read them out, I watched him, he traced each ad with a big stubby finger and I thought

(a) that I really did like him, I wished he was my Uncle or something and

(b) that I was sure I could get to him tomorrow.

Funny: as I looked at Fred and worked out exactly how to pitch it, it all seemed to matter less, like Fred radiated this feeling that you get by somehow, that here was a man who had lived all his life in and out of prison, he had never had a mortgage or a pension fund, he had probably never owned a kosher car, even, and here he was with his job and his friends and his stories and his five grandchildren already, and he would have more people at his funeral than the people who live in bungalows in Milton Keynes, and they would have a much better wake afterwards.

So it doesn't really matter much what happens to you, if you end up in Pentonville or MC Heaven, just so long as you got on with it and did the essential things, like make sure you treated the right people right and ended up with the grandchildren and the troops of friends and the respect and gave everyone a few good times over the years and a couple of decent stories to remember you with.

That old campfire again.

I decided then that I wanted to have five or six kids with Suzy, and live in one place for the rest of our lives, and never wander from job to job, I didn't care where it was, so long as it deserved the word Home.

And I still almost didn't recognize her when I saw her next.

At ten to one I could not resist going out for a pretend breath of fresh air, to make sure Suzy was really there, and there she was, on the dot, shoulders back and head up and dressed in this power-dressing soft brown tweed stuff that went right down to her ankle boots, wearing a straight brown-blonde wig and carrying an attaché case. Miss UMC-about-town, this year and every year.

She looked right through me as I passed, which was the right thing to do, it was stupid of me to go out there, but still that look put a cold breeze through me, a little sigh about the way we are all alone in the end.

(Germans like talking about things like that. Spanish people treat it as obvious, and so they think it is stupid to go on about it. Choose now which is profounder.)

At two minutes past one, Janey Herzberg came clattering down the stairs and whisked past us.

I did not go out again.

I hardly dared look up when Janey came back from lunch at half-past two, not that she would have noticed if I had, she just swept through reception like it was an empty room. Which was par for her, that was encouraging, it meant nothing much extraordinary had happened to her, like someone suddenly accosting her in the street and pretending to be a friend of a friend, and Janey not believing her, which is what would have happened if Suzy had fucked up.

For the rest of the afternoon, I sat and squirmed and smoked fags and wished there was more work to do and tried not to think about the IRA and all the other things that could go wrong with the Plan, and encouraged Fred to talk about his grandchildren.

By five o'clock, I had forgotten all that stuff about Brady and Suzy, I couldn't even think why I had ever thought it, I was longing to find out what had happened with Suzy and Janey Herzberg, but I was also just longing to see her, like I had left the battery to my pacemaker with her, and if I didn't get back soon I would just roll over and shrivel away.

It was OK, of course, Suzy was not fucking with Brady, I knew it as soon as I saw her.

I mean I knew it anyway, like you know you are not going to win the lottery, but you still check your numbers, but now I saw her I knew it really, I knew it, don't ask me how, the same way I knew I had to ask her outside that first night, body language, pheromones, eye contact, how should I know, but I knew.

She was dressed as Mr. Pink, but she had tied her shirt up under her ribs, to show off her tummy (of course, I should have guessed she would). She looked so bizarre I staggered. But I recovered quickly because I could see that she was preoccupied. Then I saw that they all were.

—How was it?

—Which bit?

—Well, Janey of course.

—Oh, fine. You shouldn't have come out like that, I nearly

fucking died, but never mind. Have you ever heard of wait-and-see pudding?

—No.

—It must be dormspeak, I think. I bumped into her and said Oh Hellay Janey and she did her trying-not-to-be-gobsmacked bit, and I just said, Ambrose's party? And she said Oh, Oh ya, and I said Well, it does rather look as if Cat is going to tell him to sling his hook, and Janey laughed all arch and said, Quite, but I suppose it's just wait-and-see pudding for us darling. And then she went.

—Did you get enough?

—Quite enough, darling, what do you take me for?

—Christ, that's Janey.

—Not quite. I just need to get her face, that's where your accent comes from, it's all in the shape of your mouth and nose. I'll get it now I know her. I have to say wait-and-see pudding tomorrow, that's great.

—So what's the problem? That's brilliant.

—The Dogging is the problem.

—What happened?

—Nothing, we got seen.

—Is easy for her, said Chicho morosely.

—Did you ride around with your shirt up like that?

—What, and show my one distinguishing mark? No way. I kept my shirt in and my beard on like a decent girl.

—Thank God. Um, look, so what's the matter?

—Is not easy for Brady, says Chicho.

We all look at Brady and I now notice that he is ominously still, he is doing his Human Sea-Slug impersonation again. I try to combat it:

—Oh. Well, look, shit, I know you've got the heaviest thing to do, in a way, I mean, I know this IRA stuff is not really . . .

—Fuck that, says Brady, that's no sweat. That's easy.

—The IRA is easy for him, says Chicho.

—Well what the f . . . what the hell is it then? I ask, I nearly yell.

—It's the Doggies, groans Brady.

—Oh shit, you said they were definitely on for tomorrow!

—Is not easy for Brady, repeats Chico, making Softly Softly gestures with his hands.

—What's not, for Christ's sake?

I look at Brady. He twitches and moans and his long legs and hands wrap round each other and unwind again like The Spaghetti From Planet X, and at last he gets it out between his big broken teeth:

—I'm just not a fucking leader of the pack, all right! I don't know if I can get the fucking Doggies to do what you fucking want, OK? I haven't got that, you know, chafuckingrisma. Why the fuck should they do what I fucking tell them to?

—But look, Christ, all you have to do is make sure they get drunk.

—But what if they don't fucking want to get fucking drunk?

—Well . . .

But that was just it.

Well what?

What the hell is charisma?

And if you haven't got it, how do you teach it?

What is it that makes some people kill the party when they leave?

—It's a fair question, says Suzy.

—Yeah, yeah I know. Look, we'll have to try a charisma workshop. Look, um, stand up.

Brady does not move.

—Come on, stand up, I say.

—Why? says Brady.

—Well, because I say so.

—So? says Brady.

—So? So I say so, so, um, well . . .

—See? says Brady.

—No is easy, says Chicho.

—Shit. Suzy, um, you try.

—Well, you have to stop saying UM for a start, she said.

—I wasn't, I said.

—You were.

—Was I?

—Yeah.

—Oh, right.

—It's down to you, she said, It's your Plan. You were good the other night.

—Yeah but that was different, that wasn't me, that was the Plan, I was explaining how to follow the Plan, I wasn't saying do this or that because, just because I say so, it was all worked out, it was just logic. You show him.

—What? she insisted.

—Jesus, how you make people do what you want.

—I don't bloody know, do I?

—No is easy.

—Thank you for sharing that, Chicho. Sorry. Oh shit. Shit shit shit shit shit shit shit.

I looked at Brady. He was curled up on the saggy armchair like a big bogridden turd in a black suit. There was only one thing to do.

Phone for Dai Substantial.

So I did.

—Hello, Battersea Dogs Home, said Dai. His voice fluted out into the room, everyone gathered round the phone except Brady, who only glared from his sick-chair.

—Dai, it's me.

—So you say, love. But can you be sure? Why, I think THIS is me, so which of us is right?

—Listen, this is important.

—Oh how boring of it.

—I need you to teach Brady about charisma.

—Oh. Well, that sounds quite unboring. I thought you were going to go on about girls with flat tummies again.

—What? said Suzy.

—Hark, I hear angelic tones, said Dai.

—Have you been talking about me? said Suzy.

—I, well, yes.

—Oh good, she said.

—This is fun, said Dai.

—Is nice, said Chicho.

—Oh, I hear the seas of the mediterranean now. Is that Pili's brother?

—Is me, yes is Chicho, shouts Chicho.

—Oh Christ, I said.

—No stress now, love, it impairs the immune system something awful. I should know. Now, tell Dai all about it.

—Well, you know Brady is a Doggie?

—Oh yes, you told me about him. (His voice sank to a low-tremulous whisper.—Is that the one with the gargantuan willy?)

—Yes, I said, unable to resist glancing over at Brady, who sulked back at me suspiciously.

—Well?

—He's going to, um, this Reservoir Dog convention, right, tomorrow, somewhere, you know, and he wants to be, sort of, the life and soul, the leader of the pack. But he doesn't know how.

—Fuck off, mutters Brady, and adds something about taking advice from some fat poof.

—Shut it, you fucking big . . .

—Well, I am, after all, says Dai, and he is going to. Hmm. You really are a hopeless liar, love, you will pay for trying to deceive me some day, but for now I assume you have good reason, and let it pass. This is most interesting. The man is a Doggie in search of Charisma, you say. Well, that is easy.

—Is it? I gasp.

—Of course, love. Charisma doesn't exist. It's a big lie, you see, it was invented by powerful people so we foolish little people would think there was some reason to do what they said. You show me a person they say has Charisma and I will show you a person who was born with status and power and knows they can always fall back on them, or one who has wheedled their way into the intimacy of people with status and power. Of course, it depends how high up the social and evolutionary ladder one is, among the sophisticated natives of my own Cwmdoom, for example, Charisma means having a lot of tattoos and a sawn-off shotgun, whereas in my present occupation it is measured by how near the front of the dress circle one is sitting and with whom, but it all means the same thing, power and status. Take me, love (not that you will, but there we are), my T-Cell count may be dodgy, but my Charisma rating among the rent boys of Covent Garden is off the scale, they hang on my every word now they are accustomed to seeing me in the company of rich and famous queens. I have to remind myself that this was not always the case, to prevent myself thinking I must be God. Or take Hitler: Hitler was in the pay of the German Army when first he made his name, and everyone knew he had powerful friends. It does help you get listened to, love.

—Dai, please, what has Hitler got to do with this?

—Nothing much, perhaps, but what about Master Tarantino?

—What, Quentin Tarantino?

—What? yelps Brady, instantly recovering human form.

—What about him? I ask.

—Gimme the fucking phone! screams Brady, and he walks straight through Suzy and Chicho and me and tables and chairs and stuff to grab the receiver.

—Fat poof advice line speaking, floats Dai's voice.

—Sorry, says Brady into the phone, going pink. (That shame again, that saving grace again!)

Then Brady listened.

He goggled.

His eyes did tangos.

He blushed and said:

—Well, yeah, yeah, yeah, yeah, yeah!

And then he put down the phone and turned to us, transfigured.—I've got to go to Camden. Dai has got the tie Tim Roth wore in Dogs! He's going to lend it to me for tomorrow. It's still got the stage blood on it! Jesus fucking Christ on a raft!!! Hey, and guess what?

—What?

—He said he can tell just by my voice that I've got a huge dick! Heh heh! Back in about two hours.

And he ran out.

We went out and watched him charging off towards Gold-hawk Road tube, knocking dumpsters aside like they were empty cans.

—Do you think that was true? Suzy asked me.

—Is true, said Chicho to Suzy, and indicated how big.

—I mean about the tie, said Suzy.

—Christ knows, I said.—But he wants to believe it and Dai will make him. OK. Shit, where were we?

My head was feeling like it was full of cotton wool, I just wanted to sit and veg out somewhere.

—Chicho's clothes? said Suzy.

—Oh yes, I said.

—Such a nice suit! said Chicho, smugly.—Armani, is very beautiful. All the policeman thinking, Oh, such a very rich Espanish man. Is very good for this gibbering. Is easy for me.

—Right, I said, hey, let's have a drink.

—Car, said Suzy.

—Eh? Oh Christ yes. What's happened?

—Is easy for us, said Chicho.

—Come on, said Suzy, and the pair of them grabbed me and frog-marched me up towards the Goldhawk Road. I felt kind of boneless, it was not just being knackered, there was more to it than that: it was suddenly such a relief to be being taken somewhere by someone else who knew what was going on and where we were going, all I had to do was go with the flow. It was like getting into a car with some people you half-know and going off somewhere, you have no idea where you are going, some club somewhere, but it is a fine night and you have money in your pocket and there is good music with a bass that shakes the plastic bits of the car, so when you watch the lights and buildings go by it looks like a film with a soundtrack, you are starring in tonight's feature presentation MY BIG LIFE, and then maybe someone passes you a joint over and you just lean back and think, mmm, yeah, Buy Buy Buy.

Eventually (I mean, it was only a hundred yards or so, but it felt good and long), eventually I thought I had better take control again.

—What's going on, hey, have you gone and got a car your-selves, or what?

—Do we look stupid? said Suzy.

—Such a nice Plan, said Chicho.—We don't mess him up.

—Are we going to Supaservice?

—We are.

—Have you already been to see him?

—Is easy for us.

—Have you got it sorted?

—A weight off your shoulders, said Suzy.

—Is easy for you now, said Chicho, and patted me on the back.

—Hello, fellow business people of W12, said Mr. Supa-service, bouncing out as usual from behind a car.—I congratulate you, Mr. Milkybar, on the quality of your business associates. These are people I can deal with. Come with Supaservice, see what the big bad weekend has brought you.

And he swung up his big four-car up-and-over door.

And there it was.

The original A-one pimpmobile.

A white Merc with fins.

Two hours later, I was being held down curled up with my face pushed into a buttock-warmed cheap vinyl car seat, and was being taken to somewhere that I knew nothing about except that it could be the end of the road.

12

THE
MIRACLE
OF PROZAC

I was trying not to breathe in crumbs off this warm plastic car seat, I could still feel where the bastard who was holding me down's hot ass had been two minutes earlier, the prop shaft sounded very close and pretty knackered, I could hear every bump in the road through the tires.

I had guessed something like this would happen the moment I walked into The Queen's Head and Artichoke up by Great Portland Street, and saw Fergal F. Fitzpatrick grinning at me.

—Hoi, the Man!

It was obviously unlikely things would all stay so warm+ friendly, and I knew I was right when he stood up straight away and said:

—Are you fit? I mean, you know, no sweat, take a pint first if you want, but if you're cool, let's head.

—Why wait? I said all nice and easy, and

—Sure why indeed? said he, but he kept his nice inviting pop-eyed look and his grin on when it was not really real anymore, and I knew it was going to get rather heavier quite soon, he was actually a bit nervous, which should have made me very nervous, because he was never nervous.

I was going somewhere where he was not in charge of the story anymore. Well, what did I expect? I was getting what I wanted.

We got into the back of a big Ford parked away from the streetlights, and I found myself grabbed by a very strong hand and had my face stuffed into what (as I said) had clearly been the other guy's seat until just then. This guy said, with no more trace of an Irish accent than I had expected.

—You try to look where we're going, I even see you trying to think where we might be going, and you're out of the door, OK?

—OK, I mumbled, and spat out a crumb of something shitty, I thought it was probably not worth bothering to ask whether they would stop before flinging me.

I was now very glad I had taken the precaution of borrowing two of Bob's Prozac before going to the pub to meet Fergal. I mean, I have never suffered from panic attacks, but this did not seem like a good time to discover them.

Even so, I did not like it. My neck was cricking like mad already, and I was having to work hard at the breathing, I kept thinking I was going to swallow my tongue or not be able to swallow, or something.

I liked it even less when I heard Fergal try to make some kind of uncool conversation with the guy who was driving, about the state of the traffic for Christ's sake, and this other guy just said all that Fergal deserved to get back, which was:

—Uh-huh?

So Fergal Fuckface Fitzpatrick was not only not in control, he was nowhere near it, he was damn near out of his depth. This got me thinking, and what it got me thinking was:

I must be bloody mad.

I want out of this.

I'll be good, I really will.

Suzy!!

And then something occurred to me that had not, stupidly, occurred to me before: that when they got to wherever they were going, they would be able to do anything at all to me, I would be utterly in their power. I had planned this and thought about it, about what I would say as negotiation, but now it was not about negotiating, it was about living.

I wanted to go back to my shed and wait quietly until tomorrow and tell Suzy it was off, and run away to be an accountant, that was all.

My blood was thudding in my ear.

So much for fucking Prozac.

I could see and hear and feel that we had come a long way along some dual carriageway, but now we were only crawling, there was traffic about and people nearby again, and different-colored light washes coming down from the window, we were back in some busy populated area, I could even hear people laughing and yelling at each other.

I felt like some sinner in Hell, with Heaven just an impossible door away.

Then I decided this would be my last chance. If they were going to do me in, I had a much better chance of getting away here than wherever they were taking me, so I thought I should try to find out what my position was exactly, so I would know if I had to really go for it right now.

—This is bullshit! I shouted.—I come to you with a fucking deal and I get treated like a gob of shit!

I finished (or rather did not finish) this outburst with my mouth being pressed more firmly into the plastic. But the unknown guy in the front spoke, he had one of those soft, country-educated Irish accents:

—I'd not make a noise if I was you, you see, my colleague in the back there with you thinks you're a stoolie, an agent provocateur, do you see?

I believed him, that was no news to me, I knew this would be the problem, but I replied:

—You mean it thinks as well? Amazing!

Now, the point of this was that by saying that I would certainly make the one in the back with me want to hit me, and if he did hit me that meant either he had the power here to do what he wanted in which case I was in trouble, or else that the one in front was telling him to hit me, which meant I was probably totally fucked.

We were still moving slowly through traffic, I saw the orange lamps of a pelican crossing flashing off the blue vinyl of the car door. I had decided that if I got hit the best thing I could do was wait until we were doing a fairish whack again, but soon, and try to suddenly jump up and grab the driver, to make us hit something or at least draw attention to us here. I assumed these people did not like attention, I thought that if I made them whack another car or do a crash stop or if I managed to kick a window out or whatever, they might let me go rather than let people see a fight going on in the car, it is difficult to grab someone in a cramped space and I reckoned I could make a job of it for them if I surprised them.

But I did not get hit.

The one up front actually laughed, which meant he was in charge and was not letting the guy in the back hit me. I took a deep breath and decided to do nothing except concentrate on how convincing and cool I was going to be when we got to wherever we got to.

Soon, the car began to roll and bounce madly about, I heard the exhaust bottom out half a dozen times as we hopped along, the springs were creaking and the seats squeaked, the noise of the car started coming back at us from something, but not like it had done when we passed concrete walls. Then we stopped, and the driver put on the handbrake nice and slow and final, like he had just finished taking his test and was pretty sure he had passed, and I knew we were wherever he wanted us to be.

There was no light from outside now, the glow of the instruments just made it into the back. Then the engine got turned off and it was all very dark and very quiet, I wondered if they were just going to do me in without even giving me a chance to say anything, and for the last time that night, I said to myself no, why the hell would they, look, this is what you wanted, you set it up, you are driving, even with your gob stuffed slobbering with warm vinyl, you are in the real driving seat, wherever we are.

Which turned out to be a wood somewhere.

Surprise surprise.

Ten thousand years later, and things like this, secrets and plotting and killing and stuff, still go on where they always did, in the woods, at night. Well, why change something if it works?

I supposed they had spades as well, for digging.

I started praying that Prozac was also a gut-gummer.

Fergal and the Boss got out of the car while the other one in the back held me down still, and then I got half-let half-shoved out of the door. The driver's door was left open, in the greeny dark the nice yellow of the little light above the front seats spread out for yards. My eyes were already adjusted for night vision, I had been staring at dark blue plastic for half an hour, I looked at the two of them as I rearranged my clothes and my spine. A big white owl floated over us in impossible silence, and we all jumped. I heard the other back door clang cheaply shut and then the dry pine needles crunched as the one from the back circled around the boot of the car and stopped. The car creaked slightly, I guessed he was leaning his warm ass against the back wing, behind me, but I did not look around, there was no point.

—Give us a fag, Fergal, I said. The sound died immediately in the trees.

The social power of fags again.

I could order Fergal to give me one, it was such a small order he could hardly say no, but it was still me giving him an order, it established things. Of course, if he had said no it would have established them even more, and the other way around, but I could see that he was watching me anxiously, like I was in some weird way deciding his fate too, no, not his fate, his status, like I was his prize dog, but one that was liable to crap on the judge's foot and blow it for him, so he gave me one without hesitating, and lit it for me, and now I was the boss of the two of us. I let them see that I could smoke without shaking.

I looked at the Boss.

He looked back, he was in no hurry. He reminded me of someone, he was about fifty, plastic-framed specs, with only thin lenses, smooth-shaven, a dimply little face running a little to fat, short but thick sandy hair, arms folded across a heavy sweater, the hand-knit sort you find in Donegal or House of Fraser, he had cords and Clarks pastie shoes. He looked like a kindish sort of headmaster, like Alan Bennett or something.

Except this man's eyes behind his almost unnecessary specs were clear and calm, they smiled, but with the far-off light of certainty, and I knew: nothing can touch this man, this is a man who is happy to be a judge, a man with a teflon conscience, this is a man who is quite sure where his tribe is waiting, and confident of his place at the fireside, as long as there are a few overheated student rebels in Dublin, a few lost young second-generation Irish in London, a few blokes who cannot imagine putting down their guns and becoming accountants, and the odd Irish-American politician who cannot resist the plug-the-brits card, this man will have a bed and an audience and a homeland somewhere. No Framework Documents and nicely cut deals will be enough for him, his shed is not full of Negotiating Positions, it has a hard bright lightbulb of absolute demands, when he splits again from whoever he is with now, it will be them that are splitting, not him, for he knows without doubt that he is guarding the True Flame. He will judge whatever he does in that pure, unearthly, magnesium light, nothing else, and if he does not believe me I will never get out of here and he will lose no sleep over thoughts of the night and the wood and the blood and the spades and the damp earth.

And now Alan Bennett spoke:

—So what first drew you to sympathize with our movement?

Fergal smiled encouragingly.

—The music, I said.—But I'm not a sympathizer now.

Fergal blanched.

—I see, said Alan Bennett.

—So warm-ass here thinks I am a nark?

—For fuck's sake, Fergal coughed.

Now I looked round. Warm-ass was actually much smaller than I had thought when he had me down on the seat, but just as dangerous, he had one of those sunless, almost green-white block-of-flats faces, lanky black hair over his collar, cheap shapeless jeans and polycotton printed shirt collar out over his sweatshirt. He had bright blue eyes that hated my guts. I knew he would have tattoos under the shirt, and I put him down as a knifeman, just like that, he just had that fast, slicing look.

—Well, says Alan Bennett, you must admit that the notion of hiring us is unusual, even, it could well be said, insulting to us.

—A hundred thousand would be a funny insult.

—A hundred and fifty, I thought?

—So it was.

We were dealing. I liked that.

Alan Bennett spoke again, just watching still:

—Mmm. It is a fair whack, a lot of collecting tins, a good few risky little bank jobs. And you did come through decent channels. Fergal trusts you. He says you knew enough years ago to make trouble for us if that was your game, but then of course Michael here (he indicated the knifeman, who was obviously not actually called Michael, because I looked around now and it was clear that he did not realize at first who was being talked about) suggested that there is such a thing as deep cover. So you see our problem. And indeed, yours. But I think all will become clear if you let us know your proposition, and then I can make a decision, yes?

I was waiting for this.

It was funny, since Alan Bennett had corrected me about my original offer, I felt kind of backlit with confidence, it was my Plan, I had thought it out and I was confident about it, I was sure rationality would win now, rationality and dealing are the same thing, the origin of rationality is dealing, so now I was just waiting to tell them and look at their faces. I took a nice drag and told them what I wanted from them, and watched.

It was worth all the ass-warmed vinyl.

—Is that it? said Alan Bennett, despite himself.

—Nothing else, I said.

Now there was a nice pause.

—Why?

—I don't think you have to know that.

—Hey, come on, my man! said Fergal.—This is too fucking bizarre, and he tries to make like it's only a joke that I'm playing hardball.

—You don't need to know anything else about me, I don't want to know anything else about you. All I want from you is what I said, and if the job comes off you get one hundred and fifty grand, you can hand it over to Dublin and be the sexiest man in IRA HQ or you can keep it for your own deals, I don't know and I don't care. If it doesn't work, you get nothing and you've risked absolutely nothing. I am offering you a one-way bet.

Alan Bennett thought. The rest waited.

—It's too neat, says Knifeman.

—Not too neat, just very neat, I say. I am now sure Knifeman can do nothing without the nod from A.B., and A.B. is thinking seriously behind those slim glasses. He looks at me hard and says:

—The idea has its attractions, I must admit. You appear to know your stuff. Let me see, what if we were to ask you for some . . . favor in the future, perhaps, perhaps a little personal help as part payment?

Easy answer. I know that if I even look like saying Yes to that he will be sure I am a plant, he will think it is all just a big set-up to get me in with them, and Mick the Knife will be carving UP THE 'RA in my liver before I could say You're on. So I make sure that I shake my head very distinctly and keep a close lock-in on his eyes:

—I only want what I said, and I am only offering you used Swiss Francs and Deutschmarks, not me, not anything else.

—I see. And yet you know Fergal, and I believe you knew Sean MacEoin's widow as well, in the biblical sense, indeed. You were, in the past, or you appeared to be, interested in our cause. Allow me to be confused, will you? Am I right to think that although this is, as you say, just business, you are still essentially on our side in what we do?

This is clearly the deciding question of the evening, I can tell because Fergal is watching my mouth like something amazing or terrifying is about to pop out of it, he doesn't dare look me in the eye, the answer is that important. But they had to ask something like that, and I know what I am going to say, and I look Alan Bennett in the eye and he knows I have something worked out too, so I don't pretend it is anything off the cuff, I just give it slow and straight:

—I would call my position benevolent neutrality.

Alan Bennett looked at me, and then he snorted.

He snorted, and then the snort went up his nose and threw his head back, and turned into a laugh. A real, loud, laugh in the night, in this forest. He uncrossed one arm and pinched his nose with one index finger and thumb and looked at me over his glasses, and it still wasn't enough, he put both hands on his hips and shook his head, he actually slapped his leg, he had to look away, I could see that he was thinking about the times he could tell this story to his friends on the Army Council of the IRA or whatever.

The only thing was, I didn't know how the story would end. He crossed his arms again, rested his chin on his chest for a minute and unfocused his eyes, then snapped them back on me, propped his chin on one palm, and said:

—Benevolent neutrality is good, I like that, benevolent neutrality. It has a fine historical resonance. Who said that?

—I did, I said.

—Very nice. So it really is just business. In one sense that is best, although we are not primarily a business organization. One can, of course, defend this sort of action as economic warfare, and all warfare is in the end both political and economic. Crime is Crime is Crime, it is all political. Well, this is all most interesting.

He just keeps on looking at me. So does Fergal, but his eyes are blank, all his senses are in his ears, he is waiting to see what Alan Bennett says. I can hear Knifeman's weight on the car shifting behind me. This is the proverbial it.

—Give the man a cigarette till I think, Fergal.

Fergal does.

I don't like the sound of this giving me a fag stuff, it has unpleasant historical resonances. Spades and holes and stuff.

I can smell myself suddenly, not the nice peppery sweat you get from sex, but a cold sour smell, like the bouquet of a wiped-out trainload of cottonrich but not cotton enough office workers in the rush hour home. The smell of stress, which is the smell of fear. But there is absolutely nothing I can do about it, so I take the cigarette and let Fergal light it.

As I take the first drag, I feel like I once felt before in my life, when I broke an ankle out on some Welsh mountain on my own. I was feeling good because I had just watched a woodpecker for a long time, I had never been that close to a woodpecker before, and then I had watched the sun start to set, and I was running down this mountainside just feeling great to be there, and I tried to hurdle a hedge at the edge of a wood, where the fields began again, and I went into the ditch the other side and I heard my ankle go pop like a shotgun. I got ten seconds of pain so bad it knocked the wind right out of me, I couldn't breathe, never mind shout, and then I was just lying there, looking up at the sky, there were all these swallows right up high, I was feeling quite calm and thinking, OK, you can't walk on a broken ankle, but you have to walk, or else you stay here and maybe freeze or get soaked and get pneumonia, and soon the pain will come back much worse, when the shock goes off, and so I walked, and the funny thing was, it didn't hurt. I mean, it hurt like hell, every step I took, I shouted out, and in between steps I roared, but in a way it didn't hurt like humans hurt, it was like being an animal, because no one could hear and no one could help, it was just me and the pain and keeping on, the pain just didn't matter, my brain was sealed off. Maybe it was just the shock, but I remember it all very clearly, maybe so much of what we call pain is to do with other people, and injustice, and thinking somewhere, deep down, if we cry loud enough, mummy, in the night, mummymummymummy! in our walk-ups, someone must, must come. It was about a mile and a half to the nearest house, I think, I had to climb over hedges and everything, and when I got there this old lady let me in, and I said:

—Um, I think I've broken my ankle, and then I fell over.

The doc who fixed me up told me about a colleague who took his own appendix out in the middle of the bush in Kenya, because he knew he would die otherwise, when his servant came back in the Land Rover with help, they found the vultures eating the appendix, and this doctor holding the final closing stitch in his hand, he must have fainted dead away the second he pulled it through.

If you can't do anything about it, you do it.

Or let it be done to you.

You know those unbearable films of people being lined up to be shot, in Poland, Russia, Vietnam, or wherever? And you always think, Christ, why don't they just scream and run about and claw at the bastards' faces or something? Why do they just stand there among the bodies, are they so blind they still hope, or what? But it is not hope that paralyzes them and not even hopelessness, it is pointlessness. If you cannot see the point, you cannot move, you just sit in your walk-up and put your head in the trough of your seat or you sit at your desk and look blankly at your papers until they have to wheel you away, or you take smack so you cannot remember what made you take it, or you just wait for your turn to walk to the edge of the trench. It is not that there are so many guards, it is not that you have hope, which means that you still have something to lose, it is just that you do not understand, it is all impossible, the world has stopped working, you do not know this story and you cannot think of one to put there instead.

I tried to tell myself that I should be listening with every ear I had to Knifeman's weight shifting on the car, I should be trying to work out exactly how far he was, how far would I have to spin if I wanted to kick him right in the solar plexus, if I crippled him first, I rated my chances with Fergal and Alan Bennett. I would jump them and tear their lips clean off their faces, I would eat their eyes out. But instead I just smoked my cigarette and wondered if they would wait till I finished it, and I thought about all the bad things I have done to nice people like Pili in my life and decided that maybe this was the right thing to happen anyway, a knife in a dark wood.

The past is only a mirror of the present: if you are in the shit, your past looks like a long, logical progression to the sewer.

I am on the fourth drag when Alan Bennett says:

—Well, you have good enough nerves.

—The miracle of Prozac, I say.

And he laughs again, and suddenly I know that I am saved.

—A quarter million, says he.

—A hundred and seventy-five, or it's not worth our while.

—Two hundred. You can't do it without us.

—Done.

—Good, says he.—So when do you want it? says he.

—Tonight, I say.—Now would be best. (My voice sounds like a hollow robot voice coming out of my throat somewhere.)—It would avoid any possibility of a fuck-up, and we wouldn't need to meet again until you come to get the money. Fergal knows where I live.

—What if he doesn't keep the deal? says Knifeman.

—Fergal knows where I live, I repeated.—He knows where my sister and my nephews live. And I know who you are and I am not that stupid.

—Right so, says Alan Bennett, and now Fergal hands the fags out all round.

Guess what?

They not only deliver, right then and there, they even give me a lift back to town.

We pass through the Lada-city wastelands of N.E. christ-knowswhat, I don't take any notice where, who cares where, I am going back and I have got it and they did not kill me. I sit in the back with Knifeman again, it is a situation fraught with the kind of social ice even fags cannot overcome, until Fergal puts on some horrible folk-rock-fusion Gaelic-electric stuff on the radio, to stop us having to speak.

—Oh Jesus, says Knifeman.—Come on Fergal, that is fucking brutal, what is it for fuck's sake?

—Runrig or some shit like that, I say.

—Yeah, says he.

He turns around, and his eyes only change after he looks round, like for a moment, in the heat of the agreement, he forgot who I was.

—Well, hey, sorry, I mean, OK, shit, what are you into lads? says Fergal.—You can have anything except A Woman's Heart, I'm not having that.

—Beethoven, says Alan Bennett, the Eroica, a revolutionary symphony, lads, from a revolutionary era!

—Save us, says Knifeman under his breath.

But God was obviously not on-line for Knifeman, so we got the Eroica Symphony all the way back into town, me and Fergal and these two IRA men who nearly killed me half an hour ago, for Christ's sake, with Beethoven pouring out of the windows, I was trying not to giggle because I kept thinking about that guy and the statuette of Beethoven, and then they let me out near Archway station, and I sat down and laughed to myself on the pavement, and then I was sick.

Maybe it was the Prozac.

Two to feel good, six for a coma, eight for goodbye: Life is a precarious little thing, a bright dragonfly hovering permanently between unbearable clarity and smacked-out deathwishes.

I went for a pint but the pub was all full of Irishmen, there was some rebel song on the jukebox, it was just too spooky, so I walked out again just as the barman was taking my order, he must have thought I was well fucked-up, which maybe I was, I was haunted by this weird feeling that it was all out of my control now, someone had clicked on the autopilot, me maybe, what difference did it make, it was up and running on its own now.

Next thing, I found myself in a taxi which for some reason— I was sure I told him Shepherd's Bush—took me to Kentish Town and put me down outside Suzy's flat, so I rang the bell, just to see.

I had never been there before without being invited. I half thought this someone would be there, and the other half of me thought what the fuck would she think of me even if no one was there, I mean, I was not supposed to be coming round tonight, I was only supposed to call from a phone booth and say it was all on, then go home, like normal, like usual, like everyday.

A shadow came up behind the door glass and someone clicked the lock open, but it was not someone, it was Suzy.

The moment I saw her face I didn't give a damn what she thought of me being there so long as she was thinking about me.

—I did it, they didn't kill me, they're on. We're on.

—God, you're white. Come in.

She stood in the middle of the room, and then she smiled slowly, and slowly raised both her arms straight out by her sides, like a scarecrow. I felt like I was on rollerskates, I was just pulled on in there, and I grabbed hold of her and put my head in her hair, and realized I was panting like I had just run a mile, I could feel my heart echoing against her chest, then she pulled my head, and said:

—Let me look at you, and put her finger on my lips to stop me saying anything, and looked at me, I could see her eyes flicking from one of my eyes to the other, all I could do was stand there and let her look in as deep as she liked, my doors were all open, I could feel her scanners lighting right to the back of my head, and then she looked at the surface of my eyes again and closed her eyes and kissed me, so I closed mine too.

So much for freedom.

Mr. J. J. O'Connor,
AUCTIONEER
MAIN ST.
CASTELBAR
CO. MAYO
IRELAND

Dear Mr. O'Connor,

I am given to understand that you are from time to time engaged in the disposal of licensed premises in the town of Castlebar. I would like to avail of any such opportunity. Please therefore send me full details of any suitable properties. I am only interested in a pub with a clientele of decent people (no tinkers) and will (God willing) very soon be in a position to be a ready cash purchaser if both the pub and the price are acceptable. I believe that you occasionally play golf with my first cousin Garda Sergeant Hugh Gallagher from Achill.

Sincerely,
Mr. Brady

P.S. Westport would also do.

Snr. Jesus Maria FERRERUELA
c/S. JUAN DE LA CRUZ 56
3° DCHA
ZARAGOZA

Dear Suso,

That you not sell the wood-fired restaurant before that you hear
of me within three days more! Tomorrow I shall be in a very
grand negotiation. Is very important for me! Many little kisses to
all the family and the friends,

CHICHO

13

THE
GAME
OF LEAVING
EARTH

Monday night still, late now, and Suzy and I were talking and smoking, I was lying resting my cheek on her hairs and drawing spunkcircles on her thigh with my finger, occasionally I looked up between her breasts, right up her nostrils, but mostly I just stayed looking at my finger on her tummy. I could feel the sweat on my head on her hairs, her calf was warm and soft on my back and her blood was thudding away gently in her flat tummy, in my ear.

Brady and Chicho were gone, and everything was arranged, the Plan was already almost out of my control.

Brady had come back from Dai's place with what Dai had told him was Tim Roth's bloodstained tie, you never saw anyone so happy, he was like some pilgrim with a piece of St. Peter's foreskin or whatever, now everything he did had meaning to him himself, he had a chunk of the big story right here in his hand, he was just shining with conviction. He also had a signed photo of Nicholas Cage, which, for some unfathomable reason, he seemed to think was absolute proof that the Tim Roth tie was the real thing.

True or not, the effect was there all right, so I suppose that made it true as well, whatever, because if something is there, working away in the world, like Brady's new confidence was, it is surely as real, and therefore as true, as any non-bouncing brick.

It took Chicho and me about twenty minutes to chill him out and sit him down and cool him off (Suzy was in the back checking out the printout of her Story) and make sure he knew when he had to have his Doggies inside the Pizza Express.

Then Suzy came and read us out the thing she had written as our cover story, so if anything went wrong she could pretend she had been trying to become an investigative journalist, Chicho was just a friend helping her and I was the inside contact she had made. It was called

MICHAEL WINNER'S PRIVATE BANK

But you know all about that anyway.

So then Chicho and Brady went off, which left just Suzy and me, which was fine. Which is where I started, lying with my cheek on her muff.

I was thinking maybe we had just made love, and the word was echoing round my head like I was in some empty airship hangar. But had we? Surely we had just fucked?

How could we have made love, because I needed her tonight.

I needed Suzy to hold me and say she would be there and fuck me to exhaustion and sleep all night in her arms, and that cannot be love, that is want and need, it is no more to do with love than just having a good time is. If you need something you need someTHING, you turn a person into an object of desire, an object, and you yourself are unfree because if you need something you are enslaved by it, but only a free person can make love. Free people make love, unfree people arrange matches, whether they know it or not. Because love is pure choice, a moment free of all deals and promises. You can only make love if you are so free you could stand up now and walk away from this person, but hope you will be with them forever, and if I had had to walk away from Suzy now, I would have curled up and howled on the floor, so how can I talk about making love?

Maybe one day you will find yourself by a glassy lake on a still, frozen day in the mountains, with blinding white sun, and the world will be so quiet that you can hear the gasjets of a single hot-air balloon, miles away against the deep blue sky and think: maybe you cannot get love, maybe you can only want it, maybe love is simply the lines of desire, that can only meet in that blue infinity.

Then Suzy opens her eyes and looks down, so I can just make eye contact either side of her nostrils, and I achieve re-entry into earth at Orgasm plus five minutes, realize I have been thinking about love and stuff on my own, as if it is something floating about, unattached and abstract, which is always bullshit, so I slide up, kiss her, light up a cigarette, pick up a pen and paper and decide that what I need is not to worry about the nature of love or whatever, but find out more about Suzy.

So I pick up a pen and paper to play the Game of Leaving Earth. The Game of Leaving Earth (it is not really a game, though, it is nothing unless you take it seriously) goes like this:

The earth is about to be destroyed, the scientists have known this for a hundred years, the politicians (incredibly enough) have actually listened and the people (even more incredibly) have turned off their TVs and deserted their shopping precincts and set about doing something about it in a philosophical manner. The human race has built a spaceship which can take one person off into space forever. It had to be one person, because if you cannot save everyone, how do you decide who to save? The only fair thing was to choose one person by a world lottery. In the meantime, the scientists have devised a wonderful machine that can extract the essence of anything and hold it in digital computer banks, in bubbles of magnetic pulses, so whenever you get lonely you can plug in and there they will be, and if you ever reach a habitable planet, you can recall these essences and they will flower out again.

You (of course) have won the lottery, you are leaving the world alone forever, and you must decide on eight things to take with you.

—OK, said Suzy.—Everything in the Universe.

—OK, I said.

—Oh. Can I say that? I was only being cute.

—Of course. Anything.

—But now there's nothing left.

—You just have to say eight things.

—This is silly.

—It always is at first. It gets better.

—OK then.

So in the end these were Suzy's eight things, the essence of which is now loaded aboard her spaceship:

EVERYTHING

THE WORLD

EVERYTHINGILIKE

MY FRIENDS

—Does that include me? I asked.

—Of course, she said.

—Oh well, I said.—Go on:

MY FAMILY

THE ECOSYSTEM

SCOTLAND

WHALES

Like I said, it always seems stupid at first.

So you are about to leave when unfortunately the spaceship is destroyed during testing. Along with the essence of everything you have already stored. But the wise scientists have provided a backup, which is, however, only half the size. You can now take only four essences with you. Four things for your trip away forever. So you have to think of four things which sum up the essences of those eight things, in pairs. See, now you have to start thinking.

Or feeling, maybe.

I am not going to tell you what Suzy chose next, I told you about the first things because everyone chooses almost the same things then, it is obvious, that is why it always seems silly at the start. But what happens when you try to think of something to express the essence, for you, of EVERYTHING and THE WORLD? I do not want to spoil it for you, if you try it, so I will just tell you one of what Suzy chose. It was A NICE CLUB.

And you have guessed what happens when you have chosen at last (the four take much longer than the eight, of course, and the more cunning you have tried to be, the more you have tried to pack everything into the eight, the more has gone forever, the more quickly we get down to it and the slower the four are). Yes. The same thing. The NICE CLUB and everything else you choose has gone. Now it has to get down to two essences which express the four. One of the ones Suzy chose was: LOOKING OUT OF A WINDOW AT THE SEA.

And now the same happens again. Now there is just one tiny little spaceship left, and you can only take one little essence, no more than half a dozen words, that will be the essence of the two things you ended up with last time. This is it, the final distillation of all your longings and hopes and feelings and memories, to sustain you in the empty eternity ahead. Most people have to have a joint or something at this stage, it takes ages, you can see them sinking into themselves and getting quiet, I suppose that is the whole point.

Of course, it is bullshit in one sense, it is trying to find out about you alone, and we are not alone, or at least we should not be, we were not made to be alone, the big secret of the western world, that is hidden by all the fantasies of Making It, is that lone-

liness is Hell. So anything you have with you is part of Hell, if
you are lonely.

But on the other hand it is not bullshit at all, maybe a person
is nothing without other people, but a person is also nothing if
they do not have that hidden place inside, a strong castle with a
deep well, that can withstand any siege if it has to. You cannot
leave the gates open to everyone, because what ceremonies would
you have left when the person you have been waiting for comes
riding up?

—You mean what is the last thing I'll be thinking about
when I die, don't you? said Suzy, and looked at me.—Or if you
leave me or I leave you, or something?

—I suppose so, I said.

—Why do you want to know that?

—Because I want to know about you.

—Have you done this?

—Oh yeah.

—What did you get down to?

—The first time I ended up with A DISTANT CAMPFIRE
BURNING and the second time I got A DRAGONFLY UN-
FREEZING IN THE SUN.

—Why?

So I told her about the time I was on a mountain in the
Pyrenees somewhere, I don't know where, near Jaca maybe, I had
been taken there by a gang of Pili's friends, I never bother much
about where on a map we are when things like that happen, and
we were all walking in these horrible dry jagged frosted-up
mountains, and we came to this village, a whole village with a
nice little baroque church and everything, about twenty houses,
totally deserted, the roofs were coming in, but you could still see

knives on the tables, prints on the walls and stuff. Then we found the only person there, an ancient woman, she said everyone had gone off to Zaragoza and Pamplona and Barcelona, the last other people left two years ago, and she wished she was dead. We camped there, it was freezing cold that night, and the next day I got up first and climbed up the rocks above the village and found this ruined castle, just a one-wall ruin over a sheer drop, there were real Spanish vultures on the top of the ruined wall, and in the shadow of the castle I found this dragonfly, a big green shiny one like a titanium model airplane kit, that had got frozen solid in the night, and I put it out in the sun and watched for more than two hours, on my own, as the frost melted on it and eventually it came alive again and flew away.

Then I said to Suzy how I really wanted to know about who this someone was. I said it before the last words of my story had died away properly, before Suzy had stopped listening.

—OK, she said, like she had been waiting for this.— It's all very simple, but simple like jumping off a bridge is simple. Simple but serious. Well: I was pregnant, he wanted me to get rid of it, I wasn't sure, he was, that was the story of our thing together, I was never sure about anything, he was sure about everything. So I agreed, just because I wasn't sure and he was, you know, I thought, anyone who can be that sure of something important has to be right, so I got rid of it, late, my breasts were already getting bigger, they were beautiful, I wish you could have seen them, but afterwards they sagged, and they've never come properly back, don't say anything fucking stupid, I know it's true, even if no one notices, I notice, so now you know about that. And then it turned out he hadn't been right, he had just been scared. And so I left him, I suppose because once I saw he was wrong and scared too, there was no point going out with someone that much older, which he was, what's the point of getting older if you don't get any better? And now he wishes I'd had it and stayed with him, but he knows I'll never come back, so he just keeps in touch to see if I ever need any help. He's 45 now, he probably won't live that much longer because of all the drugs he does all the time. He thinks he nearly fucked my life up. I know loads of people think that about other people, usually it's just crap, it's just them wanting to feel good about feeling bad about what they did, so they can feel like the center of the world. But actually, I think he's right, you know? I think he nearly did fuck me up for good, so I think about him quite a lot and I suppose I always will, not that way, once that's gone that's gone, but if I ever need help and he can help me I think I'll call him and make him do it, because he does owe me, he really does. Do you still want me to finish this game?

—Yes, I said.

—I don't know, said Suzy.—Mine sounds too sort of modern, it's like a bloody cheap film or something. I suppose that's just because so many people think like that too. That doesn't matter, an idea isn't worth less because a lot of people have it, it's worth more.

—What is it? I asked.

—Well, she said.—We eat shit and breathe shit, and read shit and watch shit and vote shit and feel like shit and we don't know what the fuck for, most of the time we even think shit, the only thing we get back for all this big shit is, we can move around like no one could ever move around before, we can get there quicker, even if we don't know where, at least we can see more of the shit, at least we know more, and go more. I suppose that has to be a good thing, doesn't it? So we might as well just stick her into D and hit the pedal.

And she shrugged her shoulders and I watched her write what the Last Thing was for her, and as I watched her write I thought about her and me and Brady and Chicho and what the hell we had got ourselves into this fuck-up in aid of, and what the hell was going to happen to them and to her and me tomorrow, and whether we would stay together afterwards, would we walk into MC Heaven together, and what I would do if we didn't and then she put down the pen and looked at me and shrugged and I read:

DRIVING WITH WIND IN MY HAIR.

14

RIGHT
BETWEEN
THE EYES
WITH A
.22 DUM-DUM

On Tuesday, at one o'clock, in a curiously furnished flat in Kentish Town (it has clothes hanging all over the walls and a standard lamp with a tutu for a shade), a young woman is preparing to make a phone call.

She is dressed in a very tight red silk dress that shows off a remarkably flat stomach, and is wearing the sort of big blonde wig and make-up that she knows makes any woman look to any man like any woman in a big blonde wig and make-up, which is why (she considers) so many men like women in big blonde wigs and make-up.

She has her eyes closed, her mouth pursed scottishly, and is frowning in concentration, so she can forget what she is wearing, and forget how she is sitting, and even forget who she is for a moment, so she can let someone else take over, she has to detach her voice from herself. Now she has got there, wherever it is: the frown smoothes out and her eyes, though they stay closed, are relaxed and still, they have found their focus somewhere deep behind her eyelids. She dials, and when the time comes, she speaks without hesitation:

—Hello darling, Janey. Ghastly, if you must know. Anyway, darling, look: you remember that Count de Giglio that came over to you a couple of days ago? Yes. Well I thought he was quite sweet. Well his nephew wants to come and see you, so I said he should pop round, is that OK, darling? Well, more or less now actually. I know, darling, but I really couldn't say no. Oh, he's appalling. Horrid and fat and flash-oid.

At this point the young woman opened her eyes and looked at the man in her room, a large young Spanish gentleman in a shiny two-tone suit. She smiled at his outrage, but did not even think about blinking or laughing, she was too deep in there by now, she was not pretending to be Janey Herzberg any more, she WAS Janey Herzberg.

—And God only knows where he picked up the tart-oid little thing he's with. Wait till you see her, darling. Indescribably awful. The tacky-oidest. And the car! No, but I won't spoil it for you: wait-and-see pudding, darling! About two? Wonderful. Dinner Wednesday? Oh, well, look, I'll have to put that on the grill and see if it sizzles, darling, let me get back to you in the afternoon, yes? Bye-bye!

Now there is a pause in the room, as the young woman sits there beside the phone. The silence goes on until the Spanish man clicks his fingers in front of her open eyes, and up she wakes.

—Oh, is Suzy back again! Is not easy for you.

—No, more like scary.

He looks at her and sits down beside her; he lights a cigarette in his own mouth and puts it in hers, then, as she drags, he fishes something out of his pocket and puts it in her hand: a cheap, red-and-blue tin Day Of The Dead skeleton figure, a red skeleton holding up a blue skull.

—Is for putting on this Mercedes mirror, like these furry dices. Is for saying: Hello Suzy, is very important and is not very important.

—Thanks, Chicho, she says. She looks at it, then at him:—Chicho, are you scared of going to prison?

—Is prison for me, here in this London with this cold and raining and no money. Or I get my restaurant in Zaragoza, or I going to prison. Is equal for me.

—Good. OK then, I'm going to tell you something.

And so she did.

At half-past one, Covent Garden mopes in slothful greed under a flat gray sky threatening drizzle, wishing for a 100% continental-style sun to warm the collective pineal gland, banish northern reticence and persuade hard currency to cavort from one warm palm to another.

The duty security man in the stage door of the Royal Opera House in Floral St. (he is subcontracted from Securicor, his name is George and he lives in Wansdyke) leans out of his door to take another look at the lovely convertible white Merc with fins that has been double-parked there for some five minutes. For many years he has watched the unnecessarily subsidized Opera-goers swanning in and out before him, his envy has become so hopeless it is almost not envy any more, it is almost more like wistfulness as he watches the car and the occupants, a flash dago and his tart, a big tall blonde in red leather, showing off her worked-out stomach, what a fuck she must be, yeah, if you had the money and the white Merc, mate, the nearest you'll ever get to that will be the scale-model cars in the back of the Sunday Mirror and the sad pics on the top shelf.

Hope she gives him the clap while he's at it. Oh, turning nicer now, rain's stopped. And here that lot come again. The fucking Reservoir Doggies, what a bunch of wankers, nothing to do all day except bloody ponce about dressed like twats, must have just come out of the Nag's Head, they look half-pissed, fucking art students from St. Martin's or something. Mind you, that one doesn't look much like a student, that big one, the leader, he looks more like a builder or something. Must be quite good fun, when you come to think about it, I like the suits anyway, those plastic guns look quite good nowadays, from a distance. Oh, he likes the Merc too, does he? Don't blame you, mate, me too.

—Nice, innit? says George.

The big man just turns his sightless shades on him, and then the rest do so too. Don't fucking look at me like that you poncy wankers, I was only trying to be civil. Fucking kill you. Fucking students. Sorry? No sir, may I see your ticket a moment, sir. Oh yes, entrance round the front, in Bow Street, sir, but I'm not sure they'll let you in this late, it is a dress rehearsal today, sir. And you, sir. Stupid bastard.

And George looks up at his TV monitor to see what is going on on stage.

Inside the ROH, Siegfried, every accountant's favorite operatic hero, has just been told by Brünnhilde that he should go off and do new Deeds to show his love, not hang around at home with her doing partnership things, which Siegfried quick-wittedly replied was just the ticket, he agrees that if he shoots off down the Rhine for a trip in search of Adventures, this will be the real proof of their undying commitment. Deep stuff, and handy for Siegfried. The resulting duet is just ending with the curious and historically unfortunate cry of Heil, Heil, HEIL!!!, which, backed by a vast orchestra with its hypertrophic brass section (the Victorian equivalent of the Xtra-Bass Woofer) attains a climax so tremendous—and so blatantly descriptive—as to leave the audience sitting straight up, blinking, hands whitening upon knees and eyes stealing pregnant glances at each other.

At five minutes to two, a large black car turns right off Russell Street and the imposing, skinheaded driver, faced with the well-known but still rather squeakily narrow alley ahead, stops lecturing his fellow passenger about how he should really find a better job, what with his qualifications and everything, and shifts down into second so he can watch his way carefully between the wall and the single cast-iron lamppost, into Crown Court WC2.

The limo burbles along, it slides between another wall and lamppost where St. Margaret's Court joins Crown Court, and so arrives, at a somehow impressively crawling speed, outside Fielding's Hotel, where it halts with no lurch beside the trellises and climbing flowers which adorn that incongruously homely establishment.

Through his shades, the leader of the black-suited gang drinking in studied silence around a large table in the superflash Pizza Express, on Bow Street, a large and gangling figure with enormous hands and wearing a red-stained black tie, sees the limo arrive. He makes his grunted excuses, picks up a slice of his pizza, and rises from the table, spilling various beers and little condiment pots, turns back, sticks a twenty-quid note on the table and tells them to order a double round of Sols, and then heads off, leaving behind him a palpable gap in the conversation, the emptiness that says the Leader has gone and no one quite knows why they are they anymore, and off he lopes across Bow Street, hops over a bollard, bounds ganglingly over the plinth of the crappy bronze dancer statue at the top of Crown Court, pausing only to slam the pizza slice up into her face to further thicken his alibi and strides to the five telephone booths that stand just behind the bollards that three quarters block the entrance to Crown Court. Only three of the booths are in use, so he chooses one of the empty ones.

He is unable to resist a quick glance around at the limo, and a quick catch of the eye with the younger of the two men who are at this moment in the act of getting out of it. Reassured, he puts on gloves, concentrates on making the strange voice that Suzy taught him to make by pulling in his nose and lowering his chin and keeping the vibrations up around his front teeth, and telephones an unpublicized number at Paddington Green Police Station to tell them to tell Chief Inspector Attercliffe that there is a 500-lb. bomb in a blue Sierra Estate parked on the corner of Bow Street and Martlet Court, opposite the cast-iron and glass gallery of Covent Garden, and it will explode in 45 minutes to show the UK Government that no True Irish Patriot will settle for less than the whole 32 counties, and fuck any backsliding ceasefires.

He then immediately calls a friend of his who worked until

recently in a big office, so that he can have a quick Stage Irish Charming Eejit chat with the receptionist, to make her laugh, to brighten her day, to make sure she recalls him having phoned.

There is no Chief Inspector Attercliffe at Paddington Green.

There is no Chief Inspector Attercliffe anywhere. The name and phone number together constitute a code which tells the police that this is a call from a serious bomber, not a fucked-up hoaxer. It is, in fact, the second-latest code used by a splinter group of a splinter group of the old Official IRA, and has recently been superseded, but it is known to have been real once, and is still warm enough to hit the bullseye. The time of forty-five minutes was chosen to make the police hurry, but not panic. As for the blue Sierra, this is just the innocent car that fate chose to be at that moment parked in the spot concerned.

The oversized caller trots out of the booth now, thinking of the merry quip from the text of the popular film Reservoir Dogs with which he will greet his dressed-up companions. As he crosses Crown Court, he cannot help casting another glance rightwards to where the limo is standing, he can see the two men standing in front of the door to the bank now, and then a further glance leftwards to make sure the white Merc with fins is already leaving Floral Street and nosing out into Bow Street, which it is. He wonders if it will really fit in between the gap left between the last bollard and the far side of Crown Court.

By now the occupants of the limo and their big sack of money are entering the first of two electronically controlled doors which give access to the Private Bank bearing the simple title No. 6 Crown Court.

Inside the bank, the larger, older and far more dangerous

looking of the two men engages in a few pleasantries with the internal guard, while the younger man sets down the linen sack of money, takes a deep breath in secret and, addressing her as Lady Caroline, enquires in a friendly and familiar manner after the health of one of the three finishing-school products whose saddle-spread backsides are perched behind large, tasteful, repro-Georgian desks stuffed with vast amounts of vulgar, radio-alarmed cash.

His question is greeted by Lady Caroline rather as if she has just received an unexpected, unwelcome and mostly incomprehensible e-mail from the planet Filth.

But Roedean and the Comtesse de Grouchy have not been wasted, and she gamely attempts a neutral reply despite her confusion. This confusion, though, is doubled when the young man asks if she fancies a drink sometime.

—A drink? she pales. Trained from young adulthood to be the Perfect Hostess and little else (her work in this private bank scarcely deserves the name, it is more an excuse to meet the kind of men she might think about marrying), she is lost: she has always been shielded from the kind of men whom one might have to reject directly, one simply does not meet them. And yet one can clearly not say yes . . .

But Lady Caroline's companions come to her rescue by ordering the young man, without a wasted syllable, to bring their money in immediately. He obeys sullenly, having achieved his goal, which was to waste a few precious moments. He snatches at the bag, in order accidentally to tip its contents (mainly Swiss Francs, today) onto the floor.

—Oh Christ, he says.

—Oh really! say the Girls.

—Butterfingers, says Fred, and does not bend to help scoop up the dough.

The younger man is indeed displaying signs of mental anguish, and no wonder: he has no way of knowing if his Plan is going as designed, he has been at work all morning, he has been unable to phone Suzy, for all he knows she never got through to the bank, or was rumbled, or whatever, the white Merc should just be drawing up about . . .

—This must be him, says Joe, at the periscope.

—Janey said it was a horrid car, calls Lady Caroline. —Is it a horrid car, Joe?

—Oh no, your Ladyship, a lovely white Mercedes soft-top.

—Oh how wonderful!

Joe continues to look through the periscope, while the Girls have to bring all of what they think of as their breeding to bear to master their curiosity. They are staring at Joe, who is their eyes. Fred too, though without much interest. If anyone were looking at the young man, they would see him twitch with excitement, but they are not.

—Joe, has it got all those sort of surfboard things stuck on to it?

—Yes, your Ladyship. The full trim pack, I should say.

—How awful! And is there a tart-oid girl with him, Joe?

—A proper cracker, your Ladyship. Oh, he's going away again. Oh no, just backing up round the comer.

(What the fuck is she doing? thinks the young man.— Will Brady still be able to see her? She was supposed to park right outside the bank, in full view, that was the whole fucking point of having the white Merc in the Plan! In full view! Jesus!)

—I simply must have a look at her, calls Lady Caroline.—
Let them in then, Joe, come on, come on, come on.

—Who's this, your Ladyships? asks Fred.

—That Italian Count's nephew. Janey said he was coming.

—Oh well, says Fred.

—OK, thinks the young man.

And the doors open and in walk Chicho and Suzy.

—Morning sir, say Joe and Fred.

—Oh, such a nice bank! says Chicho.

—Don't look much like a bank, giggles Suzy.

—Golly! whisper the delighted Girls.

The young man, with the bag of money still in his hand, as-
sumes something like an at-ease military stance, and just stands
there as if no one should notice him at all, which is apparently the
right thing for him to do, since no one does.

At that moment, George the ROH security man is buzzed by
his colleague in the main security office just inside the big wooden
gates at the Bow Street stage door.

The ROH has had to deal with five bomb emergencies in the
last ten years, and so the drill is well-known. The fundamental
point to decide, as always, is whether the house should be evacu-
ated or locked up. This depends on the location and size of the
bomb: if the bomb is likely to damage the actual fabric of the
house, the audience must obviously be got out. But if it is a small
bomb nearby, they will be safer inside. George enquires as to
which is the case this time, and the reply leaves him in little doubt:

—Five hundred fucking pounds twenty yards away? It could
demolish the bloody lot. Get them out, George, but for Christ's

sake don't send them out into Bow Street, get them into Floral Street, and down east, use the get-out doors, everything! The Met reckon we've got forty minutes, so move it.

Inside, the house lights come on as the high alarms slice through the fat tendrils of Wagner's orchestration, and bring it grinding and squealing to a halt.

With the alarms come the first sirens from outside.

Inside the Pizza Express, the Reservoir Dogs crane to see and hear.

—Keep eating! growls the big chap.—Dogs are cool.

—Yeah, say the others, happily, and munch away at their lumps of cheesy dough at their table in the far corner, while the other tables rise and go (suicidally, if they only knew) to the big plate-glass windows, to watch the forces of the State mobilizing to save them.

The leader of the Doggies can only see the front half of the white Merc, parked in the dog-leg of Crown Court beside Fielding's Hotel. He snorts to himself, since Suzy was supposed to make shagging sure the Merc was in view from the Pizza Express, and it only just is, what was the silly bitch doing parking it almost out of sight like that? Anyway, it is in place and Brady can see it is, so that is OK. Nice enough topping, this.

In No. 6 Crown Court, the bank, the young man, who feels Chicho's and Suzy's spiel nudging the bounds of credibility, has all his ears tuned to any sound of sirens, and so is the first to hear them. He drops his money bag and tells them all to listen. They do.

—What? says Joe the internal security man.

—Listen, says the young man. But now everyone can hear them, coming from every angle.

—Fuck me, says the big skinhead.—What's going on?

—Open up, Joe, let's take a look, says the young man, and the inside guard does so without thinking, it is the obvious thing to do, everybody wants to know the Story, even the Girls leave their desks with hardly a vestige of their prized insouciance. The young man runs out.

—What's going on, Geeohvahni? says the big-haired blonde.

—Is nothing, cara mia, says he, with a big, slow wave.

Inside the ROH, the orchestra is tangling its way to the stage-door exit while the audience is shuffling and queueing, trying to keep the old emotions of panic and flight pinned down. Outside, white vans crash-stop and vomit crushes of policemen busy fixing their helmets and casting about for instructions, shouting into wobbly radios, running backwards and forwards to fend away stunned gangs of foreign tourists.

In Crown Court, the slightly balding young man from the Private Bank grabs a Sergeant as he emerges from Hughes-Pritchard (Accountants) at No. 3 and is about to head across to Fielding's Hotel, to order everyone either to get out within the next ten minutes or stay put at all costs.

All around, fire bells are jangling, alarms are whooping and people in suits are scuttling about, clutching files and computer bodies. In the ground-floor window of Hughes-Pritchard, a balding man in red suspenders is desperately backing up his hard disk onto softies, clutching his hair, and screaming audibly at his machine to fucking hurry up will you, you useless piece of junk. In Crown Court, our young man asks what is going on. He is told it is a bomb, and ordered brusquely to get out of the street now. He cries that they have two titled ladies in the office over there, distant relatives of the Royal Family for Christ's sake, and some Italian Count or something.

The Sergeant stops and thinks for long enough to glimpse the fluttering coattails of tabloid fame and tells the young man to wait two secs, bursts through the door of Fielding's Hotel, tells the receptionist to either get everybody out in eight minutes, right?, or tell them to stay in and keep away from the windows. He then allows himself to be dragged along to the door of No. 6, where the two security men are watching.

Floral Street is filling with opera-goers tumbling from the doors (salesmen on Incentive Rewards and the sabled ranks of Hampstead Germans), while actors and musicians clamber and help each other from the head-high get-out doors opposite the little alley where the diners in the Jardin des Amis du Vin are deserting burgundies and entrées rather more quickly than they chose them. A group of photography-fetishist far-easterners are herded toward Long Acre with somewhat excessive enthusiasm.

In the bank, the Sergeant has explained the situation. With a respectful insistence learned from films of Edwardian England, he demands that they clear the building within (he checks his watch) the next five minutes or else stay inside at all costs and lie down and hide under tables or anything else solid. And keep away from the windows until they are advised otherwise.

—Lemmeoutahere! screams the blonde airhead. —Geeoh-vahni, gemmeoutahere!

—Oh really, says Lady Catherine, but the Girls are not that keen on lying about waiting for an explosion either, their Stiff Upper Lips are not the real Victorian things, they are pale degenerate modern versions, designed only to cope with social gaffes, not mortal danger.

—Look, says the young man loudly and firmly, and everyone turns round in surprise.—The limo's outside, we should get the ladies out of here, they'd be away in two minutes flat.

—He's right, says Fred, simply.

—My uncle is a Cabinet Minister, says Lady Caroline.

—Yeah, says Joe, who is not at all happy.—I could drive them out just like that. I mean, me or Fred.

—It's Fred's car, says the young man, putting Plan A into operation hopefully.

—I don't care who drives it, says the Sergeant.—If it's going, get it gone. Well?

—Hold on, says Fred, and goes to the nearest phone. Everyone watches, waiting in different ways for their fate.

—Hello guv, you heard about the bomb round the corner? Yeah, well the Met want us to stay in or get out now, what say we get the Ladies out in the limo and Joe stays put and locks the shop up? Yeah, OK, I'll stay, Joe'll drive. Yeah, the whole place is swimming with them.

And Fred puts the phone down.

—Right then.

—Um, you say I was driving, Fred? asks Joe.

—Yeah, go on, says Fred.—Guvnor wants me to stay here, no offense Joe, someone's got to, and it's down to me.

—No offense Fred, says Joe quickly.

The young man shifts to Plan B (codename: Fredwill). He always thought they would have to anyway. Fred is just that kind of man.

Gratefully, Joe takes the keys from Fred. The Sergeant leans his head into his radio and tells them that a VIP limo with a Cabinet Minister's daughter is evacuating out into Bow Street in two minutes. Permission comes swiftly. He turns to the Girls and almost bows:

—OK, er, ma'ams. Turn right onto Bow Street and down Long Acre, um, my colleagues will direct you.

—And what is with us? says the fat dago in the flash suit.

—Yeah what about us, mate? shouts the blonde piece.—We got our motor out there too, the white Merc round the corner, what about us?

—Oh Christ, says the Sergeant.—OK, OK, just go. All of you. Go on! and he calls again into his radio:— Victor three-four. Correction to last message: two cars coming through, a black VIP limo and, er (he takes a step out of the door and looks left), a white Merc with fins. Roger. Over and out. Get out then!

The Italian man and the blonde tart rush out thankfully.

The Sergeant hovers, ready to help, as the Girls leave the building, he puts his arms out as if he is going to pat them along on the back, but doesn't quite dare touch, and Joe leads them to the limo, shooting nervous glances around Crown Court, as if a bomb blast were something one could dodge if one saw it early enough.

—You too, says Fred. But the young man is adamant.

—I'm not leaving this here, Fred, I bloody signed for it! Not you, me! I'm not fucking leaving 153,876 quid cash I signed for, you think I'm going to be responsible for that if anything happens? They'll have me paying it off for the rest of my bloody life!

—What's going to happen to it here? laughs Fred.

—I don't care. Fred: I signed for it. I stay with it until I get a kosher receipt, mate. Anyway (he winks), if I go back they might find me something to do.

—Please yourself, says Fred.

The Sergeant, having packed the girls into the car without getting so much as a thank you, never mind his number taken for future commendation, comes back and stands in the door of the bank, full of vengeance:

—Bloody royalty my ass! Right, you two! You either get out now, or lock up and stay put! Got it?

—No sweat, says Fred.—We'll stay.

But now the cries of a serious domestic incident are heard outside.

—I gave you the bleeding keys!

—You crazy woman, the keys are with you!

—I gave them to you.

—For Christ's sake! cries the Sergeant.—Get that bloody car out of here.

—We can't find the fucking keys! spits the blonde, as if the Sergeant's intervention has made it his fault, and she bursts into tears.

—Right! That's it. Back inside, now! I said now!!

—Aaaaaah! screams the blonde.

The Italian hits her a big, slow swat across the face, she collapses, he drags her whimpering out of the car and back into the bank.

—Now stay bloody put! shouts the Sergeant.—You heard me!

—Come on, says Fred, and he helps the Italian to dump the moaning blonde in one of the chairs at one of the desks. The Sergeant looks to see, shakes his head, and runs off up Crown Court to shoo on the last people coming out of the Bacchus Wine Bar, speaking into his radio and holding his helmet on his head as he goes.

—Right, says Fred. He shuts the door and turns back inside.

—Hello, Fred, says the young man.—Have a look at this.

—What's that? asks Fred.

—What it says it is, Fred. A Will.

Among the people now being marshaled out of the door of the Pizza Express, having delayed as long as possible, enraging the police already—their lumpish Top Dog had loudly insisted that Women and Children had to go fucking first—are six drunken young idiot yuppies dressed as characters from the film Reservoir Dogs, each clutching two beer bottles. Brady sees the limo pulling away, he sees Chicho carrying Suzy back into the bank. He grabs the nearest two Doggies and whispers ferociously:

—Do what I do, and we are all going to be on the world satafuckinglite news. Are you with me?

Are a bunch of drunken film fetishists and sad poseurs going to miss a chance to appear on the World News dressed as Doggies?

Are they fuck.

Inside the bank, Fred has just found out why the hell this bloke James Andrew Marsden should be leaving his daughter, Jean Leefe née Kane, fifty grand in his Will.

—Coo, says he.

—No contact, Fred. No possible proof. I pay Jimmy cash to-morrow, Jimmy hands in his lunch bucket in six to twelve, no one knows where it came from or why it's coming to Jean and no one can ask Jimmy because Jimmy's not there to ask.

—The poor bastard, says Fred, shaking his head and still looking at the Will.

—And I'm not going to try to stitch you up. Why? Because I don't want to spend the rest of my life wondering if you might just find me one night.

—No, no, says Fred.—I can see that. Well, I never had you cut out as a big-time villain. That your mob outside with the gelly and the Merc? Nice one. Where's the shooters then?

—We haven't got any.

—What, no shooters?

—We could have, do you think I can set all this up and not get hold of a shooter? But have we? No. I don't want to use a shooter, not on you, Fred. All you have to do is let me kick you in the balls and Chicho here smack you a couple of times, there's fifty grand in it for your Jean. Why help them all the time, help yourself ! Help your grandkids!

—Is easy for you! urges Chicho.

—As soon as we're away, you hit the button, just like you should, it doesn't matter, who the fuck is going to listen to an-other alarm in all this?

Fred appears to be in a quandary.

—Nice. But you should have cut me in before, mate.

—I didn't think you'd believe me.

—I don't believe blokes, I believe Plans. Looks like you got a nice one. Very tasty. I was never any good at Plans, but I can tell them when I see them. Sweet as a nut.

—Then for fuck's sake come in now!

—You know what? You should have brought a bleeding shooter, trouble is no one will believe two blokes done ME just like that, will they? Didn't you think of that? Be serious.

—We could have taken you by surprise.

—Na, no one can take me by surprise. Haven't you even got a knife or nothing? What about him?

—No. Look . . .

—If you'd had a shooter you could have shot me in the kneecap or something.

—That's OK, you just say I had a shooter.

—Na, they won't believe it, they'll say I was in on it, they'll fit me up, mate, I know them. I can't do it.

—Fred!

—Sorry mate. I appreciate you not wanting to stiff me. Really. I owe you one. But not this time. Maybe it would work, I dunno, you see I gotta have time to think. I'll say it again just once more, you should have cut me in before, that's all I'll say, and there's an end to it.

I looked at Fred, at this solid barrel of bone and muscle and I knew he was right, I should have cut him in before. I had reckoned with everything except the simplest, most important thing: Fred's absolute sense of fair play. But we all have Ph.D.s in

Hindsight and it was no good at all now. So I let my arms drop
and I said:

—Yeah. That's it then.

I turned to Chicho and Suzy.

—That's it then.

—So what do we do now? said Suzy.

—Um, I said.

—You going to stop us? asks Suzy.

—Na, says Fred.—Fair's fair, you didn't stiff me, and anyway, I don't squeal on people. As far as I know, you're Count
whatsisface, you're his tart and you're my gofer, OK? And the
dough goes in the safe. That good enough for you?

—Thanks, Fred, I said.

—Never mind, mate. Cor, if you only brought a shooter,
eh? You got to have shooters. This your first job?

—Yeah.

—Nice try. I always knew you had brains. That's the main
thing, brains. And shooters. Here, if you need any muscle for the
next one, mate, you know where to come. If you don't like shooters, you need serious muscle, that's the thing. No offense, but you
two ain't serious muscle, see?

—Yeah. Thanks Fred, I say. I turn away, unable to look Suzy
and Chicho in the face.

Do you know what I am feeling?

Not what you think I am.

Once, when I was only about 17, I was on this cheap packed
train from Italy to Germany, I had been all night in between the
lav and the hissing automatic carriage doors, I had just found I
had lost most of my money, all I had was this bottle of red wine,

so I drank it and I gave some to this Arab who was sitting next to me. He went away, and I drifted half off to sleep, all the different languages everyone was yapping away in turned into a big porridge of sounds, in my half sleep I could make it mean anything I wanted. Two hours later, he woke me up and pulled me over quietly and made me follow him, so I did, and he took me along half the train to a compartment that had the curtains drawn and a sign in German saying it was RESERVIERT: GRUPPE POLNI-SCHER NONNEN, but there was no Group of Polish Nuns in it, just seven Arabs, and they gave me a seat and I felt like some Russian peasant who has just not been whipped for once or something, a seat in a train was more than I could possibly deserve, and I burst out crying and all these Arab men seemed to understand exactly why, they nodded and gave me fags and wine, and smiled.

That was how I felt now. I was thinking Thank fuck for that, I wanted to burst into tears on Fred's shoulder and cry Thank fuck for that, it is far more than I deserve, I just want a quiet seat and a few quid and forget all this.

I just want to go back to my shed and grow old.

I take a deep breath and look forward to the rest of my life.

I am going to apply for accountancy training tomorrow, that is definite now. Fred is right. I should be doing something decent. Hey, it's not too late: the average UK arts grad takes until 28 before they start doing what they end up doing. I am just Mr. Average, thank God. I want a Wimpey home, I want a mortgage, I want slippers and a cardigan booked for twenty years from now, and I want a wife and kids and I want them all right now.

And then as Fred turns away to pick up my sack of money and put it in the safe, Suzy looks round and this bloke I have never seen before walks in.

He is shortish and stocky, forties, dressed hippie—Mutton Dressed as Lamb in this long brown leather coat and his jeans tucked into matching cowboy boots, he looks like some DOS guru from Stonehenge, his hair is long, red and thick, tangling into natural dreadlocks, his face is lined, scarred and cokebeaten, and his eyes are very, very, very MAF, they have been blasted pale by his thoughts, they are Nature's way of putting out a health warning that says:

Be careful how you go with the owner of these eyes,

because whatever happens to him today

is nothing to what happens in his head each night.

And he flings back his coat like he has seen too many Clint Eastwood films and pulls out this silenced fucking revolver.

—Who the fuck are you? I say, but carefully.

—I am the man from the boot of the Merc, says he.—Hi.

—Who the fuck is he? I ask Suzy.

—Just Someone, says Suzy.

And then Fred says, to me of course:

—Now that's more like it! Fifty grand you said?

—But . . . , I say.

—Both legs mind, says Fred, raising a finger.—Make it sixty grand and I'll give you a clear two minutes start.

—Suzy . . .

—Done, says Suzy, and she takes the gun from Someone and gives it to me.

Me.

—Go on, neither of us can shoot, she says.

2 6 1

—One tab too many one fine day, hey, you know how it is, smiles Someone, and holds up his shaky hand.

—You told me you used to shoot rabbits, says Suzy.

—Nasty man, says Someone.

—That was a long time ago. That was rabbits for fuck's sake. Chicho?

—No, no, no, is very hard for me.

It was true, I shot many rabbits when I was a teenager in the countryside, where there is nothing for teenagers to do except drink their brains out, kill things, and dream of city nights. I stopped after the time I hit one right between the eyes with a .22 dum-dum from about fifty yards and both its eyes popped clean out, they had squeezed out so they were shaped like little gray-white eggplants. Another one for the 3 a.m. video show in my head. I forced myself to roast the bloody thing and eat it anyway, since I had killed it, but it tasted like dried cowshit.

—It's all right, mate, says Fred.—Just make sure you aim for the outside of me legs, not the inside, that's where the arteries is, see. Get me there, and there, it'll look great, that's what we always used to do. Takes me back. Is that a .22? Yeah, shouldn't do too much damage really. Come on then.

—Hurry up, says Suzy,—or Brady will be gone.

—Jesus! Who the fuck said . . .

—Cool it man, says Someone. Fucking hippie.

—Do it! says Suzy.

—Is easy for you, says Chicho.

—No it fucking well is not.

And then I do it anyway.

There is practically no kick from the gun, with the silencer it just sounds like a couple of crisp bags being burst, the bullets go straight through Fred's legs and into the desk behind him.

Fred winks at me before his legs go and his face screws up, then the messages from his two smashed legs hit his brain, and his eyes go back, he falls over, the blood doesn't splatter like in Brady's film world, it just pushes out slow and easy, it spreads like Fred's trousers were made of toilet paper, and just keeps spreading.

—Get the money, says Suzy, and she and Chicho dive for the desks. I just watch Fred, I feel the sight being welded into my brain, but it doesn't hurt, it will not burn.

—Wait, says Fred.

—What?

—It's not enough. I'll stretch out my mitt like I was trying to stop you, and you put one through the middle of it, right?

—Do you think so?

—Right through the middle, don't go shooting me bleeding fingers off or nothing. There. Come on, mate, this is fifty grand for my Jean's kids or seven years for me, do you think I care about a poxy .22 through the mitt? It's your bleeding plan! No point having the balls to think about it if you can't do it.

—OK, OK, OK.

So I do that too, I don't care anymore, I just Fire First Aim, the bullet goes right through Fred's hand, it knocks it backwards like an electric shock, and smashes a big gilt-framed mirror, this time I feel some tiny bits of Fred's hand blow back and hit me in the face, I stand and look in a bit of the mirror that is left, but I cannot see them. Suzy takes the gun from me and gives it back to Someone, who sticks it in his jeans-belt.

Now Fred is staring up at me like he is undergoing a religious conversion or something. He is hugging his hand to him and slowly tilting back over onto the floor, the blood is running between his fingers and over his groin and soaking down to meet the blood from his legs in the twenty-grand carpet.

Chicho and Suzy have a sack full of money, it doesn't look that big, but then money doesn't, and now Someone grabs me and shoves me through into the black-mirror airlock, I take one last look at Fred like in a dream, he is staring at the ceiling now, and gasping and counting half out loud: eighteen, nineteen, twenty, and then we all four of us walk calmly to the car, laughing and joking, carrying the sack quite openly.

As we get in, a couple of police at the top of the square see us, they wave madly at us, I yell at them:

—They told us to get out of here for Christ's sake! That Sergeant said we could come through!

—You were supposed to be out five bloody minutes ago!

An awkward moment?

Yes, but this is where the Plan comes in.

Because as we start the car, there is a sudden crackle of shooting and a sound of bottles and windows breaking, in this atmosphere those plastic caps cut like knives, a gang of figures in black suits and white shirts, carrying guns, breaks from the crowd moving up towards Long Acre and bursts out between the ducking police, chucking empty beer bottles around like confetti, led by a huge great bastard who is shouting:

—Let's go to work!

And every policeman for a hundred yards around dives for cover or pulls out his gun.

We pull away up the Court.

—Easy, Princess, says Someone. Some of the police see us, but Suzy waves and shouts:

—It's only us!, and Chicho shouts:

—I am finding the keys! Is easy for us now, thank you, thank you!

Behind us, I can hear the bank's alarm go off, but only because I am listening for it, there are alarms and sirens everywhere anyway, like in the Plan. I do not turn, I just keep staring at this funny thing Suzy has put on the rear-view mirror, this red-and-blue tin skeleton.

—Forty-one, forty-two, forty-three, says Someone.

But now no one is interested in us, as we approach the police at the top of the Court, almost all of them have joined in the big scrum in Bow Street, where helmets and shields and truncheons are flying, I even hear Brady's big voice yelling:

—Let fucking go of me you fucking fuck-faced fuckers! and a couple of the cops turn round and scream:

—Get that fucking Merc out of here!

But they do not stop us, because they already knew a white Merc was supposed to come through, they had all seen the car ages ago, it was here when they got here, how could you forget a car like that, some of them had seen Chicho batting Suzy about, and carrying her into the bank, how could you forget seeing some lucky dago clouting a blonde with a stomach that flat?

Just like in the Plan.

And now we slink between the bollards and the nose of the car swings right onto Bow Street, with police shouting and running towards the pile of fighting bodies and waving us on and looking nervously towards the bomb car.

Just like in the Plan. Chicho turns and grins:

—Is easy for us. Such a nice Plan!

—Fifty-six, fifty-seven, fifty-eight, says Someone.

The second rear wheel bucks down off the pavement safely and now we have all four feet on the ground, I can see Suzy champing to give her the boot, but we haul nice and slow into the middle of Bow Street, as Suzy lets the wheel spin back to center she is already putting her foot down, gently, you can already feel the slow push as we straighten and pass the Pizza Express.

On our left, we pass Brady and his Doggies buried under a heap of police just like in the Plan.

Where they fired their cap guns and smashed their bottles of beer, just like in the Plan.

Where the road is covered in broken glass from the bottles Brady and his Doggies chucked around right here, right on time, right according to what some shagging fucking stupid clever wanker (me) told them to do in his oh-so-fucking-clever Plan.

And so as we go off, so do two of the tires in the Merc, just in front of the Pizza Express, where we are (thanks to the Plan) surrounded by half the Metropolitan Police.

Nice Plan.

15

AND
SUZY
JUST NODDED

Suzy stayed icy, she slowed up nice+easy, she looked at me just once, quickly, then concentrated on not squashing the policemen who were waving us on, telling us to get out anyway, we crawled out into Long Acre, bumpa-bumpa-bumpa, where the police were still driving straggling office workers and shopkeepers away.

Chicho was thanking the police and showing them Suzy, as if it was her fault, what could a man do? and Someone was sitting with his hands in his lap to cover the gun, smiling away like the fucking Pope muttering the rosary or something, but actually saying seventy, seventy-one, seventy-two, and I was sitting on the bag of money wanting to shit myself to death and wishing to fuck I was an accountant.

—One minute thirty, said Someone.

—Oh shit, I said. Where should we be by now?

—Bottom of Long Acre at least, said Suzy.—Out of sight, at least.

—Pig Madonna, said Chicho.

—If we can get through the blockade before Fred comes out we might still have a chance, I said.

But we were still only just crawling past the armored cars down Long Acre, passing the tube station, when Suzy looked past me in the mirror and said, without turning round:

—Two minutes ten. Shit.

I looked back up Long Acre, and sure enough, there was a different wave happening among the police suddenly, an armored Land Rover moved out of sight into Bow Street.

—So Fred's out of the bank and they've seen him, I said.

—At least he's still alive, said Suzy.

—Nice shooting, said Someone.

—Is very bad for us, said Chicho.

The wheel rims were chewing into the asphalt now. We were at the blockade halfway up Long Acre. They were waving us through. But ahead lay the rest of the long street, and people crowding to see, and the place still crawling with police trying to move everyone on and cordon everyone off.

—How fast can we go? I asked Suzy without leaning forward.

—Not fast enough. We've probably got thirty seconds before they work it out, maybe a bit more with all the mess here. We won't make it to Leicester Square before they put the call out.

—Depends what call they put out, said Someone—Pull over as soon as we can. Somewhere by an alley. Here.

And Suzy did. She just did what he said, just like that, she pulled over into the crowd beside that shop with the French Horn sticking out above it, Paxman's, she slid the car nice and easy up alongside the people, so close they looked angrily at us for a second, then they turned their faces and cameras back up Long Acre in case they missed the Hollywood petrochemical explosion they just KNEW was coming.

—Get out, said Someone.—Nice and easy, go into the crowd, don't push, just melt. Oh, and by the way (he said to me, with his bleached eyes), if I thought wasting you would get Suze back, I'd do it now. Pow. But it wouldn't, so I won't. Too late. Heavy stuff, eh?

Suzy looked at him, like she knew just what he was going to do and like it was not really anything to do with the two of them, just something about the way the world is, just the only right thing to do, and like she agreed.

—Sure? she said.

—I owe you, Princess, he said.

And Suzy just nodded.

So out we all got, I slung the money bag over my shoulder like a sack of old washing.

—You can't bloody park there! shouted a cop, in between talking to his radio and shouting at other people.

—Look at the fucking tires! I shouted.—They just sent us down here, make your bloody minds up!

—Watch it! he snapped, and back he went to his radio. Chicho shouldered and bellied our way into the crowd, everyone was making way for a big Black Maria to come through, Brady must be inside there. When we were five deep into the people and just sneaking into the alley by the French Horn shop, I risked a look back and this is what I saw:

Someone was watching up Long Acre, standing in the middle of the road, and I stood on my toes and looked where he was watching, like everyone else, and I saw policemen looking around and pointing and shouting into radios and turning towards the white Merc with fins. And then Someone just strolled hippily up to the nearest bigwig cop, and flung open his coat and pulled the gun out, the silencer was off now, you could see his hand shaking from here, he fired once into the nearest cop-car hood, bwhanng!, everyone ducked and screamed, and tried to get away, then he stuck the gun behind the cop's ear and dragged him out with his left arm round his neck, he pulled him into the middle of the street, back up into the blockade, back up towards Bow Street, with a succession of cops jumping towards him and jumping back when they saw what he had in his hand besides the Superintendent, with the Superintendent alert—brave guy—but sensibly limp, and everyone around yelling and running about and Someone screaming, like some computer voice in meltdown:
Back or he fucking gets it!!
Back or he fucking gets it!!
Back or he fucking gets it!! . . .

We didn't even have to run, the crowd carried us almost as far as the Seven Dials.

By the time we gushed out there, Suzy had lost the wig and put on a pink PVC mac from her handbag and Chicho had given me his shades, we split up and I strolled along Charing X Road with my million-quid bag of washing, ambled into Old Tottenham Court Rd. and soon got to that underground car-park round the front of the British Museum, which was where Suzy's horrible old automatic mini was, where we had planned to switch cars, and dumped the trash bag, by this time I had got so used to pretending it was just any old trash bag that I believed it myself, I just slung it on the back seat and great piles of money rolled out everywhere, I had to scrabble about and get them back in, then I shut the car up and left.

Just left it there in a car-park in London?

Safe as houses.

Everyone goes on about car theft, well, what the fuck do you expect if you park a car in the street that is worth five times what your nearly-neighbors get a year? You expect to find it there tomorrow? What Planet do you come from? The Planet MC Heaven, is what. Crime is just Nature's way of rightsizing income differentials, you vote for the differentials, you get the crime. But who the hell is going to steal a horrible old automatic mini? A professional thief? No, because it is worth fuck all. A joyrider? Come on, what joyrider would court a social nightmare by turning up at Joyrider City in a horrible old automatic mini? What about a radio thief? No, because Suzy took the radio and the speakers out, any thief can see the holes where the speakers were. And the car-park is full of nice BMWs and Volvos, you could leave the crown jewels in the boot of Suzy's car here overnight, never mind for five minutes.

And anyway, as I walked out into the light, Suzy and Chicho

were just going into the car-park. They didn't see me, or maybe they were just doing the right thing and pretending not to see me, so I did too, I went to the British Museum for twenty minutes, to look at the gold and jewels they buried with some headman that died in 2000 BC or whatever, to remind myself that nothing really mattered that much, and then that started making me want to see Suzy very much indeed, I actually felt like crying in the middle of the British fucking Museum, so I went home, and waited for her to call round, just like in the Plan, and waited for my brain to settle down, and tried to stop thinking: So fucking what?

It was supposed to change everything, like when you give up smoking and everyone has gone on about it for so long that you think When I Give Up Everything Will Be Different, and actually everything is the same, your job is still shit and you are still full of fear and worry and longing, you just . . . don't smoke. Or when you are 16 and everyone has talked about fucking for so long, you think when you first actually fuck it will be like dying and rising again as A MAN. That's what I felt like. I had done it, I had just kicked the door down and all I found inside was pictures of me BEFORE and AFTER, but they were the same.

I sat there, just me and still me.

Eventually, I went and called Suzy from that phone booth in Goldhawk Road, like not in the Plan.

And guess what I got?

The ansaphone.

And guess what I felt like then?

16

THE COLLECTIVE UNCONSCIOUS OF THE CAR AGE

Those beer bottles helped save Brady's neck.

I mean, the way things turned out, the Met really went for this one, they knew there was some connection between Brady and us except of course there wasn't actually because the only one they had who they could prove was in the Gang was Someone, and Brady did not have a bull's notion who Someone was anyway, and Someone knew fuck all about Brady either, so all they did was tell the truth, and when the Met cunningly set up an accidental meeting between them in a lav, and filmed it and watched the film carefully, they could see Brady and Someone were telling the truth about not knowing each other, which confused them deeply and shook their conviction that they would get one.

At first, Brady trusted in the Plan so much that he thought

they were just trying to break him down by printing false news-paper reports about the shootings. Later, he believed them, but that didn't help them either, because then he was so pissed off with me for not trusting him with the full Plan and letting some other sod have a real gun that he was determined to get out ASAfuckingP and smash my teeth out through my asshole, so he was not shagging well going to go down for years or anything, so he clammed up. Of course, the Met did try sensory deprivation on Brady, keeping the lights on, waking him up all the time and stuff, but Brady spent the first twenty years of his life staring out at an endless bog in Roscommon and being kicked out of bed into the rain at three in the morning to deliver mutant cows or what-ever, so that was a piece of piss for him, so then they tried to just knock the truth out of him in the good old way, but Brady doesn't care about physical pain, I suppose he does feel it, he must have SOME kind of primitive nervous system, he just doesn't care, I have tried having half-serious fights with him before and I know that if it was full-serious, for keeps, you would never win by in-flicting hurt on Brady, you would have to stop him like he was a big insect, by actually taking out some large+essential moving part, so anyway, Brady just took his beating and got up and said, Have you quite finished, Gentlemen? and then the Met gave up because they couldn't go any further without seriously and visibly fucking him up, and the days when they can do that to just anyone they like are gone thank Christ, especially when half the world has seen the film of Brady in his Doggy suit with his plastic gun, looking like he was just off to accept the Nobel Prize for dildo impersonations.

So Brady's lawyer pushed the line that Brady was only being arrested because he was Irish and the Met were trying to fit any old WC paddy up yet again, and he produced all the evidence that showed that Brady was just a fucked-up bogtrotting film-head who was well-known to ride about the tube in his wank-off fantasy gear, he said Brady just got carried away when it looked like it was coming true.

But the knockout bit was when Mr. Cute Lawyer asked how the hell did the Met think Brady was part of some big Plan when it was HIS beer bottles that had crippled the getaway Merc? What kind of monumentally sad terrorist robbing gang would put that in their masterful Plan? Apparently, he had the jury creased with laughter at the thought of it.

Ha bloody ha.

That slow unplanned crawl down Long Acre meant that there were some pretty hairy video shots of us.

Chicho was OK because who in London is going to bother keeping their eyes out for Any Old Fat Wop, which was about all the pics and the descriptions really amounted to? If English people could tell the difference between Italians, French, Spanish, Portuguese, Greek, Turks and Arabs, it might have got difficult for him. As it is, all he did was hang out in the back of some friend's café down by Victoria, it looks like any old greasy cancer café, but if you know about it, and if you can ask in Spanish, you go through the door in the back and there is this little garden with two tables full of quiet Spanish men playing cards and drinking wine under umbrellas. Nice. Safe.

Suzy was OK, because the shots of her just showed a woman in that kind of big blonde wig and make-up, all Suzy had to do was lose the wig and descale her face and she was herself again, an actual person and thus a different woman, so that was OK, she could walk into a roomful of police posters and no one would look at her twice. Of course, she had to give up showing off her flat tummy for a bit, because the cops certainly got that into the descriptions, no way did the lads in Crown Court miss that. So it had to be hid. A blow to Suzy, no doubt, but she took it well, and just went into her Winter Plumage baggy jumpers early this year.

As for me, when I saw the pics, I was like a dog with two dicks: I did not look bald at all!

But seriously, I did have to lie pretty low. I look so normal and bloody ordinary, people are more likely to look carefully at what the pictures really look like, not just file them away under BLONDE TARTS or DODGY WOPS.

I had to sneak out to do my business things, of course. I paid Mr. Supaservice right away, and some days later I went down to Hammersmith Bridge with a bag full of £200,000. I kept having this paranoia that I was going to get run over and be found paraplegic with this bag of money, I crossed the roads like some poor sod nipping out for bread in Sarajevo, but I got there all right, and just waited and looked down the river and smoked a fag and did not look round once when I heard two voices drawing near. They were saying:

—Yeah, sure, right, I get it, you know, and isn't that just THE business, I mean yeah, no, let's just assume for one moment that Stalin was not just going AWOL from his brain, shall we? Is that cool?

—Mmmmmm.

—Exactly exactly exactly, and just perhaps, just maybe the struggle for control of the productive forces in the USSR involved the genuine presence of reactionary elements parading as Modernism in the guise of the Magnitogorsk technocrats, OK?

Can we shove that idea off the beach and see if the tide takes it?

—Mmmmmm.

It never occurred to me to be on guard about a knife in the back or anything, which was OK, because nothing like that happened, the footsteps hardly paused, all that happened was the money bag was whisked away from beside me and Voice #1 said:

—Hoi, the man! and they were gone.

On the way back I suddenly realized that I was thinking:

—That's OK then, I can get run over now! and so I decided I had to go and lie down straight away.

I forced myself to act normal at home.

I went up to dinner with Bob and Big Sis and made myself moan about money and jobs, like I had recently been doing, and nodded and listened when Bob told me again about how I could retrain as a lawyer or an accountant or something if I really tried, and watched him start believing it himself as he got mildly pink on the red wine, he was determined to save MC Heaven, for me and so for him, and all the time all I was thinking was: MONEY MONEY MONEY AIN'T IT FUNNY and how I did not really want a house like this after all.

After all the months I had spent being murderously jealous, now, at last, I had the keys to MC Heaven and I suddenly didn't want to join.

I went back to my shed and took up the floorboard and looked at my huge pile of money that Chicho had brought round the day after the job, and thought:

Maybe the things you have to do to get what you want change what you want?

I did not see Suzy.

I did not hear from Suzy.

Apart from her ansaphone voice.

I filled her tape for two weeks, I called her up just to hear the tape saying there was no one there, I made up Fantastic Tales to explain to myself why she had not called me back, whenever I looked up at Big Sis's house and saw her or Bob on the phone, I would start to stalk about and growl GETOFFTHEFUCKING-PHONE to myself, in case Suzy tried when it was busy. I decided she must have decided to lie low anyway, she must have gone away.

But then there was this thing on the news about how a load of tough girls with camcorders had brought Soho to a standstill, each time some of the porn barons' lowlife hardmen came up, these giant blokes in jogging suits with radio mikes appeared, and told them that if they touched the girls they would get their heads stuffed up their asses. The chief of the giant blokes appeared on the TV in his shining white steam-pressed jogging suit, a big black man, his top had SECURITY FOR THE PEOPLE 0181-777-7777 on it, and he said:

—Look here old boy, I can't tell you who hired us because I don't damn well know. Anonymous female, cash payment by post, all that sort of thing. Now, there was no violence was there? Eh? No, quite. And a bloody lucky thing for the other chaps too!

Barrington-Charrington, of course.

Suzy, of course.

So then I had to admit she was still in town, and just not answering my calls because she didn't want to.

Depressing?

Ohhhhhh no. No way.

I was that far in, I was in the horrors, I actually preferred to think she didn't WANT to see me, than think she had gone. I mean, you can change what someone WANTS, maybe, but you can't change whether they are THERE or not. So when I realized she just didn't want to see me, I was delighted, and decided that in that case I had to see her quick and change her mind before Us just faded away and she got into something new.

So one night, about three weeks after the job, I did something earthshakingly sad+stupid, I shaved my hair down to a number one, bought shades and went and hung around Filthy MacNasty's for half a whole evening, in case Suzy turned up.

Thank Christ she didn't, and see me there, doing that, maybe blowing everything out of sheer pathetic impatience. Pathetic, because all impatience is pathetic, if you are impatient it means you don't trust the future, you are scared of missing the boat, and you can be so scared of losing something that you never actually get it.

What are the three differences between a supermodel and a centerfold? Patience, patience and patience.

For days afterwards, I lay in my shed and shivered and felt sick, thinking about how many people might have seen me. I even started to think that the bald man in the walk-up across the way might have understood, maybe he was just keeping up a pretense of making his toy planes (it was a big biplane now) so I would not notice that he knew. I started to think about how I could creep up and axe the bastard and who the fuck would know or care. Or maybe follow him to the tube and just fling him. One night I realized I was actually planning it, in detail.

I needed my brain cooling so bad, I called up Greek Ted on his mobile and told him I wanted the best seat in the Dress Circle for tonight only.

Greek Ted is a top-of-the-market pusher with (of course) a white Merc, it was his car that gave me the idea, I think, and me saying Dress Circle meant I wanted a single fix of his Personal Best. I also asked him had he seen Suzy, but he said not. When I put the phone down I knew it was her I wanted, not the smack, but since when did knowing anything stop anyone, so that night I went to Greek Ted's flat, Crap Designer Heaven, I paid his minder, a wide-set guy with a roll of neck fat swamping his button-down collar, and waited with this type called Patch, a twitching UMC wreck; we sat there like people on a train who half-know each other and wish they hadn't met.

Greek Ted was cooking up over at the sink, but then he suddenly said without turning around:

—Funny, you asking about Suzy the Black Widow, Mr. Denver. You know I was next in line for her?

—Nope, I said.

Then he did turn round:

—It was a deal, you understand? I gave her good stuff way under price, man. I was next in line for her. You understand? It was a fucking deal, practically, and she never even gave me a fucking blowjob and then some cunt else stepped in the line. Some cunt. We use my personal works here, that OK, Mr. Denver?

And he took this great big shining hallmarked silver syringe out of a designer sterilizing unit, popped out a brand-new needle, screwed it in and started to fill her.

—Enough for two, said Greek Ted. Mr. Patch twitched especially strongly. Greek Ted laughed, hee hee.

—I go first, I said.

—My idea entirely, Mr. Denver. You go first. The one-off daytrip man goes first, hee hee. Patch doesn't care, do you, Patch? Patch isn't on a daytrip, Patch is slumming long-haul, aren't you, Patchy? Patch doesn't have blue blood in his veins anymore, Mr. Denver, his heart shifts pure fucking shit, hee hee. Well, here we go gentlemen, this is as good as it gets.

I had my arm pumped up already, so he took hold of it and gave me a nurselike swabbing and slid the needle in pulled the plunger back a smidge so the blood came in, and then just when I had closed my eyes and was waiting for the sunlight to hit the back of my head, he said:

—So where's Suzy?

I looked down. The needle was still stuck in there, the syringe was still full, the threads of my blood were snaking around slowly in the dull liquid, his fat strong hand still had my forearm held up by the elbow, and his thumb was still on the plunger. I looked at my arm with this needle sticking out of it and the blood starting to creep out of the hole, like it was someone else's arm, and I looked at his thumb and I could see it was very gently white with the pressure. Then I realized Mr. Blubberneck was close in behind me.

—Enough for two, said Greek Ted. That's twice too much for one, Mr. Denver, hee hee. Suzy owes me. Where is she? You been fucking her? If you been fucking her, you owe me too, see? Where is she? I squeeze too hard, your daytrip gets extended to forever.

He had his tongue between his teeth with the pleasure of it, he was getting off on the purest currency of all, power.

But to my surprise, I did not care. And to his. He looked in at me through my eyes, searching for someone to break for fun, and all he got was someone saying: So do it.

So he didn't, of course. Instead of a quick powerfuck, he saw return business, so he just nodded and pressed halfway and on the count of three my head filled with a big noise like a wave flowing back into the sea off a long pebble beach, the chemical angels lifted me softly backward. He slipped the needle out and reached it over without looking to Mr. Patch, who grabbed it with something halfway between a sigh and a yelp, like a skydiver finding his ripcord in the nick of time.

—See you again, Mr. Denver, said Greek Ted as I left.

So instead of going mad, I took a holiday, thank fuck, there are times it is best to stay and fight and times it is best to run away for a while, sometimes you need to walk away from the edge to get your breath back and have a good run-up. I got a nice little Jap car and a half-kosher inspection certificate from Mr. Supaservice—he lent it me free, like any good businessman would to a proven+profitable client—and I went to Scotland and walked about wildly in the hills and sat beside lochs and watched the sun coming through the high, fast clouds, the light came and went and ran along the heather and bracken or whatever and the dark grass so fast it looked like green and yellow searchlights were scanning the hillsides, but I knew they were not after me.

Whenever I met anyone who asked what I was doing, I just

said I was getting out of London because it was such a heap of yuppie crap, which always plays well outside ye olde S.E. of E., and so here and there I met normal people and had normal conversations, and in a little place called Kinghorn I even met a half-normal girl, one of those locals whose eyes are starting to wander, she wanted more than here could offer, she could already feel the faraway beat, the sweet track to King's X was calling her. She met me when she finished work in the bar, I was sitting on a bench eating chips and one of those sausage-shaped haggises they sell in chip shops up there, yumyum, and after a while I said, Look, I am on the rebound from this other Scottish girl I'm no good for anyone right now, especially you. And she said: Well I never even hit the wall yet and who said anything about good? So that was OK. I was very grateful to fuck with someone, but I wished it was Suzy, and she could tell that, easy peasy, and got pissed off, even though I had warned her. I said she could look me up in London and she did, but she was seriously unimpressed when she found that my shed was literal, not a figure of speech, so that was soon that, she took the opportunity to get her finishing in first, quite right, the one who actually does the finishing always feels better for it, so I pretended to be cut up, which was not hard because I was, though not really about her, just about Things, you know.

Actually, I was sick of my shed too, but I had looked at flats with tall windows and gardens and stuff, in Sheps Bush and Notting Hill, and somehow had not found anything that I could see me living in.

All I could see in them all was: me, not living.

I wondered if Brady and Chicho felt the same about their wishes-come-true, but I thought probably not.

Why?
Because they are going home, that's why:

Chicho is going over to sign the papers for half his brother-in-law's wood-fired restaurant in Zaragoza in about a week's time.
Brady is going to some pub auction in Mayo next month.
They will be cash purchasers.
Nice to be a cash purchaser.
Nice to be going home.

Fred was at home too, he was a hero in Dalston, the Daily Express collected money for him and the Villains who knew better suddenly uprated him from Mr. Muscle to Mr. Big, and when his daughter Jean Leefe suddenly got left sixty grand by this man no one knew called Jimmy that died of AIDS, Fred looked at everyone with his transparent brown eyes and said: Poor Jimmy, I never knew the bloke, but they said he was always soft on my Jean, and the Villains shook their heads in envy+admiration.

You never saw so many mallows and larkspurs at a funeral.

Jimmy's funeral was on Day Two of Dai's cycle, but naturally Dai broke the cycle, he said that was the whole point of wakes and stuff, for people to be prepared to bunk off work and ruin their livers and everything, it is a sign of respect, and more than that, it is a sign that you recognize that shit happens, that things really do get lost forever, that no amount of life insurance can ever save us, that it is very dark and very cold beyond the campfire, that all we have is us.
So afterwards we were sitting in Filthy MacNasty's and

drinking whisky and beer, and Dai made them stop playing diddle-dee-eye stuff for once and made them play Patsy Kline, thank fuck, and then, since I can tell Dai anything I told him everything.

—What we will do for freedom tokens! he said at the end.

—Freedom tokens?

—Money to you, oh brainless Saxon one. I shall demonstrate. You are, let us say, a travel agent.

—You got it, I said.

—I enter your virtual travel agency. Good virtual morning.

—And one back in the eye to you, sir.

—I think, yes I think I would like to fly to Barcelona tomorrow so I can trundle down to Sitges and sip iced manzanilla sherry when the evening starts gently to cool and the parading beach boys pass me by in their latex fripperies, in order that I may choose with whom I wish to fuck myself mad later on.

—An idyllic scenario, sir.

—How many freedom tokens will that cost me please?

—Um, about a thousand.

—But I haven't got that many. I have not been able to gather them by working or begging or borrowing or exploiting or stealing (which are the only five ways to get them).

—Well, sir, it looks black, doesn't it?

—It looks as though I am not free enough to go to Barcelona, doesn't it?

—One has that impression, sir. You could go to Reading, sir. One hears that the, how shall I put it, SCENE, is lively there, by provincial standards.

—Yes, yes, I am just about free enough to go to Reading. Let that be my epitaph. Which reminds me: don't forget, you're going to die!

—Bless me, sir, I had quite forgotten.

—So what are you going to do with your freedom? he asked, and I said I didn't really know, and he said, If you do not know what to do with yourself that means you do not Know Yourself.—But I do, he said.

—What, know YOURself?

—That as well. I have decided, lovelyboy, that you are an out-of-control fetishist. You must go with it. What you really want, in the Dark Room of your mind, is not to know what is going to happen next. Am I wrong?

So I told him that he was (as usual) probably right. I told him that I have this recurring dream, in it I am always just about to get into a car with someone I half-know and go to somewhere I do not know at all, and it is always a good dream, sometimes I wake up and feel sick because it is not true, even though I have no idea what I am missing.

—You mourn for something you never had, nodded Dai.

—Yeah, I said.—Pretty fucking stupid.

—Well, of course, our one consolation is the monumental fairness which says that it is the same for everyone, be they Achilles or a repressed accountant. All we have to fear is the inevitable, which is a pretty bloody daft thing to be scared of, it being inevitable. Thank God tomorrow is Day Three and the Lads are awaiting me. I think perhaps every day will be Day Three from now on. I have tried, I have tried, but there: Man plans, and the Gods laugh. Remember to send the occasional postcard.

—What, from Sheps Bush?

—From wherever you end up. And otherwise remember only this: that Life is not like that rather beautiful and very camp car outside. You do not need rear-view mirrors for Life, all that is coming up behind you is whatever rusty old bits of the past you have left tied on.

—What rather beautiful and very camp car? I asked, because Dai had said it with that cunning look on his face.

—Ah! he said, and he slipped gracefully from his bar stool.

I followed him out, he did not look back, he never does when he has said goodbye, and what was there in the street was

Suzy, of course.

In black leathers, of course, with her hair cropped right back and dyed jet-black, of course, and sitting in this ridiculous half-acre red 50s Yank thing with fins, not crap plastic stick-on fins like on a little pimpmobile Merc, big chrome-steel fins with lights like torpedoes. And beside her was Mr. Supaservice, counting money like a cat with a mouse.

—Hi, I said.

—Hi, said Suzy.

A pause. Then Supaservice looked up and winked:

—Hey, no need for arachnophobia, Mr. Strong-and-Tough Milkybar, Supa S. is only up here in the Northern Wastelands by way of helping Miss Silkyshift test-drive this bad-ass battleship. But she already has it caught and webbed, the Spiderwoman strikes as it thinks. Your fully legit documents, Miss Spinnerette, my cash money. Check?

—Check, said Suzy.

—Sorted! Do business with you again.

And he bounced out over the door and loped off. Another pause.

—Nice, I said.

—I thought I'd double-bluff the police, said Suzy.—It's hardly original, as fantasies go, but then what's so good about original? Original doesn't mean good. I like it because it isn't original. This is the opposite of original, this is the collective unconscious of the car age. And I got it.

—Is it automatic? I asked, not looking at her.

—They all are, she said, not looking back.

—Fifteen to the gallon or something? (ditto)

—In your dreams. (ditto)—Aye, it's kind of ungreen, I know, but don't forget: that's assuming there's only one person in it. If there's two people, well, it's really no worse than a wee accountant going to work alone in his shitbucket Granada.

—Yeah. Yeah, I said.—Where've you been?

—Here and there. Just getting my head together. You?

—Round and about trying not to lose it. Was that you that hired Barrington-Charrington?

—Who? Oh, I thought he was called Walsingham-Sandringham or something.

—Yeah, something like that.

—You know him?

—Ages ago. Nice to know where he is. You never know.

—You never know what?

—I don't know, I'm only just, you know, getting the trailers in my head. It'll come, or it won't. How's Someone?

—Well, I can hardly visit Pentonville, can I? I should think he'll do OK inside.

—They'll love him.

—He can maybe chill out. He might even live to collect his pension. And if I'm still around too, we will be just very, very old friends who nearly fucked each other's lives up, but got on with it. You have to get even, then you can get going.

—Where are you going?

Suzy shrugged. She took this thing out of her pocket, she must have snapped it off the Merc when we ran for it, I never even noticed, that shiny red-and-blue skeleton. She tied it on the mirror and tapped it so it spun:

—Oh, this wee heap of junk is made for long-distance stuff, it's way too big for London, it needs to breathe.

—Yeah. Hard to park.

—A bastard, even with the power steering. So I think I should maybe take it on a good long cruise. I was thinking maybe Berlin. Well?

I mean, come on.

TUCKAHOE PUBLIC LIBRARY

3 1884 15057345 1

HAWES   Hawes, J. M. (James
         M.)
                    FEB 28 1996
         A white Merc with
         fins.

$22.00

DATE			
JUN 7 1996			
JUN 7 1996			

TUCKAHOE PUBLIC LIBRARY
71 COLUMBUS AVE
TUCKAHOE, NY 10707

BAKER & TAYLOR